PRAISE FOR

Never a Bride

"*Never a Bride* will keep you up all night—praying for a wedding. Fresh and original and destined to be a keeper. Charming and delightful—a must-read."   —Joan Johnston

"A delightful Regency romp. You'll have lots of fun with this one."   —Kat Martin, author of *Perfect Sin*

"An uplifting, wonderfully sensual story. I hated for it to end."   —Meryl Sawyer, author of *Trust No One*

"Readers will be quickly drawn in by the lively pace, the appealing protagonists, and the sexual chemistry that almost visibly shimmers between them in this charming, lighthearted, and well-done Regency."   —*Library Journal*

"A wonderfully wrought romance full of witty dialogue and clever schemes . . . Both of Grey's vivid characters will charm readers."   —*Booklist*

"This is a very sweet story of love and trust . . . A great debut novel by Ms. Grey. Don't miss it."
—*Old Book Barn Gazette*

"A pleasure to read."   —*Rendezvous*

"Readers will find the tale charming and delightfully humorous. Amelia Grey shows promise."   —*Romantic Times*

A DASH
OF SCANDAL

Amelia Grey

JOVE BOOKS, NEW YORK

A DASH OF SCANDAL

A Jove Book / published by arrangement with
the author

PRINTING HISTORY
Jove edition / November 2002

Copyright © 2002 by Gloria Dale Skinner
Cover design by George Long
Cover photograph by Wendi Schneider

Visit our website at
www.penguinputnam.com

ISBN: 0-515-13401-5

A JOVE BOOK®
Jove Books are published by The Berkley Publishing Group,
a division of Penguin Putnam Inc.,
375 Hudson Street, New York, New York 10014.
JOVE and the "J" design
are trademarks belonging to Penguin Putnam Inc.

PRINTED IN THE UNITED STATES OF AMERICA

10 9 8 7 6 5 4 3 2 1

One

"Something is rotten in the state of Denmark" and in London, too. The Mad Ton Thief has struck again. It is reported that with more than one hundred guests in attendance at an elegant soirée in Earl Dunraven's home, the robber made off with a priceless golden raven.

Lord Truefitt
Society's Daily Column

"*I*T WAS A dark and stormy night and all the ton—"

"No, no, no, Millicent," the bruised woman said in a soft voice. "That would be the most dreadful way possible to open Lord Truefitt's column. A gossip column must start something like . . . 'It was a starry night for an elegant soirée.' "

"But it was raining," Lady Millicent Blair reminded her aunt.

The elderly woman, lying against several pillows on her bed, groaned and patted her chest with a hand-painted fan. "That doesn't matter at all, dearie. Society doesn't expect the truth. They want gossip, and they want it surrounded by beauty."

Millicent lifted the hem of her simple white gown and started to sit on the bed, but a low growl from the golden-haired spaniel curled at her aunt's feet stopped her just in time. Millicent backed away.

Hamlet was a friendly, adorable little dog except when reposing on his mistress's bed. At those times the mild-mannered pet became a devoted watchdog. Aunt Beatrice was recovering from a terrible fall, and any sudden movement brought her excruciating pain. It distressed Millicent to see her father's sister in such a pitiful state.

"Oh, Aunt Beatrice, I don't want to overtire you. Can't you see I'm trying to point out why I can't possibly do what you're asking of me? This proves I know nothing about writing a gossip column."

Millicent could have added once again that because of her own mother's heartbreaking experience with the scandal sheets she didn't think she should learn. But Millicent had tried the truth when she arrived in London yesterday morning and learned why her aunt had sent to Nottinghamshire for her. All she had succeeded in doing was making her aunt cry and call for her medication. Millicent couldn't bring herself to upset the badly injured woman again.

Her Aunt Beatrice Talbot was Lady Beatrice to her friends and members of the ton, but to thousands of readers she was the never-seen Lord Truefitt, notorious gossip columnist for the London newspaper *The Daily Reader*.

Beatrice shifted against the pillows and moaned again. Her heart-shaped face twisted in pain. One side of her mouth and chin was horribly discolored and swollen. The poor woman had tripped over her droopy-eared dog and fell, hurting her leg and breaking one of her arms, plus covering herself from head to toe with bumps and bruises. She wasn't able to do much more than feed herself.

After the accident her ladyship's servants had begged her to give Hamlet away so there would be no chance of repeating the terrible fall. Beatrice would have none of that and had shamed them all for even suggesting she abandon her beloved pet.

Emery, Beatrice's sturdy maid, walked into the room carrying a small cup on a silver tray. The buxom woman was the only person Hamlet would let near the bed.

"Oh, good," Beatrice murmured gratefully and slowly batted the lashes of her puffy eyes. "Finally, something to ease the pain. I thought it would never be time to take that wretched-tasting tonic again."

The maid stirred a spoon of restorative powder into a cup of tea and helped Beatrice drink it before retiring to a chair at the back of the room. Emery seemed the perfect person to take care of her aunt. She spoke in gentle tones and was careful not to jar the bed or her employer.

"You must do this for me, dearie," Beatrice whispered in a voice and expression meant to appeal to Millicent's softer side. "I'm loath even to say it again out loud, but I must. The money I'm paid for writing the column is what I live on. Without it, I would be in the poorhouse before I was able to walk again."

"Lord Bellecourte wouldn't let that happen."

"Oh, botheration," she murmured. "He would. He might be my nephew and your half brother but when it comes to his money he is wound tighter than a William Clement clock."

"But I'm reluctant to stand in for you, and you know why I feel this way."

"Yes, yes, but you must overcome all that." She fanned herself again. "Besides, it won't be for long. Just until I'm able to walk again and attend the parties myself. It's a simple task, really. And you won't be without my help and the assistance of my longtime friends Viscount and Viscountess Heathecoute. The three of us have been around Society long enough that between us we know everyone in Town. We've already secured a voucher for Almacks, as well as invitations for you to attend all the best parties of the Season."

"Aunt Beatrice, if Lord and Lady Heathecoute are such dear friends, why can't they write the column for you?"

She rolled her puffy eyes upward and sighed heavily. "Oh, the viscountess would like nothing better. She absolutely loves gossip. I fear if I allow her to do the job it will never be mine again. She has recently suggested it might be time for me to hand the column over to her. She is a bit younger than me, you understand. But, not only do I enjoy what I do, I must have that income."

Millicent felt her resolve wavering. Writing a gossip column? Would it be like an adventure after living quietly in the country all her life?

Shaking those intrusive thoughts away, she tried to boost her argument by saying, "But Mama and I thought I was coming to London to be your companion and help you while you recover from your accident."

"Goodness. What foolishness. What could you do for me? I have Emery and Phillips to take care of my physical needs. What I need from you is your eyes and your ears. You, dearie, have the most important job. Keeping me out of the poorhouse."

"But scandal sheets?" Millicent whispered more to herself than her aunt. She shook her head wondering how she would ever explain this to her mother should she find out. "I never dreamed you wrote tittle-tattle or that you would want to engage me in your profession."

"Don't make it sound so contemptible, Millicent. Heavens, someone has to do it and it has to be someone who's accepted by the ton. Take my word for it, if Society didn't want to read gossip, the newspapers wouldn't print it." Beatrice looked past Millicent to her maid. "Now, Emery, please ask the viscount and his lady to join us."

"Oh, Aunt Beatrice, I didn't mean any disrespect to you or what you do."

"It's truly no more than writing down a few facts and making them sound much more fascinating than they are."

"Facts? I thought most of what was written was considered rumor and speculation."

"Well, maybe sometimes, but enough of that. Remember, what is most important is that what you are doing has to be kept a secret. No one can know that you are listening to their conversations." With puffy slits for eyes, she looked at Millicent's dress, her face, and her hair. Her aunt slowly shook her head. "Oh heavens, you are too beautiful. All the beaux will want to dance with you. We must do something."

Millicent looked down at her gown. Her father had provided well for her and her mother before his death and twice a year they had new clothes made that were suitable for the county social affairs held in Nottinghamshire. Her gown was the latest fashion and the unadorned, high-waisted design suited her well. The delicate flowers in her headpiece were chosen especially to show off her golden hair and light brown eyes.

Beatrice had told her she must not stand out at the parties. "You mustn't appear so pretty that the young bachelors seek your attention, or so unattractive you are singled out and talked about as a wallflower."

"What should I do?" she asked, not wanting to displease her aunt further.

"I have just the thing. Look over there on my desk and you will find my spectacles."

Millicent's shoulders reared back and her eyes rounded in rebellion. "No, Aunt Beatrice, that's going too far. I don't need spectacles."

"Of course you don't need them, but they will help keep the young bucks from falling over themselves to dance with you and come calling. Place them in your reticule and put them on when you get there. These are wonderful parties and there is no reason you can't enjoy yourself while you're there, but remember, you are attending the parties to obtain information. Not to be pursued. And do smooth those lovely curls away from your face, dearie. You must try to look a little plainer."

Millicent brushed the sides of her hair and for the first time admitted to herself that she was not going to get out of doing this for her aunt. She picked up the spectacles and tucked them into her lacy drawstring purse but never expected to actually use them.

"What a delight you would be to all the bachelors if you could attend the Season as a debutante," Beatrice said proudly. "You would be a diamond of the first water."

"Thank you, Aunt Beatrice."

For a moment Millicent thought she might blush over her aunt's unsolicited praise, but she quickly reminded herself that she was far too sensible for something like that.

Millicent shook her head in disbelief. Was she truly going to do this for her aunt? Surely there was some way she could get out of it. She had to think of her mother and what she had been through years ago.

Millicent was the only child born to the middle-aged earl of Bellecourte and his young wife, Dorothy. The earl already had a grown son and two married daughters by his deceased wife when he married Dorothy, at the request of Dorothy's father, his longtime friend. Earl Bellecourte married Dorothy after her reputation had been ruined by a scandal in London.

When Millicent was twelve her father died suddenly, leaving his wife with a jointure more than sufficient to cover her own and her daughter's needs. Dorothy was an attentive mother and saw to it that Millicent was educated in a manner befitting the daughter of an earl.

She was given everything except a London Season.

Dorothy expected her daughter to marry a local vicar, or some suitable gentleman of means. Much to her mother's distress, at age twenty, Millicent had already refused three offers of marriage.

Her mother had left London in shame twenty-one years ago vowing never to return. When Beatrice's frantic plea came, Dorothy was reluctant to let Millicent go up to London, but having always been fond of her deceased husband's sister, she agreed Millicent would be the perfect companion to Beatrice while she recuperated.

Millicent understood why her mother had never wanted her to go to London, but her mother had no cause to worry. Millicent didn't plan to fall in love with a scoundrel and ruin her reputation.

Thinking of her mother prompted Millicent to try once more to talk her aunt out of involving her in this scheme. "I don't see how I can listen to conversations, then come home and write about them."

"Oh, heaven's gates, Millicent, don't be so puritanical. Everyone in the ton loves the gossip columns. They can't wait for the Society pages to come out each day so they can read what has been said about the parties of the night before and the people who attended."

Millicent bristled at the inconsiderate attitude of her

aunt. "It was that very same kind of gossip that forced my mother from London in shame."

"Oh fiddle-faddle. That was years ago, and it was the best thing that could have happened to her. The last I heard the man she was caught with in the garden has never married. He wanted a conquest, not a wife, and your mother was foolish enough to believe every lie he told her. But, because of that scandal she married my dear departed brother, and was, by all that I could see, very happy." Beatrice offered her a slight smile from swollen lips.

Millicent nodded, knowing that her mother and father had been devoted to each other, but her mother had paid a terrible price for the good life she'd had with her husband.

"And best of all, dearie, they had you. My brother often wrote to me what a joy and comfort you were to him."

"My father was a fine gentleman, but I'm not sure that makes up for the humiliation my mother suffered from Society when she was declared an outcast and shunned."

"True, my dear." Beatrice grimaced in pain. "Your mother had a compromising, but, I understand, not a consummated relationship with a gentleman who later refused to marry her. Society is unforgiving of such things. But it was all for the best. I know if your father were alive he'd want you to help me in my hour of need."

Millicent looked down at the vulnerable lady before her. Aunt Beatrice had finally found Millicent's soft spot. Millicent had always adored her father. Would she be honoring him by doing what Aunt Beatrice asked? Millicent wasn't shy or retiring. She knew she would be able to do the work, she just didn't like the idea of deceiving people.

"Now, before my medication puts me to sleep, let's go

over who you will most likely see and hear about tonight one more time. Start at the beginning."

Resigned to her fate, Millicent said, "Lord and Lady Heathecoute will be my chaperones and make introductions for me. I am to slowly walk around the room and listen to conversations and make mental notes of all I hear. I will accept if a gentleman asks me for a dance, but I am not to show interest or give encouragement for another dance or an afternoon call."

"Good. Now, what are the names of the people who are of special interest?"

"The notable young ladies are Miss Bardwell, Miss Donaldson and Miss Pennington. The widows are Lady Hatfield and Countess Falkland."

Aunt Beatrice tried to smile again, but her swollen chin and cut lip made it impossible. "Perfect. You are a quick learner. I knew I did the right thing in sending for you. I should have done it two days ago. Now, who are the Terrible Threesome?"

"Chandler Prestwick, the earl of Dunraven; Andrew Terwillger, the earl of Dugdale; and John Wickenham-Thickenham-Fines, the earl of Chatwin. They have been inseparable friends since Oxford."

"Splendid. The ton simply thrives on anything about those three bachelors. There are many others, of course, but none more popular with Society. So unusual, too. All three of the gentlemen lost their fathers and became earls at a young age. Perhaps that is why they are such delicious rogues and easy targets for gossip." Her lids drooped. "I do hope Emery hurries. My medicine is making me sleepy, and I must introduce you."

"Would you like me to fluff your pillows?" Millicent started to reach for the pillows, but Hamlet's head shot up in warning and she stopped.

"No, dearie. I find that no movement is best. Oh, and remember, anything you hear about the Mad Ton Thief is noteworthy. The ton and all of London are simply in a passion wanting news and information about that criminal. The thief robbed Lord Dunraven's house two nights ago." She made an attempt at a smile. "I'm sure that put his lordship in a dither. You must try to find out something about that so we can mention it again in the column. I do hope Emery returns soon with—Oh, here they are."

Hamlet stood on his short, feathered legs and barked as Millicent watched the viscount and viscountess enter the room.

"Don't make such a fuss, Hamlet," her aunt cooed to the little dog. "Be polite. You're acting like you've never seen the viscount and his lady before." Hamlet trotted up to Beatrice's uninjured side. She patted his head affectionately and he curled down beside her.

Lord and Lady Heathecoute walked directly to the foot of Lady Beatrice's bed, but no closer, and greeted her warmly. Obviously, they knew of Hamlet's protectiveness of his mistress.

The viscount was tall and lanky, but superbly dressed. His graying tufts of hair were thin and cut fashionably short. He held his chin at such an elevated level and his neckcloth was tied so high, Millicent was certain his back must be in a continuous strain.

She was surprised to find his wife was as tall as the viscount. Few women could boast such a height or such a girth. The viscountess was more than a little plump. Her rounded face was flat but pretty and attractively framed by a row of tight dark curls. She wore a green high-waisted gown that hid most of her bulk and was becoming on her large frame.

"May I present Viscount Heathecoute."

Millicent curtsied when the viscount turned to her. "It's my pleasure, Lord Heathecoute."

"Delighted to meet you," he said as stiffly as he carried himself.

"And Lady Heathecoute, who has been a dear friend these past few months," Beatrice said.

Millicent curtsied again. "How do you do, ma'am?"

"Splendid, my dear. Very splendid." Her voice was loud and throaty. Her widespread brown eyes looked Millicent over carefully. "I think the gown you have chosen for this evening is good for you, the touch of embroidery around the hem sends just the right touch of elegance. Not too elaborate to gain attention, but certainly adequate so that you won't be out of place among the ton." She looked back to Lady Beatrice. "She will be perfect for you."

"I'm glad you approve, and I'm indebted to you for watching after her for me."

Lady Heathecoute looked over at her husband and said, "We will take very good care of her, won't we, my lord?"

"Indeed, we shall." The viscount lowered his narrow light green eyes to look at Beatrice when he spoke to her, but his head remained erect. He seemed to have a pinched look to his face even when he was smiling. "The only thing you need to do is rest and get well."

"I know you will get on together. Millicent has such a pleasing disposition that she won't tire you." Beatrice cut her weary eyes around to Millicent. "They will make all the right introductions for you. Have no fear, and they will be there to assist you all evening."

"Thank you, Aunt. I shall be fine." Millicent was glad her voice sounded strong and confident, even though it was the exact opposite of how she felt.

"Excellent. And remember, dearie, young ladies like to

talk in the retiring room when they think no one is around, and at the supper table. You must not encourage a gentleman to become enamored of you. I hope you are clear on all this?"

"Yes, Aunt Beatrice."

"Good. Now go on to the parties while I sleep, and I will help you write the column when you return."

She followed the Heathecoutes out the door and down the staircase with unexpected excitement growing inside her. She tried to tamp it down, but it was impossible. She had always wanted to attend a ton party in London. She just never dreamed she'd be going as a gossip writer.

Millicent determined she wouldn't look at what she had to do as if she were spying on people concerning their personal lives. She wouldn't think about how her mother would feel if she ever found out Millicent had participated in this scheme.

She was going to look at this as if she were writing a general news column for *The Daily Reader*. She would find a way to make the column uplifting and never negative if she had any say about the final writings.

As she stepped out the front door an idea struck her that she was sure would be perfect. She would include a little Shakespeare in Lord Truefitt's column. Everyone loved the master storyteller. That should give a new dimension to the "Society's Daily Column."

Two

❧

"Modest doubt is called the beacon of the wise"—just ask any of the Runners of Bow Street. No one is escaping their questioning as they search for the Mad Ton Thief. Dukes, earls and marquesses are being interrogated like common footpads in the mad dash to catch the elusive thief.

Lord Truefitt
Society's Daily Column

IT WAS LATE in the evening and the large room was not only crowded, it was hot and stuffy with people talking in groups, laughing out loud, and whispering in secret. Millicent had been to many parties where she lived in Nottinghamshire, but she had never been to a party as grand as this. The opulence of the town house, with its crystal chandeliers, gilt fretwork and carved moldings, was magnificent. Numerous candelabra threw golden shafts of light onto the elegant stairs.

The elaborate trimming and decorations on the colorful

clothing the people wore took Millicent's breath away. She had never seen so much lace, so many feathers and such large jewels in all her life. The buffet table had been set for a feast. Beautifully arranged silver dishes were heavy with fish, lamb, fowl and vegetables and fruits of every color and season. The punch and champagne flowed without hindrance.

So this is how members of London High Society live? Millicent was awed.

The first two hours passed quickly. The Heathecoutes had been wonderful in seeing that she was introduced to the proper people at the soirée. Some of the ladies she met eyed her with reserve while others were quite warm and friendly. She had been introduced to five young men and all of them had immediately asked to sign her dance card. She had already danced with three of them.

True to her word Lady Heathecoute had not let Millicent out of her sight except to dance. Even then, Millicent was certain the woman watched her. The viscountess had remained lovely to Millicent all evening, and she couldn't help but wonder if Aunt Beatrice was wrong in thinking the lady had wanted to take over writing the tittle-tattle. Millicent had not seen a hint of envy.

Millicent's mind whirled with all the people she'd seen and met. There was no way she could remember all the names and titles she'd heard until she got home. She would have to make some notes. In order to do that she needed a few moments to herself. She remembered seeing a narrow corridor that seemed to go unnoticed by the people who passed the ballroom on their way to supper. That should be the perfect hideaway for a few minutes alone.

She quickly found the doorway and hurried down the passage, which was dimly lit by a single low-burning wall lamp. Chests, chairs and tables lined each side of the walls, making it barely possible for one person to maneuver down its length. The stagnant scents of dust, wax and burned oil tickled her nose. No doubt the furniture had been moved to the hallway to make standing room for the guests.

Little more than halfway down the corridor she saw a large porcelain compote positioned by a tall brass candle stand, and she hurried to hide between the two. Luckily, that put her almost directly under the light.

She quickly untied the ribbon of her dance card and took it off her wrist. Then, using as short abbreviations as she dared, she wrote on the back of the card with the small pencil attached to the ribbon.

Lady H. has eye on Lord Greenfield. Lord Dugdale looking make match this Season. Miss B-well will marry a Terrible Threesome, doesn't care which. Miss Chipping, unhappy with match father made would rather run away than marry elderly earl.

A shadow fell across Millicent's paper. Engrossed with her writing, she paid it no mind and adjusted the paper into the pale yellow light again. Within a moment or two, the shadow fell on her card again. Too preoccupied with her writing to look into what caused the light to fade, she turned again toward the brightness. The third time the paper went dark she took notice and looked up with a grimace of annoyance.

Her gaze first landed on a wide chest and straight shoulders covered by a crisp, white shirt that was outlined with a cream-colored brocade waistcoat, and a black evening jacket, all topped off with a perfectly tied neckcloth. The expensive material and fine cut of his clothing told her

that the man standing in front of her was no ordinary
gentleman.

So much for thinking I was concealed by the furniture.

Her gaze slowly rose past a strong-looking, cleanly
shaved chin, glided over a smooth, slightly square jawline
to lips that were so masculine and so close to her own
that her heartbeat faltered, then quickened again. She held
her breath for a moment before continuing her journey
across the narrow bridge of his nose and the well-defined
shape of his cheekbones. At last she looked into eyes so
blue she wanted to melt into them.

Thick, dark blond hair was cropped short over his ears
but fell longer at his nape. He stood perfect in stature and
impeccable in dress, letting her study him. And she did,
without guilt or shame. He was a magnificent-looking
man who, without saying a word, spoke of power, privilege and wealth.

The sharpened lead in her pencil snapped under the
pressure from her fingers.

A knowing grin slowly made its way across his manly
lips, intriguing her so she couldn't take her eyes off them.
In the depth of her abdomen a quickening started and
shuddered all the way up to her breasts and lingered there
before moving on to her throat, tightening it. Millicent
was quite sure she had never felt this way before.

He watched her, and although not one word had been
spoken between them, she sensed he knew she was not
only startled by his arrival, but was attracted to him.

With his full lips crooked roguishly into a charming
grin, she watched his gaze brush down her face and skim
over her breasts and waist before returning to lock on her
eyes. This was no shy gentleman standing so close to her
that if she lifted her arm, she could touch him.

The narrow hallway suddenly grew hotter.

Millicent took a deep breath. She must shake off her unsettling reaction to this man. She was drawn by his confidence and the ease with which he perused her. This susceptibility was the very thing her aunt had warned her against. She had to deny his strong appeal and behave toward him with the same indifference she had employed with the other gentlemen she had met during the evening.

Feeling calmer and more in control, she confidently asked, "May I help you, sir?"

"Pardon me." He bowed slightly. "I was passing by and happened to see you standing in here. I wanted to make sure you are all right."

Unlike her usual sensible self, she wondered what she should say. When she looked into his eyes, an excited, tingling sensation washed over her. When she glanced at his lips, she wanted to trace their sculpted shape with the tips of her fingers. When she stared at his chest, she wondered how it would feel to press her cheek gently against the expensive fabric of his coat and savor the warmth and strength of power in his shoulder.

But denying those wayward thoughts and using her most prim voice she said, "I'm quite well indeed, thank you."

"Have you lost your way?"

"Of course not, sir. I know exactly where I am."

"Do you often retreat to such out of the way places when a guest at house parties?"

Millicent's gaze darted around the tight space they were in, acutely aware of the cramped area they occupied and just how close he stood to her. This was not a good situation for her to be in at her first soirée.

"I suspect I retreat no more often than you happen to pass by these out of the way places, sir."

An amused light glinted in his eyes, and he nodded his approval of her answer.

"If I may be so bold as to ask, what exactly is it you are doing back here in this area of the house?"

"Oh, making notes." The instant she said it she realized that was the wrong thing to say. What had made her blurt that out without thinking? "That is to say I was writing thank-you notes," she said, trying to clarify her answer, but knew the damage had been done.

His eyes studied her face for a moment before they lowered to the card and pencil she held in her gloved hand. His lips twitched with a half grin, half smile. "Is this the new rage? Writing thank-you notes on the back of a dance card?"

He was not helping her cause. "Oh, no. I'm sure it must look that way. But you see, I meant to say, I'm only making notes of things I want to include when I write them. I didn't get all my thank-you letters finished today, and I was trying to catch up."

She stopped, realizing she was making the matter worse, not better. Ordinarily, Millicent was not one to ramble, babble or stutter incoherently, but this man had her behaving like a drunk ninny.

She looked down at her broken pencil lead and wondered where she could find another. All the names her aunt had given her were mixing with the names of people she had met over the course of the evening. She would be completely useless to her aunt without notes.

Millicent noticed that the gentleman's gaze was on her dance card and broken pencil, too. Angels above! She opened the fancy-laced reticule that dangled from the drawstring handle on her wrist and slipped the card and pencil inside with the unused spectacles before continuing.

She wasn't sure there was any way to keep him from thinking she was an imbecile, but she had to try. "I do believe you startled me so that I wasn't thinking properly."

"That wasn't my intention."

"I'm sure. Let me say, I was writing down ideas for the thank-you notes that I will write tomorrow, when I have proper paper, quill and ink." That sounded better.

He reached into the pocket of his frock and extended to her a stubby pencil.

She cleared her throat and said, "Oh, no, I couldn't take your writing instrument."

"You must allow me to do this. After all, it was my fault the lead broke in yours."

"What do you mean by it was your fault?"

"For startling you."

"Yes, of course. But no, I don't need it. As you can see, I've finished writing and have put my notes away."

He continued to hold the pencil out to her. Worse yet, he continued that knowing grin that should have irritated her but instead, thoroughly intrigued her. Heavens, could he possibly know that she had been completely enchanted by him?

Millicent tried to take a step back but was brought up short by the wall.

"I insist," he stated again.

In an effort to hurry him along, she kept her voice level and said, "All right. Thank you."

She took the pencil, and as she did his fingers boldly caressed the inside of her palm. Even through her gloves and his a shiver of awareness shuddered inside her. Her breath snatched in her throat. The touch was no innocent, accidental brushing of her hand. He had orchestrated it so that she would be certain it was a brash, deliberate act and not an unintentional one.

Millicent did the only thing a proper young lady should do. She pretended not to notice the contact and gave him the benefit of the doubt. She was, however, truly grateful to get the pencil so she could continue making her notes. Not that this man would ever know that.

Eager to change the subject, she quickly said, "Now that I've given my perfectly reasonable explanation for being in this hallway, tell me what brought you to this secluded section of the house."

He took his time in responding to her, and when he did, it was with a question of his own. "Were you forthright in your answer to me or did you color the truth a little?"

His question was direct and the implication was clear, so she answered honestly. "If I colored it at all, sir, rest assured it was only with a hint of shading and not with a painter's heavy brush."

His smile deepened, lightened. "I thought as much and to answer your question with the same dash of shading, I was looking for someone. I thought I saw a person turn down this hallway. Obviously, that was you."

"Yes, it must have been me for there are no others here that I am aware of."

He leaned forward just a fraction and lowered his voice as he said, "You're the only one I see."

No doubt as handsome as the gentleman was he had planned to have an assignation with a young lady. Millicent had heard that secret liaisons were quite common among members of the ton. But she couldn't afford being caught having one. Either the lady hadn't arrived or she had seen Millicent and hurried away. In either case, Millicent did not need to be seen in the dim hallway with a dapper gentleman. That would surely bring the attention her aunt insisted she avoid.

"Well, no doubt she will be along shortly, so if you will excuse me, I'll take my leave so you can have the privacy you desire."

In a gentle, fluid movement he placed his hand on the candle stand, preventing her from passing. His head dipped lower, bringing his face even closer to her eyes, her lips, her nose. They were so confined she felt his warm breath, heard his shallow breathing and caught the masculine scent of him.

This time, his forward behavior should have frightened her or at the very least upset her, but it didn't. He tantalized her in a way that no man ever had. In another time or place she would have been eager to match wits with his mischievous deportment, but here in London, doing her aunt's work, she could not.

In a low-pitched voice that sounded far too intimate, he smiled ruefully and asked, "What makes you think I was looking for a lady?"

Feeling no need to cower or back away, Millicent looked up into his unbelievably blue eyes. She didn't even hint at a blink as she said in a far too sensible voice, "You are quite handsome, sir, it would be a shame if you were looking to meet secretly with a man."

For a moment surprise gleamed in his eyes, then he threw back his head and laughed softly, genuinely. It was a wonderful, infectious sound that made him even more charming, if that were possible.

"Indeed, it would."

Millicent found herself smiling at him, knowing she would like to continue the conversation with him, but she'd already stepped too far over the line of propriety in even speaking to a gentleman who hadn't been properly introduced to her. And his motives were highly suspect because in the short time they had stood there, he'd crossed the lines of gentlemanly behavior more than once.

"I've never seen you before," he said, "yet, you don't look like—" He paused abruptly as if catching himself before saying something he shouldn't say.

"I don't look young enough for this to be my coming-out year," she finished for him. "And I am not, sir, but you are correct in that you haven't seen me before. This is my first visit to London."

"Then I feel free to say that you are far more beautiful and discerning than any girl fresh out for her first year in Society."

"I can see you are skilled at flattery, sir."

"You wound me. I speak the truth. Flattery is what you bestowed on me."

Oh no. I was being honest. He is by far the most handsome man I have ever met.

Quickly she said, "Tell me, will you be able to obtain another?"

His expression questioned her before he asked, "Another lady?"

Millicent was pleased to give him a knowing smile and held up his pencil in front of his eyes. "I would hate for you to miss the next promenade because you couldn't sign a dance card."

He nodded and gave her a grudging smile. "I think I can find another."

"In that case, perhaps now, if you will excuse me, I believe I promised a gentleman the next dance."

His gaze swept over her face once again before he placed his open gloved hand to his lips. He kissed his palm then slowly blew toward her.

An unexpected thrill of desire rushed through her. She

couldn't have been more surprised if his lips had actually brushed hers.

Millicent gasped.

Keeping an indulgent gaze on her face, he slowly, reluctantly removed his arm, freeing her.

Millicent hesitated for a moment longer than she should have, then she darted past him.

She didn't look back. Oh, but how she wanted to.

Three

"To be, or not to be, that is the question" on everyone's mind as Miss Elizabeth Donaldson declines another marriage proposal, and Lord Dunraven loses patience with the uninspired efforts of the Bow Street Runners. The earl declares he will find the Mad Ton Thief himself and recover the missing Dunraven raven.

Lord Truefitt
Society's Daily Column

CHANDLER PRESTWICK, THE earl of Dunraven, sat at a table in White's furious over what he'd just read. He wadded the evening paper with a jerk and a curse.

"Damned gossips," he muttered aloud. Must they put his name in every column!

Tossing the newspaper aside, he picked up his drink and looked at the amber-colored brandy that covered the bottom of his glass, and as easily as night slipped into day, he thought of the woman he'd met last night.

The liquor was the color of *her* eyes. They were the

first thing he'd noticed about her when she faced him. Stunning, intriguing, golden brown eyes that were full of dancing lights. He had startled her, but only for a moment. She'd recovered quickly and looked him over carefully, fully, before letting her gaze settle on his face.

Who was she? He was sure he had never seen her before and just as sure he wanted to see her again. She was lovely with trim, slightly arched brows the same flaxen color of her thick, neatly arranged hair. The style was too tight and severe for her, but it didn't take away from her classical beauty. Her lips were full, exquisitely and temptingly shaped, and the color of a dusky pink flower.

He remembered thinking she was trying to play down her loveliness, and he couldn't help but wonder why. Most young ladies in High Society went to great lengths to enhance their beauty.

The gentle allure in her face wasn't the only thing that drew him, or the inviting curves of her womanly body. He was charmed by how quickly she'd regained her confidence and her sharp wit. Hellfire, he was drawn to everything about her. He even approved of the way she'd handled herself in a most inappropriate situation. Proper but not stiff, excited but not emotional.

And she was daring, too. Yes, uncommonly bold to remain in his presence and talk to him so long when it was obvious she was a young lady of quality. Most of the gentlewomen of the ton would never have spoken to him without benefit of proper introduction for fear of their reputations being ruined beyond repair. She had no such compunction. That was a very good indication she had no idea who he was.

Some young ladies tried to gain his attention by fluttering their lashes or fans, dropping their handkerchiefs or talking in a voice so soft and low he could hardly hear them. But this enchanting lady was so confident in herself that she was willing not only to talk to him but to challenge him with her wit. He felt certain she wasn't in any way trying to gain his attention, but that is exactly what she had done.

Chandler knew she liked his looks by her bold appraisal of him before she'd been confident enough to tell him she thought he was handsome. She had sent heat flashing through him like no other woman had. He could tell by her approving expression when her gaze skimmed his face that she appreciated his features. Chandler smiled to himself, remembering how it had pleased him and astonished him at the same time. Who was she? And was she the kind of lady he had been looking for to share his life?

Chandler shook his head, not ready for where his thoughts had taken him. It was way too soon to start asking himself questions like that about a lady he didn't even know by name. He would admit there had been too many things to like about her, but that was as far as he wanted to go with that idea.

After they had parted, he noticed her more than once during the remainder of the evening. She appeared poised and self-assured when she talked with people but not forward. He wasn't sure he wanted to admit even to himself that he'd actually been watching her.

Now here he was sitting at White's, waiting for his friend and thinking about her when he should have been concentrating on the damned thief who had stolen the raven. The solid gold bird had come from the tomb of an Egyptian pharoah and had been a part of the house since the Dunraven estate was built, close to one hundred years ago. He refused to be known throughout all time as the earl who had lost the most precious family heirloom.

Chandler swirled the brandy in the glass and forced

himself to shake thoughts of the young lady who had caught his attention so effortlessly during the evening— for now. He would see her again. If she didn't see to it they were introduced in the next night or two, he would. He would find out who she was. He'd make sure of that.

He leaned his head back and relaxed in his comfortable high-backed chair. The sounds of the club surrounded him—muted conversations, loud laughter and the clank of heavy glass hitting wooden tabletops. He listened to the noise for a moment before he shut it out and let his mind drift back to the events in his life that had led to the theft of the raven.

Chandler had inherited the title earl of Dunraven at age fifteen. As head of his family, he took his position seriously and finished his education at the top of his class. He quickly became a good steward of the vast holdings his father had left him and had added to his wealth each year.

Over his mother's strident objections he decided to see his three younger sisters properly married before he considered marriage for himself. He contented himself with enjoying his ever-changing mistresses.

After his youngest sister had married, his mother told him he could wait no longer. He must marry and produce an heir to ensure the title. Since that time, Chandler had resisted all her attempts to marry him off to a suitable young lady.

Chandler found that his first complete year without a sister to escort to ton parties and to Almack's was like sprouting the wings of an eagle. With his two good friends from Oxford, John Whickenham-Thickenham-Fines and Andrew Terwillger, he drank too much, gambled too often on cards and horses and dallied regularly with more than one mistress at a time.

That he was a constant feature in the gossip columns irritated him. Most of the information written about him and the other two members of the Terrible Threesome, as the tiddle-tattle liked to refer to Chandler and his friends, was untrue. Chandler had never bothered to dispute any of the absurd claims until about a year ago when he was very nearly brought to dueling over a story published in one of the columns.

There was nothing he would like better than to know the identity of the person who spied on unsuspecting people and wrote those wretched things.

He couldn't deny the debauchery of his late youth and his enjoyment of it, free from responsibilities, but recently his carefree lifestyle had lost its appeal. He had slowly, confidently let go of his wild days.

Chandler had finally admitted to himself, but to no one else, that his mother was right. It was time for him to take a wife and beget a son to carry on the Dunraven title.

He didn't want his friends to know he was searching for a bride. They would badger him without mercy, and the matchmaking mamas would be lining up to parade their innocent daughters before him. No, he had long ago realized he had no desire for a giddy girl right out of the schoolroom.

Chandler's mother had not held a party in their town house since his youngest sister married. This year she had broken her vow of staying in Kent and had hosted one of the first parties of the Season, hoping to encourage her son to pursue thoughts of a wife.

The morning after the party Chandler was stunned and outraged when his housekeeper had informed him that the Mad Ton Thief, as the London papers had dubbed the robber, had stolen his family's priceless heirloom, the golden raven, from its place of privilege on the tall mantel in Chandler's library.

Thoughts of finding a wife had vanished. His mother had announced she was taking up residence at their home in Kent, and she intended to remain there until he became serious about choosing a wife.

He was serious about finding a wife. It just wouldn't consume him until he caught the Mad Ton Thief and reclaimed the golden raven for his family before it was sold or melted down.

The sound of billiard balls smacking together broke Chandler from his reverie. He sipped his drink. The only thing his mother's party had done was allow the Mad Ton Thief entrance into his home to rob him. He had not seen one woman, innocent or widow, who caught his eye. No lady had enchanted him like the young lady last night since his brief but fervid affair with the beautiful Lady Lambsbeth.

As the tiddle-tattle had indicated, he was damned unhappy about his unsuccessful meeting with Mr. Percy Doulton of the Bow Street's elite Thief Takers, who were investigating the rash of thefts in London's finest homes. But how had the scandal writers known that?

Doulton was Bow Street's number-one member of Thief Takers and so far he and his Runners had made no headway in finding the Mad Ton Thief. All they had succeeded in doing was making most of the members of the ton feel as if they were under suspicion by inappropriate and inane questions about the stolen artwork and jewels.

Chandler agreed that it was most peculiar there had been a theft at three different homes and that not one person had admitted seeing anyone who remotely looked suspicious. But as he reminded Doulton, one seldom saw a pickpocket nab a man's coinpurse.

Criminals were skilled at such behavior. The strange and difficult thing was that almost all the guests who attended the parties were known to someone in Society. Few, if any, strangers attended the private parties of the Season. That meant there was a robber among them passing himself off as a gentleman.

"Good. You've ordered a bottle. But what's this? Only one glass? Did you forget I was joining you? How quickly we neglect our friends."

Chandler looked up into the dark brown eyes of his longtime friend John Whickenham-Thickenham-Fines, better known in Town as Lord Chatwin. Fines was a tall, handsome fellow with thick hair as dark as his eyes. Like Chandler, his friend was broad in the chest and shoulders. He carried himself with just the right amount of self-importance, and he had a smile that made all the ladies swoon.

"Actually, you are so late I thought you had decided not to show. I was just thinking about calling it a night."

"Sorry to be delayed."

"No harm done," Chandler said. "I thought you must still be dallying—I mean dancing with the young ladies. There seem to be more of them this year."

Like Chandler and Andrew, Fines worked at seeing how many of the coming-out ladies he could convince to take a forbidden walk in the garden with him. No matter how bad the Threesome's reputation got, there were always one or two new ladies each Season who couldn't resist them.

"You must be deep into your cups, man. It's near dawn. All the parties were over hours ago. I truly thought you'd be long gone but had to check just in case you were here, and it's a good thing I did."

Fines looked around the room, spotted a waiter and

motioned for a glass before he plopped down in the seat opposite Chandler and made an attempt to loosen his neckcloth.

Chandler shifted in his chair and looked around the dimly lit room. Most of the tables in the taproom were empty. No doubt the gaming rooms would have thinned as well by this hour, with only the stout gamblers and drinkers around to see the morning break.

"Well, I didn't realize I'd been here that long, but perhaps I have."

"Sounds to me like you have been woolgathering."

Fines knew him too well, and Chandler wasn't sure he was as pleased about that as he once was. "Don't make me sound as if I'm in my dotage."

"A year ago, I would have found you gambling at a table, not sitting drinking here by yourself."

"I was merely relaxing with my drink. So tell me, where have you been while I've been patiently waiting?"

"Impatiently is more like it, ol' chap. Don't try to fool me. I know you too well." He cleared his throat and sniffed. "I just came from Anne's. Sorry to keep you, but I was in the mood and didn't want to lose it, you know."

Chandler felt a twinge of envy. He hadn't felt in the *mood* to see his mistress lately, which was why he had dismissed her with a considerable sum not more than a month ago. In years past he would have been into another relationship before the day ended, but he was restless and felt he was looking for something more or different.

"So tell me, was there a jewel you danced with this evening who put you in a strain to see Anne?"

"All of them." He laughed. "You know how I love beautiful ladies, and I would take every one of them to my bed if I could."

"You love all women, Fines, not just the beautiful ones."

"True. I rather like changing my affections from one lady to another. It would be positively tiresome to settle on one, don't you think?"

Tiresome to settle on one lady? Chandler used to think so, too, but now he planned to do just that after he apprehended the thief.

"Hmm. It's not something you are trying to accomplish, is it?"

"Damn, no, Dunraven. Don't startle me this early in the morning. I'm not up to it. Me make a match?" He shook his head. "The devil take me if I do." Fines picked up the bottle of brandy and poured a generous amount into the glass that had been set before him.

Chandler laughed. "Nothing would please me more than seeing a young lady sweep your legs right out from under you and land you prone at her feet."

Fines grimaced. "What a horrible thought. I'd just as soon grovel at the king's feet. No doubt Andrew put such a foolish notion in your head. Just yesterday he said to me that one of us should start acting respectable before Society gives up on us and no longer seeks us out for their daughters. Can you believe such poppycock?"

"He mentioned something similar to me, but I doubt that will happen."

"So true." Fines sipped his drink. "It's a damn good thing titles and money wash away a lot of past bad deeds. No doubt, the young ladies will be standing in line with their dowries ready when we give the signal."

Realizing he wasn't up to Fines's line of banter tonight, Chandler drained his glass. "I think I'm going to give up the night."

"I just got here," his friend complained. "And where is Andrew, the devil?"

"No doubt he has given up the night as well. As you said, it's almost dawn."

"You're still depressed about the missing raven, I gather."

Chandler forced his face not to betray him with anger or frustration. "Not so much," he lied.

"Truly?"

Leave it to Fines to press the matter. "I feel sure I'll find the man who is stealing sooner or later."

"Yes, but later could very well be too late for you. It's rather easy to melt down gold into an unrecognizable shape, isn't it? And then the raven would be gone forever."

Chandler gritted his teeth before saying, "How nice of you to remind me of that."

"Facts are facts, Dunraven, and can't be denied." He drank from his glass rather than sip and savor the fine brandy. "Actually, it might already have been done."

"You really know how to lift a man's spirits."

"There is one good thing. It's not a piece that could be easily sold to a trader or collector. Too recognizable."

"That's true."

"They'd have to melt it."

"Damnation, Fines, enough of it."

"I just don't want you having false hopes."

"Certainly no chance of that with you around."

"How long has the blasted thing been in the family anyway? Must be more than a hundred years or so."

Fines never did know when to quit. Chandler pushed back from the table and rose from his chair. He said, "Long enough that I'm going to do everything in my power to find the person who took it and recover it."

"Don't go off in a huff," Fines said. "I haven't finished my drink."

"But I have."

"I can see you're ill-tempered because I went to see Anne and kept you waiting until all hours."

Chandler smiled. "I'd never begrudge friend or foe a rendezvous with his mistress. You know that. I do, however, have an appointment early in the afternoon."

"Speaking of Anne and mistresses, have you found a new one yet?"

"No, still looking."

Chandler realized that he had lied again. He wasn't looking for a mistress, but he didn't want to explain his business to Fines. He wasn't exactly sure when it had happened, but he was beyond sharing all his thoughts and deeds with his friends.

"You always were the picky one, Dunraven."

"No, Fines, it's that you have never shown much discretion."

"There's never been a reason to. I think it best to sample them all. Short, tall, thin, young and older." Fines smiled wickedly at Chandler. "They're all delicious in different ways. I'll let you know if I hear of anyone who is available."

The last thing Chandler wanted was his friend's help in finding a mistress, but he answered, "Do that," before he walked away.

"IT IS THE best and the worst Season for London Society. The ton flourishes with the indulgence of elegant parties while reeling in shock from having a mad thief in its midst."

"Heaven have mercy, Millicent, you do try me. Why, in heaven's name, would you think our readers would appreciate an opening like that?" Beatrice sighed heavily and slowly brushed Hamlet's coat.

Millicent had no idea how her aunt could be so coherent at this time of the morning. It was dawn and here they were in her aunt's bedroom with lamps turned high, putting the finishing touches to Lord Truefitt's column so that it could appear in the afternoon paper. Millicent thought her opening had been a perfect depiction of the events of the Season.

It would be best for her to cajole her aunt and not try to upset her. Millicent would tweak the writings before putting them in an envelope to be taken to the address where her aunt dropped off the column each morning.

"Truly, Aunt, don't get upset. Remember it concerns Hamlet when you fret. I forgot that you said the readers of the gossip sheets don't like too much reality in the columns. Not to worry, I'll change it."

"Thank goodness." She patted Hamlet's head affectionately and he licked her hand noisily. "You're here to help me keep my column, not see to it that I lose it. Worst of times, indeed! We must write only what our readers want to read. They don't refer to them as scandal sheets because we write about weather and politics."

"I understand. I won't forget again, and I'm pleased you didn't have a problem with the line from Shakespeare that I added at the last minute."

Lady Beatrice seemed to consider her answer before saying, "No, I must admit that it didn't bother me. In fact, I thought it rather clever. I've always enjoyed his writings. Especially the sonnets. That's why I've sent you so many copies of his work over the years. But, you should have obtained my permission first."

Millicent took the reprimand silently.

"The wording seemed to fit what we wrote. I suppose it was all right, but you really must not add things like that, dearie, after we have finished a column, without consulting with me first."

"I'll remember that."

"See that you do."

"Now, you are certain you heard Lord Dunraven is personally looking for the Mad Ton Thief."

"Yes. Although I didn't meet any of the Terrible Threesome earls tonight. There was plenty of talk about them at both parties we attended."

"There always is, and I'm sure you will meet them soon enough. Most evenings they leave early to gamble or go to private parties where not even I can gain entrance. Listen to anything they have to say, but do not let any of them talk you into agreeing to a private meeting with them."

"Oh, I wouldn't, Aunt. You can trust me on that," she said, feeling somewhat guilty, since she'd just this evening been alone with a handsome gentleman. She must make sure that didn't happen again.

"I'm sure you will behave splendidly, dearie. But it is interesting that Lord Dugdale might be thinking about settling down and making a match. I do wish I could be out and about myself. I know just the questions to ask that wouldn't raise suspicions."

"I was careful."

"I know. It's always such a delight to hear what is going on with the earls."

"From what I heard, Aunt Beatrice, it's clear Lord Dugdale is paying more attention to the young ladies at the parties this year and staying later for dancing at the balls."

"Oh, it would be so delicious to have one of them finally wed. Maybe now that the earls are reaching their thirties they are finally growing up. But it will be such a shame to lose them. They've been splendid to write about all these years, but not a person among the ton will care a pence about them once they are married."

Millicent watched her aunt's expression soften as she talked about her work. "You seem to actually enjoy what you do," Millicent said.

"Dearie, I do. I do. I can't imagine what it would be like not to have my column to write. It's my life. Now, did anything else interesting happen?"

Millicent immediately thought of the gentleman she'd met in the hallway in an unused section of the house. She had been drawn to him in a way that excited her. She had never felt the least brazen in her life until she looked into his eyes. He was the only gentleman she had met since coming to London whom she would like to talk to again.

She had been enchanted by his unbelievably blue eyes, the tilt of his head and the way his friendly, disarming grin fascinated her. She couldn't forget the way her skin prickled when his unveiled gaze swept up and down her with appreciation. And then offering her his pencil before letting her go.

But, was he a gentleman or a rogue?

Millicent mentally shook herself. What was she doing daydreaming about him? She was at the parties to do a job for her aunt, not to get starry-eyed over a courtly rogue who dared to be so forward as to detain her, then caress her hand and blow her a kiss so tantalizing she could almost feel its softness land against her cheek. Besides, he could be a married scoundrel for all she knew.

Several handsome young gentlemen in her village had

tried to persuade her to accept their marriage proposals, but Millicent was waiting until she met a man she wanted to be with every day for the rest of her life.

Millicent wondered if she could feel that way about the nameless gentleman she had met last night. Already she wanted to see him again. She wanted to know if she would have that same sensuous experience of breathless wonder when she looked into his eyes the second time.

Her father had provided well for her and she had no need to marry for financial security. She wanted to marry for love.

But, Aunt Beatrice had made it clear that she was here to do an assignment. If she enjoyed a little of the Season along the way, so be it, but that was not her primary responsibility. Still, Millicent couldn't help but think about the upcoming evening and look forward to it with a very different attitude than she had the previous evening of engagements.

"Come, come, dearest, don't take so long over your thinking. We must finish this before I sleep. Did you hear anything else that we need to write about?"

"No, nothing other than what I've already told you. I'm sure I'll do better tonight."

"It does take a certain aptitude to listen to conversations and glean what is good gossip and what is mere talk, not worthy of print. Now, don't hurry with your rewriting of this so there will be no mistakes in the column, and see that Phillips delivers the package on time."

"Consider it done."

"Splendid." Beatrice's eyes closed. "Now leave me, Millicent. I need to rest." Her eyes popped open. "Don't forget to seal the paper with Truefitt's crest."

"I'll take care of everything," Millicent said softly, wishing she could bend down and place a tender kiss on her aunt's forehead, but with Hamlet curled beside his mistress that was not going to happen.

"Go on to sleep, Aunt Beatrice, and dream of pleasant things. All will be well."

Millicent tiptoed out of the room and softly closed her aunt's door. She walked down the shadowed hallway to her bedroom and, after sending her maid, Glenda, downstairs for tea, Millicent shut herself inside. She turned up the lamp on the small desk that had been put in the room for her and sat down to start the painfully slow work of rewriting the article, making all the corrections her aunt had suggested, thankful that the gossip column wasn't very long.

She picked up the quill and dipped it into the ink jar, but the sharpened nib didn't touch the vellum before she replaced it on the stand. Instead, she picked up her reticule and opened it. She shook the contents down onto the desk: handkerchief, spectacles, dance card, a satin ribbon and two pencils.

Her stomach quickened when she saw the pencil the intriguing gentleman had insisted she accept. She picked it up and squeezed it in her fist, then slowly she opened her hand and rolled it back and forth between her fingers. An unexpected pleasure filled her.

She remembered how she had felt when he'd deliberately let his fingertips brush across the inside of her gloved hand, soft but firm enough she would know he'd stepped outside the boundary of propriety. What daring. He had no idea how she would react, yet he took the chance she wouldn't scream for help or box his ears. And he was right. Surely the man was an unscrupulous rake to be so forward to a lady he had never been introduced to.

As a proper young lady, she should have given him a snub for such ill-mannered behavior, but that thought had never entered her mind. And as a proper young lady, she should never allow herself to write such things as tittle-tattle. Perhaps she should feel heavy with guilt for what she was doing, but for some reason that emotion hadn't entered her thoughts either.

Millicent shook her head. She must banish the stranger from her mind. No doubt he had deliberately set out to make himself unforgettable so she would wonder who he was and seek him out so that appropriate introductions could be made. She wouldn't allow herself to think about him again. She had too much work to do and very little time.

She picked up the quill again determined to do her work. She wrote *What's in a name?* before her mind betrayed her and turned to dreamy blue eyes, a knowing smile and a forbidden kiss blown across the air.

Four

꧁꧂

"What's in a name? That which we call a rose
by any other name would smell as sweet," but
not according to Miss Pennington. She was
overheard saying she could never marry a
man named Longnecker. One wonders what
the eligible marquess had to say about that.

Lord Truefitt
Society's Daily Column

CHANDLER WATCHED HER. Dancing. Gliding across the
floor with ease through the steps, the turns and twirls. She
was a natural beauty, slim with delicate bone structure, a
small waist and slightly rounded hips.

The neckline of her flowing gossamer gown was higher
than most fashions of the day and showed only a mere
hint of the swell of breasts which lay beneath her clothing.
That disappointed him because he very much wanted to
see that gentle swell. Again, he had the feeling she was
deliberately trying not to draw attention to her beauty by
wearing severe hairstyles and modest clothing.

Chandler had noticed more about her than he should have, but something about her beckoned him. He desired to get closer to her and see her mesmerizing golden brown eyes again, which he had decided were really a glimmering shade of dark, speckled amber. He wanted to engage her in conversation again, but for now he was content to ponder and watch her.

She was polite to her dance partner but not overly so. She smiled at him, but it wasn't the encouraging smile of a young lady who wanted to gain the gentleman's attention. It seemed to be more of a "thank you for the dance" smile. That pleased him, too.

"Do you know who she is?"

Chandler turned to see that his friend Andrew Terwillger, who was more notoriously known throughout Society as Lord Dugdale, standing right beside him.

It bothered Chandler that Andrew had caught him watching *her,* and it bothered him that *she hadn't* noticed him observing her at all.

His friend's appearance reminded him he was supposed to be watching for suspicious-looking characters and following men who wandered off alone. That's how he happened upon the young lady last night. Chandler had little faith that the authorities in charge of finding the Mad Ton Thief would be successful. He felt it necessary to do some investigating on his own.

The thief was daring enough to have already stolen from three different homes. He had been so successful in stealing right out from under the eyes of the owners and guests, there was no reason to think he wouldn't continue to pilfer the homes where he was a welcomed guest. Chandler wanted to catch him, and to do that he had to watch the doorways for any man who might wander off alone.

"Haven't got the foggiest clue who she is," Chandler finally answered his friend. "Do you know?"

"Me? No, I haven't met her, but—" Andrew paused.

"But what?" Chandler was forced to ask, knowing that his friend wouldn't quit the subject until he did.

"After I noticed that you couldn't keep your eyes off her, I made an inquiry for you."

"For me?"

"Did I not just say that?" He grinned playfully. "I dare say you'd be damned perturbed at me right now if I'd asked about her for myself. Right?"

Chandler frowned and turned to his friend. "Surely, I wasn't being that transparent?"

"Only to me. I know you so well."

"Obviously, too well," Chandler grumbled under his breath while throwing a sly glance toward his friend. "Or perhaps, after all these years, I'm losing my touch."

"Let's pray it's not that. Possibly for the first time in your life you are actually interested in a lady of quality rather than a dutiful mistress."

"It would be a damn nuisance if that were true, wouldn't it?" Chandler said

"Damn nuisance, indeed."

"But it's nice to know I have a friend like you who is looking out for me, just in case I decide to turn from my wicked ways."

"You know you can depend on me, Dunraven. I've always been there for you, always will."

"That is a comfort, Andrew."

"I find that I'm looking the ladies over more carefully this Season, too."

Chandler's eyes strayed to the dance floor. "I believe you mentioned that."

"I passed thirty this year, you know. I guess it's time

to think about setting up a nursery. I wouldn't want to pass the title on to my brother's little hellion. My father would rise up out of his grave in objection."

Chandler smiled and nodded a greeting to a gentleman who passed by. "Your nephew is still a babe, isn't he?"

"Four, I think."

"He'll grow out of his fits of ill-temper."

"God help us all if he doesn't. I'm told by his father that no one can bear to be in the same room with the child but his mother."

"There is plenty of time for you to have an heir."

Andrew was shorter and slimmer than Chandler and his medium brown hair had started thinning on top. Recently Chandler had noticed that his friend's middle was getting pudgy, too, but he'd thought better of teasing him about it. Maybe Chandler should suggest they get back into fencing and riding like the devil was after them. None of them were as active as they used to be. It was as if a change had taken place over the past year or two without either of them realizing it.

"Tell me, Andrew, has any of this year's bevy of young ladies caught your eye?"

"They've all caught my attention at one time or another, Dunraven."

"Of course. You've now looked them all over carefully and narrowed the list, I presume?"

"Exactly." Andrew nodded and asked, "What do you think of Miss Bardwell?"

"Truthfully?"

A rueful smile lifted the corners of his lips and he sniffed quietly. "We don't know any other way to be with each other, do we, Dunraven?"

"I think not," Chandler said, but silently wondered.

That used to be so, but Chandler knew it wasn't anymore, at least for him. Recently, he was keeping things from his friends. He was becoming more evasive and private about his personal thoughts and life. He'd lost the desire to be with them day and night laughing, talking, drinking and gaming.

"Well, what do you think of Miss Bardwell?" Andrew asked again.

Chandler hesitated before saying, "Since you asked for honesty, I think her father's purse is bigger than her heart, and a January day would be warmer than her bed."

Andrew laughed. "It's no wonder we have gotten along so well together these past years. We think so much alike. She does remind one of a cold cod with her pale complexion, light blue eyes and blond hair. You know, according to the tittle-tattle, she's determined to capture one of us this Season."

"Be my guest," Chandler said, knowing it best not to make a further comment about the young lady. Andrew could be seriously considering her for a match. "And tell me, since when do you know what the gossips say?"

"I read them from time to time just to see if they still think I'm worth writing about, and so do you. Don't try to deny it."

"I read them in hopes there will come a day I won't find my name printed there."

"The day they stop writing about us will be when we're dead or married, and I'm sure they don't care which comes first. Better they talk about us than forget about us. They were rather vicious to you about Lady Lambsbeth and her husband, but since that time, it hasn't been so bad, has it?"

Chandler didn't want to go down the road that led to Lady Lambsbeth again so he took the conversation back to where it had started. "Don't worry, Andrew. More desirable young ladies than Miss Bardwell have tried to catch us and failed. Keep the faith."

"Hmm. There have been a few ladies over the years who have tried to entrap us. Some of them have been quite delightfully clever."

"Some have been beautiful."

"Some wealthy."

Chandler's eyebrows shot up. "Are you, by any chance, hinting that Miss Bardwell might have had reason to have made such a brash statement that she intended to marry one of us this Season?"

"Maybe. Maybe not, but I don't think there's anything wrong with a lady having more money than heart. After all, a good mistress can make up for the warmth that's lost in the marriage bed. That is what lovers are for, isn't it? An acceptable wife gives a man children, and a mistress gives him pleasure."

How had they become so cynical?

Somehow Chandler knew he didn't want what Andrew just described. "Maybe it works that way for a desperate man."

"Which neither of us are," Andrew added.

"And may we never be."

It was all the rage for members of the peerage to seek the arms of a mistress, but Chandler knew he didn't want another woman in his bed after he married. Although he wasn't going to admit that to anyone other than himself. And he certainly wasn't going to admit he was interested in taking a wife. It wouldn't be worth the raucous remarks he'd have to suffer. He was surprised Andrew was letting it be known that he might actually be pursuing the idea of making a match.

Chandler turned his attention back to the young lady

with the golden eyes. The dance had ended and she was being escorted off the crowded floor. He watched her until she was returned to Viscountess Heathecoute. No doubt the tall, buxom lady was her chaperone for the evening and quite possibly for the entire Season.

"What do you think about Miss Pennington?"

Preferable to Miss Bardwell.

Chandler looked back to Andrew. "She appears to be a favorite among the younger bachelors this Season. I hear she's enjoying the attention of all of them, accepting four and five calls in an afternoon."

"That many?"

"From what I hear, but we both know how unreliable gossip is." Chandler smiled ruefully at his friend. "I think she's already rejected two offers of a match, including Albert Longnecker."

"Yes, I heard. He didn't take kindly to her open rejection, and neither did his father. The duke was furious about what she said about his name."

"Only the gossips reported that, and I certainly don't believe everything that's written in them. You'll have to arrive at a party early in the evening to find an empty space on her dance card."

"I know." Andrew clapped Chandler on the back of his shoulder. "And I do believe my dance with her is coming up next."

He started to walk off, but Chandler stopped him by putting a hand to his upper arm. "Andrew, aren't you forgetting something?"

His friend rubbed his chin and gave a mock expression of deep thought. "No. I don't believe so."

"What did you find out about her?" He nodded toward the dance floor.

"Who?" Andrew asked with a fake expression of seriousness.

"You know who," Chandler said impatiently.

A wicked smile spread across Andrew's face. "Oh, yes. I almost forgot. We were talking about Miss Bardwell, right?"

Chandler's eyes narrowed. "Don't lead me, old friend. We've been together too many years for that."

"Damn shame. It would have been such fun." Andrew's smile turned mischievous. "At least now I know just how interested in her you are."

"You only know I asked about her."

"Twice." He held up two fingers as if Chandler couldn't hear him.

"You know nothing more than that."

"Then let me put you out of your misery. Viscount Healthecoute and his lady are her sponsors for the Season, and she is staying with Lady Beatrice, who I believe is ill at the moment. They aren't saying too much more about her except she's the niece of a friend. They felt she was deserving of a Season in London so they agreed to be her chaperones."

"And?"

"And that's about all I know."

"About all?" Chandler questioned. "So there is more—like her name?"

"Good lord, you don't miss a thing, do you? I believe you are still capable of obtaining an introduction to a lady, if you are truly interested enough."

"Then I'll take it from here."

"Friendly warning, Dunraven."

"After fifteen years by your side, do I need one?"

"Perhaps this time you do," Andrew said. "I've never

seen you look at a lady quite the way I saw you looking at her tonight. I know fascination when I see it. I have to admit you have me a bit worried."

Chandler smiled to cover the truth of his friend's words. "Fascination? You jest. Slow down on the champagne, Andrew, it has gone straight to your head."

Andrew smirked. "Don't change the subject. Look all you want, but do not touch."

"Why the stern warning?"

"No doubt you are just the kind of man she is looking for. Handsome, wealthy and titled. She's probably some farm-poor knight's daughter, and her family is hoping she's pretty enough to catch some man's eye and land a titled gentleman and be set for life."

"You could be right," Chandler said, considering Andrew's words.

Would that be so bad if the lady was enchanting?

"Did I hear a long, silent 'but' at the end of that sentence?"

Chandler drew in a deep breath and started to say more, but instead he said, "No. You heard the call for the next dance. You don't want to be tardy."

"I'll be off then." He pointed a finger in Chandler's direction. "Forewarned."

His friend walked away, leaving Chandler curious about his own feelings where the mysterious young lady was concerned.

A giggle sounded behind him, and he turned to see Miss Bardwell and Miss Donaldson standing before him. Both young ladies looked hopeful and giddy with big smiles on their faces. Their dresses were cut far too low for their tender age, but it was the fashion.

Chandler smiled more to himself than at the ladies. He

used to think the lower cut the neckline of a gown the better, but recently he found their ploys to get attention didn't intrigue him like they once did. Now he was more interested in a lady who was a little, but not too much, older and more communicative.

"Good evening, ladies." He bowed, then took both their hands in his and divided one kiss between the two ladies's hands. He would not fall for the trick of favoring one lady over the other. Long ago he had realized the gossips who circle among the ton see from the backs of their heads.

"Shame on you, Lord Dunraven," Miss Bardwell said in a provocative tone with a flirtatious smile on her too thin lips. "You've been avoiding all the young ladies at the ball this evening. Why attend a party if you don't mean to dance with at least two of us?"

Miss Bardwell was not coy.

Chandler looked at the pale, blue-eyed beauty. She was fetching and intelligent enough, he supposed, but there was nothing about her that he found appealing enough to encourage her approach. He didn't even want to pay her an obligatory call.

He looked from Miss Bardwell to the prettier, but quieter, and more reserved Miss Donaldson and said, "May I assume you two young ladies would be willing to see to it that I'm not left a wallflower tonight?"

Miss Bardwell giggled and flapped her fan a couple of times. "You have only to ask."

Chandler relented and said, "In that case, ladies, I should like a dance with each of you if you haven't promised them to other gentlemen."

While he waited for them to produce their cards he turned and searched the room for *her*.

She was nowhere in sight.

"*IT WON'T WORK* you know."

Startled, Millicent jumped at the sound of the woman's voice coming from behind her. Someone had caught her again! Angels above, was there no safe place where a lady could make a few notes?

Millicent turned around from the darkened corner of the buffet room and faced a tall, buxom, dark-haired lady. Millicent's eyes were immediately drawn to a brownish-red disfiguring birthmark that covered the lower half of her left cheek and spilled just under the line of her jaw.

Not wanting to stare, Millicent quickly focused on the young lady's pretty green eyes and asked, "What makes you so sure it won't work?"

"Oh, I've tried it."

Millicent wasn't sure exactly what this young lady thought she was doing, so she merely stated, "You have?"

"Oh, mercy, yes. Many times." She sighed heavily. "I finally gave up and you should, too."

"And why is that?"

The young lady walked closer to Millicent. Even though she was a large young woman, she moved with the regal grace of a lady of breeding.

"You can fill in names on all the blank spaces but sooner or later the other ladies in attendance will talk about why your dance card is always full, but you are never seen on the dance floor."

Relief. She thought Millicent was filling in gentlemen's names on her dance card. Thank goodness. For a moment Millicent had thought the lady might actually have some idea of what she was writing.

"I'm sure you are right about that," Millicent said. "Thank you for the warning."

"I am perplexed about something, though," the young lady continued as she looked down at Millicent's card.

"What is that?" Millicent asked as she slipped her dance card into her reticule.

"There should be no need for you to have to write down gentlemen's names. I've seen you on the dance floor a respectable number of times this evening. And you are much too pretty to end up a spinster like me. Why would you be adding names?"

Millicent relaxed and smiled. She liked the friendliness she saw in this young lady's eyes and didn't want to mislead her, but there was no way she could be completely honest with her or anyone else.

"That's most kind of you to say, but I guess we all want to be more sought after than we are. Human nature, you know."

"I used to feel that way, too, but I don't anymore," the young lady said with resignation. "After four years I realized that no man was going to marry me because of my birthmark. The few gentlemen who danced with me only asked me to please their mothers, who felt sorry for me, or to show other young ladies they were nice enough gentlemen to marry because they would dance with someone who looks like me."

Millicent wanted to dispute what she said but knew she probably spoke the truth. She didn't understand it, but she believed beauty meant more to a man than loyalty and love.

"I'm sure you are shortchanging yourself unduly."

"No, I'm not. But I've found other things that give me pleasure. I enjoy reading and writing poetry. And I'm very good with a needle."

"Those are good things to do. Perhaps you didn't give

the gentlemen in your life a chance to get to know you."

"You are just being kind," she said wistfully, "and that is very nice of you." She smiled sweetly at Millicent. "Let's break the rules and pretend we've been properly introduced. Do you mind?"

"No, of course not."

"Good. I'm Lynette Knightington, the youngest daughter of the Duke of Grembrooke."

Millicent curtsied. "It is my pleasure to meet you, Lady Lynette. I'm Millicent Blair." Millicent didn't add that she was the daughter of an earl. It was Aunt Beatrice's desire that her true identity not be revealed. No one was to know her heritage, and considering what she was doing, that was the way Millicent wanted it, too.

"I've not seen you before."

"Lord Heathecoute and his lady have graciously agreed to sponsor me for the Season," Millicent said with ease. "And I'm the houseguest of Lady Beatrice."

"How very generous of them. I'm not surprised, since they never had children of their own. Lady Beatrice is usually at all the parties, but I haven't seen her recently."

"I'm afraid she had a rather bad fall and is laid up. She won't make any of the parties this Season."

"That does sound serious."

"She should be fine soon," Millicent answered just the way her aunt had instructed.

"Please tell her I asked about her."

"Yes, I will. I don't want to keep you from the party. I appreciate your excellent advice about the dance cards, Lady Lynette."

"You would have figured it out, and please call me Lynette. I'd like us to be friends."

"I think it would be lovely for us to be friends, and please call me Millicent."

"I shall. I've been around so long that I know everyone. I can tell you which young men to accept a second dance from and which to avoid. I know all the young ladies, too, but I'll let you make up your own mind about them. Most of them don't even realize I'm around."

"I will be sure to solicit you."

"Thank you."

She smiled and Millicent realized that when she was talking to Lynette she didn't notice the birthmark on her face at all. She was an intelligent and cheerful young lady who appeared to be in need of a friend.

"I'll look forward to meeting you again. Enjoy the rest of your evening."

Millicent watched Lynette walk away and thought that she would enjoy being a friend to Lynette, but she hesitated over getting too involved with anyone. She didn't think her aunt would approve. Besides, no one would ever be her friend again if it was discovered that she was gathering information on people to write about them in Lord Truefitt's column. According to Aunt Beatrice, everyone in the ton wanted to read the tittle-tattle, but no one wanted to be written about in them. And Millicent had no doubt that members of the ton would never associate with anyone who wrote them.

"There you are, Millicent, dear. We've been looking everywhere for you."

Millicent turned at the sound of Lady Heathecoute's loud voice, but instead of seeing the large woman, she looked straight into the sparkling blue eyes of the handsome gentleman she'd talked to last night. Her breathing kicked up a notch and her throat went dry.

The handsome gentleman had sought her out.

"May I present Chandler Prestwick, the earl of Dunraven."

Five

"I do desire that we may be better strangers" or the Mad Ton Thief will not be found this Season. But not to worry, while we wait for the robber to be apprehended, we can expect wedding parties for Miss Watson-Wentworth and the marquess of Gardendowns.

Lord Truefitt
Society's Daily Column

MILLICENT CURTSIED LOW, hoping to hide the shock in her eyes and slow the hammering of her heart at hearing his name. Angels above, Lord Dunraven was one of the Terrible Threesome her aunt had warned her about. Not only was he one of the most eligible men in Town, he was one of the most scandalous, if what her aunt said was true.

He was just the kind of rake who had ruined her mother's reputation. He certainly wasn't the kind of man that Millicent should lose her senses over. And to think she had dreamed about him last night and had wanted to meet him again.

She rose from her curtsy determined to find a way to deny his strong appeal. "How do you do, my lord," she answered, her tone cool now that she knew who he was.

"Lord Dunraven, this is Miss Millicent Blair, the niece of a dear friend from the country. This is her first visit to Town."

His shining blue gaze brushed lingeringly down her face before lighting on her eyes. Unexpected pleasure filled her, and excitement at his presence grew inside her despite her resolution not to be affected by him.

"Welcome to London, Miss Blair. I trust you are enjoying yourself."

"Very much, thank you. I find London and its people fascinating."

"That's good to hear. We do take great pride in our fair city. I'm sure Lady Heathecoute is seeing that you are attending the best parties and luncheons and taking calls from only the most respectable of gentlemen."

Millicent glanced at her chaperone, who wore a delighted expression on her face. "You have no need to concern yourself on that account, sir. Her ladyship and the viscount have been dedicated to me."

"No doubt you have many thank-you letters to write," he said with a hint of a devilish grin attractively lifting one corner of his lips.

Millicent cleared her throat. He dared to bring that up, obviously in hopes of provoking her to blush. He was a rake of the highest order. The smile on his roguish lips and the sparkle in his intriguing eyes made it clear he was having a wonderful time at her expense. She should be outraged, but she wasn't. She was pleasantly puzzled by his attention.

"Yes. I believe I'm up to date on all my notes, Lord

Dunraven. I'm flattered by your interest, considering I'm a stranger to you."

"Not that we've now been introduced. With Lady Heathecoute's permission, perhaps there's room on your dance card for me, if it's not filled with notes—I mean names."

Millicent had to think quickly. The last thing she wanted was Lord Dunraven looking at her card. She didn't want anyone looking at it.

No wonder he was considered one of the Terrible Threesome. He was a scandalous earl. He was openly flirting with her in front of the viscountess at one moment and trying to get her into trouble the next—proof that the earl of Dunraven was not a man she could afford to have anything to do with—no matter how utterly charming he was.

"How very kind of you to offer, my lord, but I'm afraid I can't accept any more invitations tonight. I believe her ladyship is eager for us to go on to the next party she has planned for us this evening."

"Balderdash, Millicent, dear," Lady Heathecoute cooed as softly as was possible given her strong voice. "We'll forego the next party if we must. Have a dance with the earl. That's what the Season is for, isn't it? Dancing the night away. In fact, I believe the next one is about to start. Is this dance taken, dear? Let me see. Where is your card?"

Millicent clutched her reticule tighter and smiled sweetly at her ladyship. "Ah—no. There's no need to look. I'm sure this dance is open."

"Then it's settled, if you are free, my lord?" the viscountess said.

"Indeed, I am." He extended his arm for Millicent. "May I have this dance?"

Not trusting herself to speak, there was nothing for her to do but graciously agree with a slight nod. She lightly placed her hand on the crook of his arm and walked with him to the dance floor.

"It's impolite to decline a dance with an earl," he said.

Millicent turned to look at him and saw by the glint in his eyes and the half grin on his lips that he was teasing her, not reprimanding her for ill manners.

She lifted her chin a notch. "Not when the earl's flagrant reputation precedes him."

"So you've been in London long enough to hear all the tittle-tattle."

"Surely not all there is, but enough to make me wary of you and a few others. Besides what I've heard about you, I have firsthand knowledge of your abilities."

"My abilities, Miss Blair?" he questioned. "I'm not certain which abilities you are referring to."

"Your roguish ones, sir."

He smiled again, one that was full of genuine amusement. It should have irritated Millicent immensely that he found such pleasure in her discomfort, but for reasons unknown to her his attitude didn't bother her.

But she wasn't prepared to let him know that. "You were positively forward last night when you happened upon me in that darkened hallway."

"Forward? Did you think so?"

"Certainly."

"I thought I behaved like a perfect gentleman."

They walked by a group of people and Millicent noticed that every one of them watched her as they passed. Her aunt would not like it that she had this kind of attention. Oh, how had she caught the eye of one of the Terrible Threesome? And what was she going to do about it?

She drew in her breath with a soft gasp and asked, "Perfect?"

"Yes."

"A gentleman?"

"Yes."

"What rubbish you speak, sir. It was unquestionably bold of you to have brushed my hand when you gave me your pencil last evening. A true gentleman would not have allowed that to happen."

He turned to her, a well-pleased expression on his face. "I didn't think you noticed."

"How could I not? It was so—unexpected," she said, remembering the delightful tingle that jolted through her at his brief touch.

Lord Dunraven nodded to a beautiful woman and a gentleman dressed in a military uniform before answering her by saying, "And we were both wearing gloves. You are obviously a very sensitive woman, Miss Blair. I shall remember that."

Millicent could have bitten her tongue out for even bringing up the incident. It was clear she would not get the upper hand with this man. Why had she mentioned that touch? Because she hadn't been able to forget about it. The contact was no more than a butterfly's brush, but she had felt it all the way down to her toes. He was right, she was sensitive to everything about him. His mere presence had her senses on alert.

"I said nothing because I was sure you had touched me by mistake, and I didn't want to alarm you."

"It would take a great deal more than a brush of hands with a beautiful woman to alarm me, I assure you. How thoughtful of you to think of my feelings, but no, Miss Blair, I caressed your hand by design not mistake."

He smiled that knowing smile as they took their places

on the crowded dance floor and waited for the music to begin.

"You are no gentleman, sir."

"Sometimes. I thought you would pretend forever that I hadn't touched you. You surprise me, Miss Blair, and I like surprises."

"You wear your title of rake well, my lord. Not only did you stroke my hand, but you deigned to blow me a kiss. It was most inappropriate for you to do so."

"I thought it dashing."

"Dashing? I believe mischievous is the word you meant to say, for surely it was."

He laughed softly, attractively. Once again Millicent felt a strange fluttering sensation in her stomach. As much as she hated to admit it, there was something remarkably appealing about him. No matter how hard she tried, she couldn't make herself be truly angry with him. Oh, yes, knowing how she responded to his charm and his gentle touch, she believed he was a scoundrel of the highest order.

"You are not only a lady of great beauty, Miss Blair, you are a lady of delightfully quick wit. I haven't been called impish in years. I'm impressed."

"It's not my desire to please you or to entertain you, my lord. I only want to be done with you."

He laughed softly. "Tell me, would you believe me if I told you that most of whatever you may have heard about me is not true?"

"I think that would make your integrity as suspect as your flattery."

The music started and the dance began. Millicent didn't have time to think. She could only fall into his rhythm and step and let him lead her through the dance steps. When his hand touched hers, the tingles skittered up her back as if she weren't wearing gloves at all.

He picked up the conversation where they had left off and said in a low seductive voice, "In that case, Miss Blair, I won't bother to deny a single word you have heard about me, and you can assume it is all true. How's that?"

"Perfect," Millicent answered as she yielded to his expert leading in the dance.

"I can see I've made you happy."

"I would have been happier had you not sought an introduction. Something tells me you somehow knew I would be free to accept your invitation of this dance."

"How could I possibly know that? I would have to be a wizard."

"Perhaps you are. I've heard you have great power over young ladies and that you can make them endanger their reputations and lose their heads over you."

"The gossips give me more credit than I deserve, Miss Blair. I simply wanted to meet you and dance with you. I had no idea what dances you had free."

Millicent felt her hand tighten in his, and she was certain he put emphasis on the word *what*. He couldn't possibly know what she was doing, could he?

"I've not seen your card. You could have already promised this dance to another."

"Yes, of course."

If Millicent wasn't careful, her guilty conscience was going to make her say the wrong thing and make him suspicious of her. She didn't need anyone asking her too many questions.

"So you are only in London for the Season?" he asked after a moment of silence.

"Perhaps a little longer, I can't be sure right now."

"And where do you call home?" he asked as the tips of his fingers once again stroked inside her hand.

"Where my mother lives," she answered and easily changed the subject to say, "I haven't met either of your friends, Lord Chatwin and Lord Dugdale."

"Does that mean you want to meet them?"

"Certainly not. I was merely making conversation."

"Good. I would think you'd react to Fines and Andrew much the same way you have to me."

"No doubt."

"You have been filled in on the gossip about all three of us, I see."

"It didn't take much. I think the three of you must try to do things that make people want to talk about you and make the scandal sheets want to write about you."

"Perhaps we have. What would you say if I told you that we were thinking of mending our ways?"

"Probably that it's too late to make a difference. The damage has been done."

Millicent was close to being in a dither. The lazy stroll his fingers made on her hand was making her crazy with need to return the sensuous touch. She was supposed to be too sensible to fall for his persuasive machinations, but she was finding herself quite susceptible to him.

She had to do something to break the spell he'd cast on her. No matter how special his touch made her feel, she had to remember that with this man she was just another young lady in his arms and therefore he felt free to trifle with her. He was a rogue's rogue.

"Do you caress the hands of every lady you dance with?" she asked.

His blue eyes darkened. "With all that you've heard about me, I'm surprised you have to ask."

"I wanted to know if you would tell the truth or fill my head with the silly notion that I'm the first."

"You are far too clever for me to tell you anything silly."

Another thing to like about him. "Thank you."

"You're welcome."

"Now, would you please stop? I find your brashness very disconcerting." *But pleasing.*

"I thought I was being quite restrained, when what I really want to do is pull you into my arms and kiss you."

A stunned gasp rushed past her lips. "You forget yourself, sir."

"No, but there are times like these when I'd very much like to."

He guided her into a twirl under his arm and brought her to face him again without missing a step. There was a gleam of amusement in his eyes, though he was discreet enough not to show it in his polite smile.

"You have that affect on me, Miss Blair. But I will change the subject so as not to further offend your sensibilities. So where does your mother reside?"

Millicent took a deep breath before saying, "In the country. So tell me, if what is written about you is not true, what is?"

"That's a rather broad question for a lady who only gives the narrowest of answers."

Millicent stared directly into his intriguing blue eyes, sparkling with immense pleasure. For the first time since beginning their dance, she couldn't help giving him a genuine smile as she said, "Surely a lady is not supposed to tell everything during a first dance, my lord."

"Careful, Miss Blair, you are about to ruin your reputation."

Undaunted, she asked, "How so?"

"I believe that remark was the first thing you have said to me that could be considered flirtatious."

"Then I must be more careful. Flirting with you is the farthest thing from my mind."

"I fear the lady doth protest too much, methinks."

Millicent's eyes widened in surprise as a warm feeling flooded her. "You've studied Shakespeare?"

"Studied? No. I've simply read some of his work."

"He was a very clever man with words."

"Is that a hint of how I might find my way past your head to your heart, Miss Blair?"

Millicent tingled and tensed at the same time. He was so bold. He was so charming she easily forgot who he was and eagerly engaged him in pleasant conversation.

"Certainly not."

"I should like to call on you tomorrow afternoon, Miss Blair."

"That wouldn't be convenient, Lord Dunraven."

"The next afternoon, perhaps?"

Lord Dunraven lifted his arm and led her into a slow twirl as the dance ended, far too quickly yet not fast enough. He gently squeezed her fingers again, let go of her hand and bowed.

Millicent curtsied on weak knees. He kept her constantly on her wits. "I'm sorry. I fear my afternoons are full."

Chandler extended his arm for her, and Millicent graciously accepted. "I do believe you are rejecting my advances, Miss Blair."

"That's exactly what I'm doing, sir."

Quietly they walked back to the perimeter of the room where Lady Heathecoute was waiting for her. Millicent's heart beat faster than it ever had, and the speed had nothing to do with the dancing. Lord Dunraven's touch sent her heart rate spiraling out of control, and her common sense took leave.

As they neared the viscountess, Lord Dunraven turned to Millicent and softly said, "If clever words won't win your heart, Miss Blair, then I shall have to keep looking until I find what will."

AFTER DUTIFULLY DELIVERING Miss Blair back to the lady Heathecoute, he watched them leave. When she turned away from him, Miss Blair was still wearing the stunned look she gave him when he told her he would find a way to her heart. He had shocked himself, too. He hadn't been this interested in anyone since Lady Lambsbeth sank her claws into him.

He'd been with Miss Blair twice and he hadn't heard her giggle once, an annoying habit of most of the young ladies at the parties he attended. Funny, the batting of eyelashes and fluttering of fans never used to bother him, but now he found them quite irritating. Thankfully, Miss Blair hadn't even carried a fan. He wasn't sure he even saw her blink. She was too in control of herself.

Chandler needed to get himself a drink and search the room again for anyone who looked like he didn't belong.

Miss Blair was certainly the most intriguing young lady he'd ever met. He wasn't so sure he should let her know of his interest so soon. He learned early not to act interested in a young lady even if he was. But tonight he'd indicated he wanted to find the way to Miss Blair's heart. He had never said anything like that before. What was he thinking? He couldn't have sounded more oafish if he'd been a common schoolboy getting his first glimpse of a paid mistress.

Damnation! He'd spent enough time pondering Miss Blair. He had to catch a thief. It was time he watched the doorways, roamed the rooms and searched the crowds, or he would never find the man he sought.

Chandler stopped and chatted with the duke of Grembrooke and asked about his daughter Lady Lynette, but his gaze continuously searched the room, looking for a man who didn't quite fit in with the group. He spoke to Sir Charles Wright when he passed him, nodded and smiled to a group of ladies and snubbed a gentleman who once tried to call him out over a misunderstanding.

After slowly walking through each room twice, Chandler concluded that all the men looked alike. If one was suspicious looking, then they all were. And to make matters worse, he realized he knew most of the men by name and wouldn't consider any of them a robber. Still, he told himself, the thief would have already been caught if he looked like a beggar among the ton.

"Dunraven, hold up."

Chandler swore under his breath and kept walking, never changing his stride. He wasn't up for another conversation with Andrew. With any luck someone would stop his friend and waylay him before he caught up with Chandler.

But seconds later Andrew fell in step with him.

"Dunraven, I'm glad I found you. I saw you dancing with her. How did it go?"

Chandler ignored Andrew's last question and turned to greet his friend with a smile and gentle clap on the shoulder. "You found me just in time. I'm on my way to get a drink. Care to join me?"

"Yes, but let's quit this party and head over to White's. It's early enough for a game or two of whist."

"I can't, old friend."

"Why not? She's gone. I saw her leave."

His relationship with Miss Blair was off-limits. Chandler turned to him and asked, "Who?"

"Who indeed?" Andrew said impatiently. "Miss Blair, of course. It's not as if we didn't spend half an hour talking about her earlier."

"So you did know her name when we last spoke?"

Andrew gave Chandler a shrugging gesture and a smirk. "Yes of course I did. I wanted to know if you were interested enough to find out about her for yourself. I got my answer when I saw you dancing with her."

"And I saw you dancing with Miss Pennington. I hope she met your expectations."

"I'm still thinking about that. She seems terribly young and goosey."

"Maybe it's you getting old."

"What a damning thought that is. I'm finding all the young ladies that way this Season." He shook his head in disgust. "It's damnable getting old, isn't it? Come on, let's head over to White's, have a drink and talk about it."

"I have a dance with Miss Bardwell coming up in a short time."

"Truly?" Andrew eyed him suspiciously. "You didn't sound the least interested in her when we talked earlier."

"I'm not. A situation came up that made it impossible for me to get out of asking her without being rude." She'd obviously learned how to be forward from her mother, Chandler thought, but only added, "As bad luck would have it, I had to invite Miss Donaldson to dance as well, so I will be here a bit longer than I intended."

"You must have been cornered by them."

"That's a mild way of putting it."

"The hopefuls are getting braver every year. Remember how timid they all were just ten years ago?"

"Yes. Didn't you just recently refer to them as the 'good old days'?"

Andrew laughed. "I must have been well into the bottle."

"I think we both were."

"But we're mending our ways, right?"

"That remains to be seen," Chandler answered as honestly as he could, considering he was no longer willing to share every thought with his friends.

"So tell me, did Miss Blair meet your expectations when you danced with her?"

Oh, yes, Chandler thought but eluded the direct question by saying, "I find that tonight I'm more interested in catching a thief than a pretty lady's attention."

"Hmm, I guess that means she was quite unremarkable."

No, quite the opposite, Chandler thought and kept walking through the crowd.

If Chandler had only pondered it before, he knew for certain that there came a time in a gentleman's life when he became his own man and not part of a threesome.

Six

"Therefore, since brevity is the soul of wit . . .
I will be brief" and report how remarkable it
is to see Lord Dunraven, Lord Chatwin and
Lord Dugdale dance with so many young ladies in one evening. And all three of the gentlemen danced with Miss Bardwell last night.
Could it be that after all these years we are
going to see the Terrible Threesome fighting
over the same young lady?

Lord Truefitt
Society's Daily Column

MILLICENT SAT ALONE in the dining room of her aunt's
town house finishing a meal of cheese, cooked figs and
fresh-baked bread. Even at half past two in the afternoon
it was still difficult for her to clear the sleepiness from
her eyes.

Thankfully, Aunt Beatrice's cook sent up hot tea to
Millicent's bedroom each afternoon to help her wake up.
She had not had a proper night's sleep since she'd arrived
in London several days ago.

Millicent didn't know how her aunt had kept such extended hours for all these years. The pace was grueling.
After attending two and three parties each evening until
the early morning hours, Millicent would go straight to
her Aunt's bedroom when she returned home and the two
of them would discuss the night's gossip.

Millicent would take notes about what Aunt Beatrice
wanted her to write in the column, then, retiring to her
room, she would begin the tedious task of making a leg-
ible copy for Phillips to deliver to *The Daily Reader*.

She hadn't gone to bed until after daybreak since the
first day she arrived in London.

While she sipped tea out of a dainty china cup, Millicent's gaze drifted to the garden outside the window to
where the primroses, crocuses and tree shrubs bloomed in
pinks, yellows and white. Emery was out cutting flowers
for Aunt Beatrice's room, and Hamlet sniffed the ground
around Emery's feet.

Millicent didn't know why the dog had taken an instant
dislike to her. She was usually very good with animals.
She could only attribute it to the fact that Hamlet didn't
seem to like anyone but his mistress and Emery. Aunt
Beatrice had suggested it was because he was getting old
and grumpy, which was more than likely the case.

As Millicent watched Emery and Hamlet, her thoughts
faded back to what Earl Dunraven had said last night just
before he returned her to Viscountess Heathecoute. A sudden expectancy filled her.

Millicent was shocked, and her aunt would be mortified
if she knew the earl had indicated he was going to pursue
her. She must stop his interest in her, but for some reason
she was reluctant to do that. Even though he was a High
Society rake, she found her attraction to him was too powerful to ignore. She had tried. Her only hope was that he

would soon tire of her and go on to pursue some other young lady.

A smile lifted the corners of her lips just thinking about how gently yet commandingly he'd touched her while they danced. She loved the feel of the strength in him when he caressed her hand. Oh, and he was so handsome and debonair. He was intriguing and as fascinating a gentleman as she had ever met.

But, and it was a huge *but,* she had to remember that was exactly how he had earned his reputation for being one of the Terrible Threesome. He knew how to enchant young ladies and make them desire to see him again. She had to remember he liked the chase and to pay suit to young ladies only to go no further than a few dances and paying a call or two. Her smile faded.

She was not one he could trifle with for two very good reasons. Aunt Beatrice had brought her to London to safeguard her position at *The Daily Reader*, and it was a man comparable to Lord Dunraven who had made her mother an outcast in all of London. If the dashing earl approached Millicent again, she would have no choice but to rebuff him—no matter that she wasn't inclined to do so. She would not end up like her mother.

Millicent looked out at the lush garden again. It was too beautiful a day to stay inside. Maybe a leisurely stroll among the flowers and shrubs would free her mind of Lord Dunraven. She should join Emery and Hamlet outside in the fresh air and spend a little time thinking up new quotes from Shakespeare to use in the column.

She could always resort to looking through her aunt's books on Shakespeare's writings, and reading his works was never a chore, but she rather liked the idea that she could remember so many of her favorite lines without lifting a book or turning a page.

She finished off her tea, then headed toward the rear door. Millicent stepped out of her aunt's house and into the lovely formal garden. She'd been told that her aunt's flower garden was one of the largest and most beautiful in Mayfair, and looking at the splendor before her she could believe it. The enclosure was alive with color.

Tall, thick yews formed a hedge that was at least eight-feet high and completely surrounded the garden on three sides. Separate beds of flowers had been arranged so that there would be some flower or shrub blooming from early spring until late in the autumn. At the end of the garden stood a larger-than-life-size statue of Diana, the Huntress. The goddess held a cluster of arrows in one hand and her trusted dog stood by her side. It was easy to figure out why her aunt picked that piece of statuary, given her love for her own pet.

Emery and Hamlet met her at the bottom step on their way back inside.

"Good afternoon, Miss." Emery greeted her with a pleasant smile.

"And the same to you, Emery," Millicent said, peering down into the maid's basket. "You picked beautiful flowers for Aunt Beatrice."

The maid's eyes brightened at the praise. "You think she'll like them?"

"I'm sure of it."

Emery smiled and said, "Thank you, Miss," then headed up the steps to the back door.

Millicent turned to the spaniel who was still looking at her with curious eyes. "What about you, Hamlet? Would you like to stay out here in the garden with me for a while?"

The little dog barked once. Millicent thought that meant he would stay outside with her, but as soon as Emery opened the door, he scampered up the steps and rushed inside just before the maid shut the door.

So much for trying to make friends with him, Millicent thought as she made her way along the stone path that led to the back of the garden. It was a beautiful day bright with sunshine, with a clear blue sky and a gentle breeze to rustle the leaves. The foliage was a lush shade of green from the early spring rains and their wet winter.

Millicent's modest afternoon dress swished across the tops of her satin slippers as she bent down to smell a pretty pink flower.

"Millicent."

Rising up, Millicent thought she must be going daft. She could have sworn she'd heard Lord Dunraven call her name. She looked around the grounds from corner to corner and saw nothing. She shook her head and smiled to herself. How unlike her to have such fanciful notions about a gentleman. Probably because she couldn't get the dashing scoundrel off her mind.

She continued her lazy stroll.

"Millicent."

This time she stopped with a jerk and looked around again. She wasn't hearing things. It was Lord Dunraven calling her name.

"Over here by the statue."

She slowly walked toward the statue and, when she moved to an angle at the far right, she saw Lord Dunraven, crouched down low and hidden behind the large statue. He was motioning for her to join him.

He was unbelievable.

She looked at the back door where Emery and Hamlet had just entered. There was no sign of them, Phillips or any of her aunt's servants. It was inconceivable that he'd made it into the garden without anyone seeing him.

Millicent knew she should just ignore him and rush back into the house, but she couldn't. Curiosity got the better of her and she started toward him. She took her time walking over to where he was hidden in the back center of the garden where the statue stood. When she was close enough to talk to Lord Dunraven, she stopped and pretended to look at a cluster of daisies but had her gaze on him.

"You, sir, are astounding."

He winked at her. "Thank you."

"How did you get into this garden?"

"Through the hedge."

She looked at the closely cropped, thick hedge that stood just beyond the garden and didn't see a break or even a ruffle of disturbance in the primly cut yew.

"Impossible."

"Miss Blair, have you never heard the old adage, 'where there's a will there's a way'?"

"You sir, are an extraordinary magician if you indeed came through that thick hedge."

A roguish smile played on his lips and melted any hint of anger toward him. "I've had plenty of practice over the years, but I do have to admit that I am a bit rusty." He grunted and adjusted his position on the ground to a sitting position. "I haven't slipped into a garden to meet a young lady in years."

"I should think not," she admonished him. Although she was appalled by his brash behavior, she was also excited by it. "You are much too old for such pranks."

He grimaced as he touched a slight scratch to his cheek. "I agree. They used to be such fun, and it is quite nice to know I can still do it."

"I'm not surprised to hear you have done this sort of thing before."

"I would rather you had allowed me to call on you properly."

"Sir, I thought I made it clear I didn't want you to call on me at all.

"I'm sure you believe I'm living up to my reputation."

"Indeed. You could have been caught slipping in here." She stopped. "What am I saying?—I could be caught standing here talking to you and be scandalized. Emery and Hamlet were just in the garden."

"I saw them and waited for them to leave. I'm always careful. I've been hiding on the other side of the hedge for some time now hoping Hamlet wouldn't detect me and that you would come out into the garden this afternoon."

"Really? Why?"

"I wanted to see you. You wouldn't give me permission to call on you properly, so I shall call on you improperly. Now, come a bit closer so we won't have to talk so loud and alert one of the servants."

Closer? She shouldn't be talking to him at all. But . . . rake that he was, with him there was always that *but*. She wanted to talk to him.

She walked closer to the statue and sat down on its base, right beside Lord Dunraven, who sat on the grass. She looked over at him. His hair was ruffled and had bits of shrub in it. The shoulder of his jacket had a small tear, and his white shirt had grass stains from the hedge. There was a small scratch on his cheek below his eye. He indeed looked like a gentleman who had just stolen into a garden to see the love of his life.

Suddenly she laughed softly.

"And what is so funny?" he asked as he leaned against the back of the statue.

"You."

"Me? I hoped to impress you, not make you laugh at

me. Where did I go wrong?" he asked with a teasing grin.

"I was just thinking that it is no wonder you have the reputation you do. Coming here like this was very risky for both of us."

"I learned early in my youth how to steal into gardens, climb houses and crawl into windows without being caught."

"Stunts like that could easily fool most young ladies into thinking you were absolutely, madly in love with them."

"Most?" he questioned. "I guess that means you are not included in that number."

"Certainly not."

"But you aren't upset I came to see you."

Oh no.

"Of course I am," she said with little conviction in her voice. "It is very foolish. If you were caught here, my reputation would be ruined forever."

"There should be some comfort in knowing that I've never actually been caught."

"Obviously not. You would have been wed."

"Which is the reason I'm always careful."

"But you did say you were *rusty*."

"Did I say that? Surely not. But, let's see."

In one fluid motion, he gently took hold of her wrist and pulled her down into the grass, half beside him and half on his lap, and covered her lips with his in a quick, soft kiss—but to her it was a powerful kiss that sent her head spinning with tantalizing sensations.

Millicent was too stunned to move or to say anything. She looked into his gently smiling eyes and felt no fear, no remorse, no shame. How could that be? It went against everything she had been taught.

He reached up and caressed her cheek with his fingertips and asked, "Have I lost my technique?"

"No, sir, you are very adept."

She was almost sitting on top of him. He held her but with no forcing pressure. She could easily rise, scream, or even box his ears, but she remained where she was without moving.

He raised his lips to hers again for another gentle kiss. Her stomach quivered. His lips were warm and moist as he gently taught her how to return the kiss. It would be so easy to give herself up to his touch and simply enjoy this man, but she couldn't. She must take control of him and herself and not allow this to continue.

She pushed against his chest and the kiss ended. "You have proven your point, Lord Dunraven. You are a rake of the highest order."

"Should I consider that a compliment or insult?"

"You should consider it the truth. Now, I really must go before someone sees us."

"May I call on you tomorrow?"

She rose from the ground and looked down at him. "I can't allow that, sir. Please turn your attentions to someone else. Now, leave the way you came while I watch for you."

He grinned and blew her a kiss.

The back door opened and Hamlet rushed out. He stood on the top step and barked a couple of times before he came running down the steps at top speed toward Millicent. Her heart jumped to her throat.

"Hurry, Lord Dunraven. Hamlet knows you are here," Millicent whispered to him but he was already disappearing through a small opening he had made in the bottom of the shrub. It closed back together as soon as he was gone.

Hamlet headed straight for the hedge where Lord Dun-

raven had disappeared. He sniffed around the ground and
barked.

Millicent looked back to the rear door saw that it was
her own maid, Glenda, standing in the doorway. Millicent
flinched. She wondered how long Glenda had been standing there. Could she have seen Lord Dunraven from
where she stood? Would she say anything to her aunt if
she had seen him or would she consider it none of her
concern and remain quiet?

A small young lady with large dark eyes and sallow
skin, Glenda was the quietest person Millicent had ever
known. She could enter a room without anyone ever
knowing she was there.

"Miss, are you all right?" she called.

"Yes, Glenda," Millicent answered and without looking
back toward Hamlet, she started walking toward her maid.

"You have a visitor."

"No, no, I don't have a visitor," she fibbed, trying not
to sound or act nervous, but wasn't so sure she managed
it. "I don't know what Hamlet is barking at. Maybe a
rabbit or a cat."

She could strangle Lord Dunraven for putting her in
this awkward position.

Glenda walked down the steps to meet Millicent. She
presented Millicent a card on a silver tray. "No, Miss, I
mean you have had a visitor call on you. A young lady."

"Oh, yes. I see. Thank you." Millicent tried to calm her
breathing as she picked up the card and read. "Lady Lynette Knightington." She looked up at the maid. "Is the
lady still here or did she just leave her card?"

"She's in the front parlor, Miss, but says not to bother
you if she's called at an inopportune time."

Millicent wiped her lips with the back of her hand,

remembering Lord Dunraven's kiss, wishing she had more time to ponder why he was pursuing her.

She would think about him later.

This pleasant day had certainly turned into an exciting one. Should she greet the young lady who had been so friendly the night before or should she tell Glenda to say she was unavailable?

Millicent threw down the card on the tray. Angels above, her aunt couldn't expect her to attend two and three parties each evening and not develop at least one friendship.

"Tell her I'll be right there, then ask the housekeeper to speak to the cook about a fresh pot of tea and sandwiches."

"Yes, Miss."

"Lady Lynette, how kind of you to call," Millicent said a few moments later as she entered the front parlor. Her off-white day dress swept the floor, and her steps were soundless in her comfortable satin slippers.

Lynette turned from the fireplace, where she was looking at the painting of a much younger Lady Beatrice that hung above the mantel. She smiled graciously at Millicent. "I'm so happy you were available to see me on short notice. I promise not to stay long."

"Nonsense. Stay as long as you like. I'm having some tea brought in for us."

"Thank you. And remember to call me Lynette. We are friends now, and there should be no formalities with us."

"All right. Please sit down."

Millicent motioned for Lynette to take one of the twin burgundy-colored settees that were placed in the center of the cozy room. Matching gilded armchairs flanked each end of the settees, and a satinwood pedestal table with alabaster inlays stood between the settees. Burgundy-and

green-striped velvet drapery panels had been pulled back
from the windows and daylight lit the parlor with brightness.

Lynette was an imposing young lady, tall and robust.
Her sapphire-blue walking dress spread out over the small
settee as she sat down on the edge. Her matching bonnet
had a wide ribbon sash tied under her chin that covered
most of the birthmark that spilled over her cheek. Millicent noticed that Lynette's face was really quite lovely
when the dark red birthmark was covered.

Millicent took a deep breath, smiled and sat in the settee opposite the other woman.

"How is Lady Beatrice feeling?" Lynette asked.

"A little better each day, but I'm afraid she's not up to
visitors."

"That's quite all right. I understand. Please tell her I
asked for her."

"I shall be happy to. I'm sure she'll be disappointed
she wasn't able to see you."

"I saw you dancing with Lord Dunraven last night."

Millicent suddenly became wary. Was there any way
Lynette could have seen Lord Dunraven sneak into the
garden? Millicent remained calm and said, "Yes, that's
right."

"I talked with my mother about it at breakfast this
morning."

That was rather presumptuous, but Millicent decided
not to take her to task—just yet. She would wait and see
where the conversation was going. She answered, "Is that
so?"

"Yes. I explained you had been recently introduced to
me and that you were here only for the Season. Since you
are new in Town, my mother and I felt I should take it

upon myself to come and warn you about Lord Dunraven."

"Warn me?" Millicent asked but felt sure she knew what Lynette would say, and she was a little perturbed at how quickly the subject changed from pleasantries to what must have been the real reason for Lynette's visit.

Lynette rolled her eyes upward and smiled. "To be sure he's the most charming of the Terrible Threesome, and most young ladies think the most handsome, too. But if you came to Town looking to make a match you would do well to forget about Lord Dunraven and concentrate on someone else."

"It was only one dance, Lynette. And he was not the only gentleman I danced with."

"I know, but he is the only one that you danced with who is unattainable. Over the years so many young ladies have lost their hearts to him only to be disappointed. I think you should take more interest in Sir Charles Wright or Viscount Tolby. Both are handsome and either would suit. Lord Dunraven's interest in any young lady is not to be taken seriously. I could tell you stories about him that would—but you don't want to hear things about him, I'm sure."

Oh, but I do.

She saw this as her opportunity to find out more about the dashing rogue who was so daring as to go so quickly from merely caressing her hand and blowing kisses to sneaking into the garden, pulling her down on the grass beside him and kissing her on the lips.

"Oh, no bad things, but I would like to know a little more about him. I keep hearing about these earls who are called the Terrible Threesome. What exactly has Lord Dunraven done that makes him such a scoundrel?"

"I thought you'd never give me permission to tell. Now

that I'm older, most of the friends I have are married and
are not into hearing the gossip about the bachelors." Lynette smiled waggishly and moved closer to the edge of
her seat but held her tongue as Glenda came in with the
tea.

Millicent had to smile at how young Lynette suddenly
looked. She probably hadn't reached thirty yet and right
now she looked more like seventeen. No doubt Lynette
would relish telling every word of gossip she knew. Her
eyes fairly sparkled with enjoyment and her strong facial
features turned playful.

As soon as Glenda left the room Lynette said, "Everyone in Town thought Lord Dunraven would marry as soon
as he finished his education because he had already inherited the title. All the young ladies and hopeful widows
set their caps for him that first year he was eligible. But
no, word got out quickly that he would see all three of
his sisters wed before he took a wife. Naturally he was
then considered unattainable."

"And that made him all the more sought after?" Millicent asked, while she poured tea for Lynette.

"Indeed. It's been that way for at least ten years—for
all the Terrible Threesome."

Millicent said, "Cream or sugar?"

"Plenty of both. Lord Dunraven dances, charms and
calls on many of the ladies each Season. And from what
I've overheard, he has certainly stolen more than his share
of kisses. He's never offered for the hand of any lady. I
don't believe he's ever called on a lady more than three
times in a Season."

"Why is that?"

"One never knows for sure because Lord Dunraven
hasn't spoken about it to anyone as far as I know, but I

would assume it's because he doesn't want any fathers forcing his hand about his intentions."

"Yes, I suppose he'd be serious if he called on the same lady more than three times."

"Everyone assumes he prefers to spend his time with his friends racing fast horses during the day, gaming in the evenings and gambling into early morning hours. Mama says that some gentlemen never settle down and take wives."

"Well, that doesn't sound so bad," Millicent answered as she handed Lynette a blue cup with a pink flower painted on it.

Lynette accepted with her gloved hand as she leaned forward and whispered, "You won't tell anyone what I've told you?"

"No," Millicent assured her.

"Good. I don't usually talk so much, but then I don't usually have anyone other than Mama who wants to listen to me."

"You can feel free to call on me when you want to talk. I'm enjoying hearing about Lord Dunraven—and other members of the ton," she added quickly.

"One time I overheard a young gentleman say that Lord Dunraven was keeping four mistresses in Town. All at the same time."

Millicent's eyes widened. "My goodness. That many?"

"Astonishing, isn't it?"

"I would think so. That does sound like four too many."

"And sometimes he would see all four of them in one evening and I've heard more than one at a time," Lynette added in a softer whisper.

Shocked, Millicent lowered her cup back to the saucer. Did she dare believe that of Lord Dunraven or was it mere gossip? Four women in one evening and more than one at one time? If only part of what Lynette said was true then his reputation was well deserved. But . . . he had indicated that everything that was said about him wasn't true.

"I'm sure I don't know what to say to that except, perhaps I've heard enough about Lord Dunraven and his mistresses."

Lynette paid no mind to Millicent's subtle suggestion they move on to another topic of conversation and added, "He's noted for stealing kisses at any opportunity and then not offering for the lady's hand."

Lynette said the words as if it were the most dreadful thing that could happen to a young lady. Millicent had been kissed a couple of times on the cheek, and she had wondered what was the harm in a kiss or two, but not anymore. Those kisses had been most uninspiring. But Lord Dunraven's kisses this afternoon had left her head spinning and her lungs breathless.

"On the few occasions he calls on a lady, he always brings the same gift without fail," Lynette continued.

It was clear Lynette was not ready to change the subject, so Millicent said, "Really? What would that be?"

"Apricot tarts. His chef is said to make the most delicious tarts in all of London." She bent closer to Millicent. "If he brings you any, you will save one for me, won't you? I've always wanted to taste them."

Millicent faltered for a moment, but quickly said, "Of course, but truly, Lynette, I gave Lord Dunraven no encouragement whatsoever. I do not expect him or any other gentleman to call on me."

"He might. He danced with you."

"And so have many other gentlemen. Let me assure you Lady Heathecoute set up the dance between Lord Dunraven and me. He was but a reluctant participant. You have no cause to worry about him putting me under a magic spell."

"If he doesn't, you will be the first. Just last year Lord Truefitt suggested in his column that Lord Dunraven was seeing Lady Lambsbeth. It turns out he was seeing her in secret while her husband was in France."

Millicent gasped. "A married woman?"

Lynette nodded once. "I'm sure by now you know that Lord Dunraven is quite hard to turn down."

Oh, yes, I know.

"Lord Lambsbeth heard about it when he arrived in Town. He marched into White's, drew his sword against Lord Dunraven, demanding a duel."

"What happened?"

Lynette sipped her tea again before saying, "Lord Lambsbeth's friends grabbed his arm and forced him to put away his sword. Everyone knew he was much too old to challenge such a young man. I heard he and his wife immediately went back to Paris without further incident. There are always rumors about Lord Dunraven's mistresses, stealing kisses in gardens, but nothing has ever upset him like the time he was linked to Lady Lambsbeth in the gossip columns."

"It's no wonder. Seeing a married woman. It could have cost him his life." This was more proof that Millicent had been right in being so cautious where Lord Dunraven was concerned.

"Every year there is always a young lady who decides she can snare one of the earls. This year it is Miss Bardwell."

"Yes," Millicent said. "I've met her."

"She tricked all three of them into dancing with her last evening. She does seem to be more forward than previous young ladies, and her father allows her wild behavior.

And poor Miss Donaldson is heartsick. She fears her father wants her to marry an older bachelor who is determinedly courting her, and she is not at all delighted with his attentions."

"How do you know all this?" Millicent asked, surprised and curious as to why Lynette knew so much about what was going on in Society.

"I've told you. I listen to what is being said around me. I'm usually very careful not to repeat what I've heard, but for some reason you are so very easy to talk to. I hope you don't mind that I've sought you out to talk to."

"No, of course not."

"Perhaps I've confided in you because you told me you will only be here for the Season. It would be a shame for you to set your heart for a gentleman who is beyond your reach."

"You're quite right," Millicent agreed, but inside she knew she had enjoyed Lord Dunraven's attention, even if he had done the same thing to a hundred young ladies before her and even though he was risking her reputation.

As Lynette sipped her tea, Millicent looked at her and realized that the young lady was a wealth of Society information. Millicent could almost write a gossip column just by listening to Lynette. And that was good to know.

C*HANDLER SHOOK RAIN* from his coat, then strode with purpose into the dark tavern located near Bow Street. The evening crowds hadn't arrived, so even in the dim light it was easy for him to spot the man he was to meet.

The short, slim-built man rose from his chair at the

table when Chandler approached. "Lord Dunraven, I didn't count on you wanting to see me again so soon."

"Doulton. I expect you shall see me every day until I hear from you the thief has been caught and the raven has been recovered."

Chandler picked up the bottle of port from the table and poured a splash into the glass that Doulton had pushed over to him.

"Tell me, what can I do for you today?" the man said.

Chandler's eyes narrowed. "Why don't we start with you telling me what your men discovered yesterday."

Doulton clasped his hands together and laid them on the table in front of him. He blinked slowly. "Well." He cleared his throat and shifted in his chair, causing a loud squeak. "I told you yesterday I have two of my best men interviewing guests who were in attendance at all three of the parties where there have been thefts. Someone was bound to have seen something or someone suspicious, but there are hundreds of people to talk to. That takes time, Lord Dunraven."

"Then maybe you should have more than two Runners doing the questioning."

"Perhaps I could spare more. I'll look in to it."

"Today?"

"Yes, today." He shifted in his chair again. "You know that more and more people are considering the notion that it is a ghost committing the robberies."

"A ghost?" Chandler gave him a curious stare. "Where did this come from?"

He blinked faster. "I'm not sure where it started, but it is queer that no one has seen anyone walking out with the missing items. And no one has reported seeing a stranger in any of the homes."

"Don't tell me you think there's any possibility there's a ghost doing this."

"No, no, not me."

"Good, because I can assure you it wasn't a ghost who stole the raven. Damnation! One of the scandal sheets probably started this outlandish rumor, as they did with calling him the Mad Ton Thief."

"Yes, now that you mention it," Doulton said nervously. "I believe that is where it started."

"Thank you for reassuring me you, at least, are sane. The jewelry could have easily fit in a man's coat pockets, and the raven could have been held under a man's waistcoat. Ghost indeed. Pickpockets can take your coin purse right out from under your nose without you realizing it. Does that make them a ghost?"

"No sir. But you must admit that the whole affair with this thief is rather strange."

"No, Doulton. It is not strange to have a thief on the loose among the ton. The strange thing is that he hasn't been caught and neither you nor the authorities have a suspect yet."

Doulton sniffed uncomfortably and moved in his chair again. "I only meant that no one has seen anyone who looks like a thief."

"Right, because a beggar would be easy to spot at a dinner party. It means they are damn good at what they do, so you have to be better."

"Yes, quite right and so we are." Doulton rose from his chair. "The only problem is that we haven't had enough time. You must give us more time. We have to interview everyone. Even the smallest clue might help us identify the thief."

"There are other things that need to be done. I suggest

you station a couple of Runners at each party to watch for suspicious-looking characters."

"But that would cost a lot of money, sir. I'm not sure we have the authorization to do that."

"I'm quite friendly with the lord mayor. If you need more money or men to help you accomplish this, tell me now, and I will speak to him. He will know how to go about seeing to it that you have more men on this case. And you need to have someone checking with all the known traders to see if anyone has shown the missing items."

"That's a very good suggestion. No reason for you to bother the lord mayor or anyone else. I'll speak to him and see what can be done. And give me a few more days to look over all the information that my men have obtained so far. I'm sure we'll come up with a suspect."

Chandler didn't know how many days he had. Even now someone could be melting the raven into a lump of gold. The only thing he knew for sure was that it wasn't a ghost who had stolen the raven.

Seven

꧁꧂

"Things without all remedy should be without regard, what's done is done"—just ask Miss Donaldson. It's reported that her father will soon make an announcement about her upcoming engagement. Miss Pennington danced with Lord Dugdale twice last night. Hmm. Are there bets the earl will be the fourth gentleman to offer for her hand this Season? And what is being done to find the Mad Ton Thief, or should he now be called the Mad Ghost Thief?

Lord Truefitt
Society's Daily Column

SHE WAS EASY to identify in the flowing white gown and crown of small white flowers in her hair. The modest, round neckline of her evening dress was held on the shoulders by small capped sleeves and gold satin bands. Gold-colored bullion fell from the shoulders down her back like a shawl. A small band of gold satin fit snugly underneath her breasts. Chandler watched as she calmly made her way through the crowded room before being stopped by two older ladies of the ton.

He wanted to get closer to Millicent Blair, talk to her again, ask her to dance. But that wasn't all he desired. He wanted to pull her into his arms and kiss her tempting lips as he had this afternoon in Lady Beatrice's garden.

He was quite proud of himself for not getting caught by that meddlesome dog. It was close, but thankfully he made it through the hedge, but not without wounds on his hands and a scratch on the side of his neck that he was able to hide with his neckcloth. Though, he admitted to himself with a smile, all the wounds were worth the kiss.

But, he must remain at a distance tonight. He had overplayed his hand last night in telling her he planned to discover the way to her heart. And perhaps he should have waited a few more days before trying to see her, but he hadn't been able to stay away. He had needed to see her.

What had happened to the man who used to be so aloof?

What a sentimentalist he must have sounded like last night. He might as well be wearing his heart on his sleeve, but she intrigued him. That was all. She had been deliberately evasive to his questions just so he would want to seek her out again and again to know more about her.

And he had fallen for it. Hard.

Chandler shook his head. He didn't know if he had ever been so charmed by a young lady who seemed to have no interest in him whatsoever.

He walked closer to her as he greeted friends and acquaintances in the crowded room. She was nodding, listening intently to the lady who was speaking to her. She looked sweet and pure, as if only thoughtful and congenial things would come out of her mouth, but he knew without a doubt that she could be direct or difficult, whichever suited her purpose.

Over the years, many young ladies and his mistresses, too, had excited him, but there was something different about Miss Millicent Blair.

Never had he met a lady so enchanting and so clever in avoiding his questions. Was she playing him in hopes of getting him to ask for her hand or was she truly not interested in him? Could it be that his reputation was so marred by his youthful indiscretions that now that he was interested in a proper young lady she feared he would only trifle with her affections?

She had been surprised to see him in the garden today, but she hadn't been angry. He liked that about her. And she was very slow in rebuffing his attentions, allowing him two kisses before she retreated. Obviously she was not afraid of him.

He wondered why she was so secretive about her family. That certainly put credence to what Andrew had said about her being from a poor family and only being interested in making a wealthy match. It wasn't unusual for a lovely country girl to come to Town hoping some young buck would become besotted with her before he probed too deeply into her family's background. If that was the case, it was no wonder she wasn't interested in him. Anyone in Society could tell her that he had never given serious consideration to marrying any young lady.

Chandler's intuition was usually sharp, and he had a gut feeling that there was more to Miss Blair than simply looking for a suitable match. But what?

A gentleman Chandler had never seen before caught his attention, and he let his gaze stay where the fellow lounged near the front door. Suddenly Chandler's senses went on alert.

The man was properly dressed in evening attire like every other gentleman at the party but something about the man made him appear uncomfortable and out of place. This was just the sort of fellow he suspected the Mad Ton Thief to be, a man who obviously knew how to dress like a gentleman but didn't look at ease being one.

Chandler decided to walk over and present himself to the man and find out who he was. He turned back for a quick glance at Miss Blair.

He liked the way she remained serene and gave her complete attention to the ladies. Her eyes didn't search the room looking for a distraction or a reason to move on to someone else. That was an admirable quality. He had decided a couple of nights ago there were too many things to like about that intriguing young lady without adding more to the list.

"Good evening, sir," Chandler said as he approached the gentleman. "I don't believe we've met before. I'm Chandler Prestwick, the earl of Dunraven."

The tall, sturdily built man bowed graciously, then said, "I'm pleased to meet you, Lord Dunraven. I'm William Hogarth, in the employ of Mr. Percy Doulton. We're here watching for suspicious-looking characters."

Chandler smiled to himself. Hogarth *was* the suspicious-looking character.

"Good. I'm glad to see Doulton acted promptly in securing men to be available at the parties."

"Yes, sir. He went right to work on that. There are two of us at several of the homes where there are more than fifty guests attending this evening."

Chandler was impressed at how quickly Doulton had acted and that there were so many new men added on such short notice.

"Have you seen anyone or anything out of the ordinary?" Chandler asked.

"My partner and I have everything under control. He's watching the rooms where the guests are, and I'm looking over everyone who leaves by this door. If a gentleman tries to walk out with anything bulging from his pocket or his coat, I have orders to politely stop him and search him."

"Thank you, Hogarth. It seems like you are handling everything adequately."

Chandler nodded to the man and started to take his leave.

A feather brushed across the back of his neck and, before he could turn around, he caught sight of a woman from the corner of his eye as Lady Lambsbeth stood before him. A chill of warning flashed down his back.

Chandler folded his arms across his chest and said, "Lady MacBeth—" he cleared his throat and irreverently added, "That is to say, Lady Lambsbeth."

She smiled cunningly at him and slowly batted her long lashes. She was beautiful, with large, expressive blue eyes that seemed always to be beckoning. Curls of shiny blond hair framed her round face.

"My, but you are so delightful when you're cruel. You used to call me Olivia, Chandler. Why so formal?"

"I want it that way."

"I'll have to change your mind. I've missed your charm."

"I doubt that."

She stepped closer to him. "What a devil you are. You wound me with your words."

"Has your husband died again this Season, or perhaps Paris is too hot for you this time of year?"

"Nothing could be as hot as your arms, dearest Chandler." She smiled seductively. "And, yes, it just so happens I am a widow—this time. Truly."

Chandler looked around to see if anyone could see him talking to her. Thankfully there was no one else near the front door but the Runner he had just left.

"My condolences," he said with no concern in his voice.

"I know you have no reason to believe me, but it's true. My husband was killed in a carriage accident shortly after we returned to Paris last year. I'm surprised you haven't heard."

"That is of no concern to me. If you've come back to create more mischief, you'll have to find some other willing soul. This one is not available."

She breathed deeply, lifting her ample breasts, which showed from the low-cut gown she wore. "Tsk, tsk. You're still angry with me for lying to you."

"I don't care enough to be angry."

"My but you've grown a hard edge, Chandler." She reached up and pretended to straighten his neckcloth. "I like it. It could prove interesting in bed."

Chandler stepped away from her and said, "Excuse me, I'm meeting someone."

He started to pass her, but she grabbed his arm and stopped him. She gave him a beguiling smile, showing beautiful white teeth. Chandler was reminded of why he once wanted to possess her. Her skin was soft, her body beautiful, and she adored being touched and worshipped by a man. She was a skilled lover . . . and a practiced liar.

Chandler forced his gaze to slide past her face, down her slender neck, over her full breasts to the long feminine fingers that gripped his arm like a vise. Animosity caused his muscles to work involuntarily beneath her hand. He stared down at her firm grip and then up to her lascivious expression.

His eyes narrowed and his mouth tightened.

Slowly she relented and let go of him. "How distasteful of you to hold a grudge, Chandler. We'll kiss and make up." She lifted her face toward his.

He never had been downright rude to a lady, but tonight he was tempted to tread those uncharted waters, for surely no other woman deserved it more. It was on his mind to tell Lady Lambsbeth what he thought of her, but the last thing he wanted was to be seen talking to her.

"You are beautiful, Lady Lambsbeth, but your mind and your heart are deceitful. I no longer have an interest in you."

Her eyes narrowed. An attractive pout formed on her full lips, puckering the corners. She should have been furious about his nasty remark, but she didn't even blink an eye. She was a coldhearted woman.

"I know you think I'm the one who let it slip to the gossip sheets about our love affair, but I swear it wasn't me. I don't know who found out about us. I was going to tell you the truth before my husband came to Town. It was not my desire for him to catch us in bed. Henry would have killed us both had you not escaped in time."

He didn't even like to hear the word love come out of her mouth. "So whoever told him wanted to see only me dead? That's comforting. I don't care if it was your personal maid who betrayed you. What's done is done. My affair with you is over."

"If that must be so, I will accept it, but dance with me and let's show everyone there are no hard feelings between us."

"Oh, but there are. You no longer captivate me, Lady Lambsbeth. Find someone else to believe you are a lonely widow. I'm not a taker this time. Accept it, I've had my fill of you and I'm no longer interested." He turned and walked away.

Chandler realized that he felt damn good as he eased back into the crowd gathered in the front parlor. He picked up a glass of champagne from a tray and took a sip as he kept walking. He had wanted to tell Lady Lambsbeth what he thought of her since he found out she had lied to him about being a widow.

He was no saint. He'd done his share of slipping into gardens, parlors and bedrooms, but he'd never knowingly taken a married woman to his bed. He had his own code of honor and he didn't knowingly step over it. There were too many available ladies eager for his attentions. He had no desire to pursue another man's wife.

He stopped, took a deep breath and smiled. He was glad he no longer desired her. There was only one set of lips he desired beneath his, and they were on the lovely face of Miss Blair. He had every intention of finding her again before this evening ended.

Minutes passed as he wandered from room to room. He brushed elbows with a duke, smiled at Miss Pennington, nodded to a duke and duchess and greeted friends as he searched the crowd for Miss Blair. He knew she had to be at the party because Lord Heathecoute and his lady were still in attendance. Miss Bardwell caught up with him again, but he was clever enough to avoid asking her to dance. He ducked into a packed room to avoid being seen by Fines.

Chandler continued walking and eventually found himself in what appeared to be a deserted section of the house. He stood at the beginning of a long, narrow corridor that had several doors opening from each side. Oil lamps on the wall lit the passageway, and at the end of the hall stood a tall clock with a large white face.

"Time changes a lot of things," he said softly as his thoughts drifted to the past.

Just after the Season ended last year he began his torrid affair with Lady Lambsbeth. He'd met her at the last big ball of the Season. She had told him she was a widow who was back in Town after several years in Paris. She invited him to call on her and he did so the very next day.

He'd had his chef prepare apricot tarts, thinking to enjoy them with a cup of tea and a smile from the beautiful Lady Lambsbeth. He had no idea that he would spend the entire afternoon in her bed with not a sip of tea or a bite of food. And her bed is where he'd spent every afternoon for the better part of three weeks.

Until rumor of their liaison ended up in the "Society's Daily Column." He'd like to personally strangle Lord Truefitt, and would if he ever discovered the true identity of the gossip writer.

Chandler had been in the columns for years and he didn't let the rumors keep him from visiting Lady Lambsbeth, but it was hardly a week later that her husband unexpectedly and miraculously returned from the dead while Chandler was in her bed.

He had to jump from her second story bedroom with his clothes in his hand. An evening or two later, he was in White's when her husband stormed in with his sword drawn. Chandler would be missing an arm, if not his head, had not some of Lord Lambsbeth's friends held him down and relieved him of his weapon.

Chandler was forced to do the only thing a decent gentleman would do. He denied ever being in Lady Lambsbeth's bedroom, and his friends, who had gathered round him, offered their support of his lie. He'd never seen her again until just a few moments ago. He was glad to know he had no desire to see her again.

Chandler put his glass to his lips and found the glass was empty. He hadn't even realized he'd drunk the champagne while he relived the past. He looked down toward the clock again and noticed the shadow of a person moving in the room at the end of the hallway.

A wary feeling washed over him. Someone was in that room. But who? The master of the house or the Mad Ton Thief? Chandler had to know. He silently placed his empty glass on the table beside him and slowly, as quietly as possible, moved down the hallway. He peeped around the door and was surprised to see Miss Millicent Blair.

She stood in front of the fireplace looking up at a painting over the mantel, then wrote on her dance card. Was she making notes again? Thank-you notes? He grimaced. Surely not. He wasn't falling for that explanation again.

Hell, no.

Chandler stepped backward away from the door. She was alone in a private study. Clearly a place that wasn't usually available to the ordinary guest. Should he let her know he was present?

Suddenly a thought struck him like lightning streaking across a dark gray sky. Chandler's body went rigid. He didn't want to believe what his thoughts were suggesting. But he couldn't keep the idea from taking shape in his mind. Could Miss Blair be making notes about valuable objects in the house in preparation for stealing something?

He refused to consider that, but he couldn't deny the possibility that she might be jotting down notes and relaying them to an accomplice. Things that might be easily taken out of a house without anyone seeing them.

He didn't want to believe it. But what else would she be doing in an area of the house where she shouldn't be, for the second time, writing on her dance card? She had been making notes the first night he saw her. His mind continued digging up facts. Last night she refused to let Lady Heathecoute see her dance card.

No one knew much about her. She certainly hadn't told him anything about herself. Damnation, he didn't like the way things were adding up. He couldn't believe she was stealing things from the homes, but she could be someone's accomplice.

If that was true, it meant Millicent Blair, the beautiful young lady who had him mad with desire, was partners with the Mad Ton Thief.

*M*ILLICENT REJOINED THE party feeling quite satisfied that she had written down enough gossip for Aunt Beatrice. She had filled the back of her dance card with notes and was in the process of trying to retie it to her wrist with one hand as she walked back into the crowded room. Most of what she had written had come from Lady Lynette. After just a few minutes with her new friend during the evening, Millicent had plenty of news for her aunt's column.

She was surprised that Aunt Beatrice or the viscountess hadn't already realized that Lady Lynette knew more gossip than any of the scandal sheets reported. Millicent supposed it was exactly what Lynette had suggested. She was easy to overlook by everyone in Society because they all wanted to pretend she wasn't around so they wouldn't have to look at her birthmark.

It was such a shame. Lynette was a lovely person and

obviously starved for friendship. Millicent made a mental note to call on—

A bump from behind jolted Millicent forward. Her pencil and dance card went flying from her hand as she stumbled to catch herself from falling forward. Strong, heated hands grasped her upper arms and kept her from hitting the floor. She didn't have to see his face or even hear his voice to know that it was Lord Dunraven who had saved her from tumbling onto to her face.

"My sincere apologies, Miss Blair." The words were whispered close to her ear as the guiding hands turned her to face not her guardian angel who saved her from a spill to the floor, but her nemesis.

"Some ill-mannered oaf knocked me right into you. Are you all right?"

"Quite," she answered breathlessly and smiled, realizing several people were staring at them and wanting to minimize the attention to herself.

"I didn't mean to crash into you."

"Of course, you didn't," she said, but could have sworn she didn't see any real expression of regret in the depths of his blue eyes. For the first time she felt a distance in him.

He looked around the room. "I haven't the faintest idea who the devil was so clumsy."

"It's quite all right. Really, I'm not injured and you don't appear to be."

"Not at all."

"Good. Don't give it another thought," she said and immediately started searching the floor for her dance card and pencil. All she saw were polished boots, satin slippers and the hems of dresses.

"Did you lose something? A piece of your jewelry?"

"No, no," she said, determined not to panic. Instinctively she reached up and felt for her pearl earrings and necklace and found everything in place.

"I dropped my pencil and dance card."

"Allow me to find them for you."

"No, no. I'll find them."

But Chandler was already in motion. In a courtly manner, he asked men to watch their steps and ladies to move to the side. Within a few moments, he reached down and picked up her dance card and pencil.

Cupping both in his gloved hand he returned to Millicent and said, "How have you been, Miss Blair?"

She was surprised and apprehensive when he didn't immediately return the card to her. However, she couldn't let him know how desperate she was to get those notes back in her hands.

Politely she brushed her hands down the sides of her dress and answered, "Very well, sir. And you?"

"Same, thank you. I've been to three parties this evening looking for you."

"Well, it seems you finally ran right into me."

His smile was more than a bit roguish as he answered, "Yes. I apologize again for such a brutish greeting."

"No need. Thank you for finding my dance card and pencil."

She held out her gloved hand palm up, but again he made no offer to give them to her, and she was forced to lower her arm because some guests continued to stare at them. It was clear he was going to hold her things hostage until he was ready to return them.

"I should like to call on you tomorrow afternoon, Miss Blair. Would that be acceptable?"

His question was so unexpected she just looked at him for a moment, but regained her wits and said, "No, I don't think I should like that, sir."

His eyebrows shot up in a challenging manner. "Do you find me unattractive, Miss Blair?"

"No, you are quite aware that the opposite is true. You are a most attractive man."

She watched as his gaze swept down her face and back up to her eyes. Something inside made her yearn to give in to his wishes and for a moment it was difficult to catch her breath.

"Thank you. Though, I wasn't soliciting compliments. I'm trying to understand why you consider me an unacceptable suitor?"

She looked away for a moment before turning back to look into his eyes. "Unacceptable is too harsh a word."

"Then I'm confused. Explain why you won't agree to receive a call from me?"

Millicent had feared something like this from Lord Dunraven after this afternoon. If not for how she was helping her aunt she would be thrilled to accept a call from him, even knowing he was a rake and a scoundrel not to be trusted. It was because he was a man who flirted with a lady's emotions that she must rebuff him.

"I'm quite busy enough, but I do thank you for your kindness in wanting to call on me."

"You thank me for my kindness. That's not what I wanted to hear. Are you so busy receiving calls from other gentlemen that you don't have time for me?"

"To be perfectly honest, Lord Dunraven, we really don't get on together very well. And I see no reason to make us suffer through an afternoon together."

He questioned her with his eyes. "Surely that is not an honest answer, Miss Blair."

No it wasn't.

"A gentleman wouldn't challenge a lady's honesty, sir?"

"I'm not feeling the gentleman right now."

"I noticed." Millicent was very close to being flustered, and she never became flustered. She took a deep, steadying breath. "I really don't see the point in carrying this conversation any farther, Lord Dunraven, but, yes, I do thank you for asking to call on me."

He stepped closer and lowered his voice so those who were standing nearby would not hear him. "It's not as if I'm asking you to marry me."

"I should think not."

"You sound as if the very idea horrifies you."

"What? You calling on me?"

"No, the idea of marrying me."

Her eyes widened. "Sir, are you asking me to marry you?"

"Damnation, no," he said too loudly, causing a few glances their way.

Several people stared at them, and Millicent noticed frowns on the faces of the men and shocked expressions on the faces of several ladies.

"I apologize for my manners, Miss Blair, but I'm finding you extremely frustrating at the moment."

"In that case, return my card and pencil and we will bid our farewells."

"Not so fast and not until I get a reasonable answer about why I shouldn't call on you tomorrow afternoon."

Millicent had to remain firm, no matter how she felt to the contrary. She had no doubt that an afternoon with him would be thrilling, but she couldn't afford the attention Lord Dunraven would bring to her.

"Very well, I tried to spare you, but if you must know the truth, not only am I quite aware of your reputation among the ton, I have experienced it firsthand. I don't feel it would be in my best interest for you to call on me."

"So, you refuse to believe my reputation might have been exaggerated by the gossips?"

"No, I believe some of the rumors have been overstated," she said, remembering the things Lynette had said. "But the fact remains that an association with you could ruin my reputation and I'm not willing to chance that. I would like for you to return my dance card and leave me be."

An unfamiliar wrinkle formed in his brow. "So you have no desire to get to know me better."

Millicent hesitated for a moment but finally said, "That's right. That is exactly what I want."

"Not to know me better or for me not to know you better?"

She took a deep breath. "You are far more frustrating than I am, sir. Either or both will do, Lord Dunraven. Let me see how much plainer I can be on this subject. I have no wish to associate with you whatsoever. Does that make it clear enough for you?"

For a moment he looked wounded, and she hated that she was so harsh. If only he knew how much she would enjoy getting to know him better.

"Yes. I believe I'm clear on that now and so is everyone else in the room."

Millicent glanced around, and suddenly it looked as if a thousand eyes watched her. She willed her cheeks not to flame red. Aunt Beatrice was going to consider her an utter failure. She would be sent packing to Nottinghamshire in shame just like her mother and all because of this handsome rogue.

"I didn't mean to be so loud or so harsh. You've forced me to be that way by insisting you want to call on me when I've tried politely to discourage your interest."

"I do believe I understand now. And I know exactly what I need to do."

She took a deep breath. "Good. Now would you mind ever so much returning my dance card and pencil so that I might take my leave?"

"Certainly." He pulled his hand from behind his back and laid the items in her outstretched palm. She quickly folded her fingers over them.

"Here they are. Why don't you put them inside your reticule? That's where you like to keep your dance card, isn't it?"

"Yes. Yes, that's a very good idea. I—I find it easier to keep up with it."

"Easier than tied to your wrist, Miss Blair?"

An odd feeling shook Millicent. Sometimes he said things that made her feel like he could read her mind and knew what she was doing for her aunt.

"Millicent, dear, how are you? Are you hurt?" Lady Heathecoute came rushing over to her as fast as her large frame would allow her to move. "I just heard you were knocked to the floor and trampled upon and Lord Dunraven was kind enough to help you up."

"Angels above, my lady, where did you hear that? I was only lightly bumped. I didn't fall and I certainly wasn't stepped on. I am fine."

"Are you sure? You do look a bit flushed in your cheeks. Do you need smelling salts?"

"No. I'm positive, I'm quite all right."

When the viscountess moved from in front of her, Millicent saw that Lord Dunraven had disappeared and there was only a crowd of strangers standing around her.

She should have been relieved that he was gone. Any kind of relationship with him would only mean trouble for her. She'd had an unexpected kiss from him. That should have been enough, but instead, she found it only left her wanting more.

Eight

"Conversation should be pleasant without scurrility, witty without affectation, free without indecency, learned without conceitedness, novel without falsehood," which is why this one only seeks to provide information so that you might be the judge. Lord Dunraven was seen having a tête-à-tête with Lady Lambsbeth last evening. After the scandal they caused last year, one has to wonder what they discussed.

Lord Truefitt
Society's Daily Column

CHANDLER WATCHED MISS Blair leave the party with the Heathecoutes and took a deep breath. He slipped his hand into his jacket pocket and felt for the dance card. It was safely tucked inside.

Good. It was almost too perfect how his plan had worked.

He really hated having to bump into her so hard, but

when he saw her taking her dance card off her wrist, he knew what he had to do. A slight bump would not have accomplished his goal. It was still unbelievable to him that she never even looked at the card he had given her—a blank card he had borrowed from a dowager duchess who had always liked him. Thankfully, she hadn't asked him any questions.

Now that Miss Blair was gone, he could find a quiet place and read the card. He'd been able to keep her mind off the card by talking about calling on her. That had worked well, too. He didn't understand his feelings for Miss Blair. She could be responsible for the stolen raven, she rebuffed him at every turn, but she intrigued him. Her notes intrigued him.

Chandler desperately wanted to find the thief, but he didn't want to turn Miss Blair's dance card over to Doulton's elite Thief Takers first thing tomorrow for inspection. Clearly she was taking notes when he saw her. He no longer believed her story of making thank-you notes. She had to be writing notes about valuable art objects to hand over to an accomplice.

He walked over to a candle stand and took the card from his pocket and read:

Lord D-dale asked Miss B-well to dance twice.
Lady H. left suddenly for Kent. Miss D. refuses to
attend more parties until father relents

Chandler skimmed the rest of the notes and then skimmed them again. There was nothing but snippets of news on the card. Where were the notes that had information about expensive art objects?

Perhaps there had been two cards on the floor, and he'd picked up the wrong one. Had he somehow kept the wrong card by mistake? No. The dowager had given him a blank card and he had written in a few names for the dances himself. He turned the card over again.

He'd only seen Miss Blair's writing once before, at a distance that first night he saw her, but the writing seemed to be the same beautiful script. He put the card to his nose and inhaled. Oh, yes, it was Miss Blair's.

He studied it for a moment, trying to figure out a logical explanation. Maybe because she was new in Town she was making notes about people to help her remember their names. Considering the number of people in Society, that was highly possible.

Chandler took an easy breath. Yes, that did sound plausible. She didn't grow up in London, so she might have difficulty remembering young ladies and titled gentlemen. That had to be the reason she was making notes. How could he have ever suspected she might be an accomplice to the Mad Ton Thief just because she arrived in Town about the time the thief had arrived?

Relief washed through him. Millicent had nothing to do with the robber.

He had obviously wanted to recover the raven so badly that his mind was going wild with possibilities. Now that Doulton had added security at all the parties, maybe they'd catch the thief in the act. And perhaps he should ask to look over the information that Doulton had received so far. He wasn't sure he trusted the man not to miss something important.

Chandler put the card back in his pocket. The evening was already spent. He'd go home and—

"You've been avoiding us, Dunraven."

Damnation! Andrew and Fines. One at each elbow. Suddenly his two best friends were feeling decidedly like his two worst enemies. He didn't want to talk to them

right now. He wanted to hurry to the privacy of his home
and reread Miss Blair's writings.

"We thought we'd head over to White's for a game and
a drink? Come join us."

"Not tonight, fellows. Some other time. I was just on
my way—"

"We think it's best that you leave right now," Fines
said and took him by one arm. Andrew took hold of the
other and they started leading him toward the doorway.

Chandler pulled his arms away from their grasp and
stopped. "Damnation! What the hell are you two trying
to do? I bloody well don't need an escort."

"We're trying to keep you out of trouble," Fines said,
looking him directly in the eyes. "Keep walking. I just
ran into Lady Lambsbeth. I'm sure she is the last person
you want to see tonight."

"Especially after the rather playful conversation you
just had with Miss Blair," Andrew said before Chandler
had a chance to make a response.

"It was anything but playful," Chandler muttered.

"Exactly."

The three of them began to walk again. "What conversation? What do you mean?" Fines asked. "Who is Miss
Blair?"

"A young lady new to Town this Season," Andrew told
Fines, then to Chandler he said, "She didn't look too
happy with you, Dunraven. And no wonder. I hear you
knocked her silly. Are you losing your touch when it
comes to ladies of quality?"

"I thought we were talking about Lady Lambsbeth?"
Fines grumbled.

"We are."

"No, you were talking about a Miss Blair."

"Her, too," Andrew needled him. "Is it too difficult for you to keep up? We can talk slower."

"Blast it. Could we just please talk about one lady at a time?"

"My, my, what's this? There was a time when you had no problem dealing with two ladies at a time and taking care of both of them quite well."

"We're not talking about me and my ladies. We're talking about Dunraven and his ladies, and I prefer not to handle them at all."

They continued to walk through the crowd of people with Fines and Andrew talking to each other, not giving Chandler the opportunity to say a word to either of them. Not that he wanted to. He didn't want anyone to know that he had spoken to Lady Lambsbeth tonight. And he certainly didn't want to discuss Miss Blair with these two.

"I saw you talking to Miss Blair, but you didn't dance with her tonight," Andrew said. "If you are not going to pursue her, Dunraven, do you mind if I ask her for a dance?"

That got Chandler's attention. Andrew? Dance with Miss Blair?

No.

Yes.

Hell no!

"Don't test me on this, Andrew. I'm in no mood to challenge you over this."

He chuckled. "I just wanted to know where you stood with her, that's all."

The gentlemen stepped outside. Andrew looked to where the drivers and footmen were standing. He pointed to all three of them, signaling for their carriages.

"Who is this Miss Blair you two are talking about?" Fines complained again. "We are supposed to be talking about Lady Lambsbeth. Remember the married lady who almost got Chandler killed last year?"

"Yes, we were talking about her, but, Miss Blair, too. She is the lady who had Chandler's head spinning the other night. Pretty enough, but no one knows much about her. You know what that always means. He would do well to keep his eyes on someone like Miss Bardwell or Miss Pennington."

"Miss Bardwell? That cold fish?"

"I'm told that a generous dowry can make a very warm bed," Andrew said with a sly grin.

"What's this? We're now talking about Miss Bardwell? Could we please talk about one lady at a time?"

"Let's not talk about any lady," Chandler said, realizing it was past time for him to speak up and stop the bickering. He'd had enough from both of them.

"That's easy for you to say, Dunraven. Seems you have two ladies after you tonight. I'm only trying to figure out why."

"You are ready to settle down, Andrew," Fines said. "Why not admit it?"

"Why not have my boot up your arse?"

"You want a fight?" Fines asked. "Tell me when and where. I'm available starting right now."

Chandler saw his carriage pull up. This was his chance to escape. "It was really good of you two to get me out of the party so fast, but I'm going home, not to White's."

"Don't be a spoilsport, Dunraven," Andrew said. "It's not late and the three of us haven't been together to talk about the young ladies since the Season started."

"Let him go. He's been a bore ever since the raven was stolen," Fines said.

"There are times you seem to be more worried about the missing raven than I am."

"It's been in your family for a hundred years. I'd think you'd feel positively dreadful about having it stolen right from underneath your nose."

Chandler bristled. He did feel terrible about it.

"Why should I feel so pained about it when you seem to feel wretched enough for the both of us?"

"No, no. You're all wrong, Fines," Andrew jumped into the conversation gain. "I think it's Miss Blair who has him in a snit. He obviously asked her to dance tonight after he nearly knocked her to the floor, and she refused him. It's put him in a foul temper."

"Good Lord, Dunraven, why did you knock her to the floor?" Fines asked.

"I didn't," Chandler said, holding his teeth together in an attempt to hold on to his anger. "I merely bumped into her."

"Perhaps the fact that he hasn't had a mistress for more than a month has made him clumsy."

"Going that long without a mistress is enough to make a weak man ill-tempered. Damnation, Dunraven, why didn't you say something?"

"It's not the sort of thing a man mentions," Andrew answered for Chandler.

"I'll see if I can help you find one, Dunraven."

Chandler held up his hand. "No, thank you. I'm perfectly capable of finding my own mistress when I'm ready. I'm going to bid my farewell for one reason only: I've had enough of you for one evening and I'm ready to go home."

"If you must go, go. Are we still on for the races tomorrow?" Fines asked.

"Not me," Andrew said, taking a step back. "Count me out. I have other plans."

Chandler and Fines looked at him.

"Sorry." He shrugged his shoulders and smiled sheepishly. "I'm taking Miss Pennington for a ride in the park tomorrow afternoon."

"You cur." Fines grinned. "You are positively smitten by the beautiful lady, aren't you?"

Andrew frowned. "Smitten? Good Lord, no! I'm just checking the ladies over more carefully this year. And if you two would look at yourselves in a mirror once in a while you would do the same. In case you haven't noticed, you're not getting any younger."

"Now, see here," Fines complained. "There's no call for that kind of talk."

Chandler gave up on his two friends and walked off.

THE MOON WAS high in the sky when the Heathecoute's carriage let Millicent out in front of her aunt's town home. They waited until Phillips opened the door and let her inside before driving away. Hamlet started barking before Millicent made it to the top of the stairs. He didn't bark when any of the servants headed to the upper floors, and Millicent hoped he would soon know her footsteps as well.

She stopped outside her aunt's partly open door and knocked lightly. She always waited until she heard either her aunt or Emery reply before she walked inside.

At the response to enter Millicent stepped through the doorway. The heavy odor of lamp oil mixed with the strong scent of liniment hit her like a blast of tepid air. Much to Millicent's surprise her aunt was sitting propped up in bed against several pillows with Hamlet curled and watchful next to her hip. For the first time since Millicent had arrived at her aunt's house, the lamps were brightly lit. Millicent could see her aunt's face clearly.

"Aunt Beatrice," Millicent exclaimed with a smile. She walked closer to the bed, even though Hamlet growled a warning. "You are looking wonderful this evening. I mean morning." Millicent had lost all track of time with the exhausting hours she kept.

"How can you say that, dearie?" her aunt complained with a wave of her uninjured hand. "I feel so absolutely wretched. My head is spinning."

Beatrice was a comely woman—when not injured. She was small in stature and looked much younger than her age of fifty-five. Millicent could see how her friendly manner had served her well, considering what she had been doing for all these years. Her dark brown hair was lightly streaked with gray and fell in soft waves down her shoulders. The swelling had gone down around her eyes and mouth. Her face was regaining its shape.

"I say it because it's true. You are beginning to look like the beautiful aunt I remember."

"Go on with that nonsense talk," she said, but lightly touched the skin around her eyes and her mouth.

"It's not nonsense. Most of the puffiness has gone down in your face and the bruising has faded from a dark purple to a light pink and yellow."

"Don't say any more, please. That sounds positively horrible. It's been well more than a week now since I fell and it still pains me to move."

"That's because your body is still healing. It takes time for broken bones to mend. Don't fret. You'll be taking Hamlet for walks in your beautiful garden and be back at your work before you know it."

"Not soon enough for me," she grumbled.

"Everyone I've met who knows I'm staying with you sends greetings and good well wishes."

Aunt Beatrice sighed and pulled at the neckline of her night rail. "I'm sure I won't make it to return at all this Season."

Her aunt couldn't get well soon enough for Millicent. "Let's not give up hope until we have to, shall we?"

"My face doesn't feel as tight today." She reached up and lightly patted her palm to her cheek. "Perhaps, I look a little better, but I'm by no means ready to be up and about."

Millicent moved a step closer. Hamlet's head popped up, and he watched her with big, dark brown eyes, but he didn't bark or growl. Maybe she was making progress with him. She smiled at him before returning her attention to her aunt.

"You're sitting up, which you haven't done before, so I see that as a good sign that you are now on the mend."

"I suppose you are right. Let's get on with the article. What do you have for me tonight?"

Millicent took her reticule off her wrist and opened it. She pulled out her dance card and turned it over to read her notes on the back, but the back was blank.

Blank? Angels above! How could that be? Frantic, she searched her reticule for another card but found nothing. Still not believing her eyes, she turned her small purse upside down and emptied its contents on the foot of her aunt's bed. Hamlet rose and walked over to the things lying near her aunt's feet. He quietly sniffed the pencil and barked once, then moved on to her handkerchief.

Oh, no!

She looked at the front of the card and realized that Lord Dunraven had mistakenly picked up someone else's card from the floor! What rotten luck! Hers was probably at this moment being swept into a trash heap by the servants while she stared at a useless card.

"What could have happened?" she whispered softly to herself as her hands clutched into tight fists.

"Dear girl, what is it?" her aunt questioned. "You seem distraught."

"It's nothing." Millicent couldn't let her aunt know what had happened. "I was just looking for something. Never mind. It doesn't matter." She wasn't covering for herself very well. How could Lord Dunraven pick up the wrong card?

"Now, what did I discover tonight? Let me think for a moment."

Millicent put her finger to her lips and pretended to do some serious thinking. Her mind was as blank as the useless card in her hand. What had she written down when she was in that reading room?

She couldn't remember anything but the expression on Lord Dunraven's face when he handed her the dance card. Had he known he had the wrong card? No, that would have been impossible. She watched him reach down and pick it up. It looked like her card, but then most of them looked very much alike.

Lord Dunraven had caught her once before making notes on her dance card. He had even teased her about it later, but she was sure there was no way he could have seen her making notes tonight. She'd been so careful to be sure that no one had followed her to that back room.

"Millicent, you are taking too long with your thinking. We don't have that much time."

"Ah—I think the most important gossip I heard tonight was that Lady Lambsbeth is back in Town."

"Are you sure?" Aunt Beatrice leaned forward. Having

lost interest in the contents of Millicent's reticule, Hamlet snuggled back against Aunt Beatrice.

"Quite." Millicent felt sure she could trust anything Lynette told her.

"That sounds delicious. If this is true, it's worth reporting. Who was she dancing with?"

"I don't know, but she was seen having a secluded tête-à-tête with Lord Dunraven." Millicent blurted out the bit of information Lynette had whispered to her as she was leaving the party with Viscountess Heathecoute.

"Are you sure about this? Did you witness their intimate conversation?"

She hadn't, but she was sure. She'd been attacked with something that felt very much like jealousy when Lynette had whispered the information to her.

"Goodness no. I have no idea what Lady Lambsbeth looks like. I received this information from a very good source as I was leaving the party."

Aunt's Beatrice's eyes suddenly looked glassy. "If it is true, this is just the sort of thing our readers like to read about."

A lump formed in Millicent's throat. She was a bit concerned about how interested her aunt was in this particular information. Her eyes were flashing with excitement.

"Millicent, I need to know who told you about this clandestine meeting. We can't publish a word of it unless we are sure Lady Lambsbeth is in Town and that she attended at least one party that the earl attended."

Millicent wrinkled her brow. She had a sinking feeling that it might have been better had she kept the information about Lady Lambsbeth and Lord Dunraven to herself. But it was too late for recriminations now.

"So whether they actually had a conversation is not important?" Millicent asked.

"Of course it is. In a small way. It is perfectly all right to assume that if they, indeed, ended up at the same party that sometime during the evening, they had a conversation—given their past relationship. It would have been so delicious to have overheard a word or two of what they said. Now tell me, who gave you this information?"

"I'd rather not say, Aunt Beatrice. My source believes she talks to me in secret."

"And she does. The same as I talk to you and you to me in private. Good heavens! Do you think I'd ever reveal where Lord Truefitt's information comes from? What a ninny I would be if I did that. And if anyone finds out I am Lord Truefitt, I'll leave Town in shame."

"I understand that. I'm certain that she would not tell me something that didn't happen. She is most reliable."

"I'm certain of that, too. Heavens, Millicent, I've been doing this for over fifteen years and I've trusted no one with the information but my contact at *The Daily Reader*, the Heathecoutes and now you."

What her aunt said was true and gave Millicent some reassurance, but this made her certain she'd never like writing about other people's personal lives. What if Lord Dunraven didn't want anyone to know he had talked to Lady Lambsbeth?

"Very well," Millicent relented. "My informant is Lady Lynette Knightington."

"Hmm. The one with the birthmark?" Aunt Beatrice screwed up her face in thought while Hamlet licked her hand.

Millicent nodded.

"Her father being a duke, she's always at the best parties. She's usually quiet. Spends most of her time just watching other people. I seldom see her talking with anyone."

"Maybe that's because no one takes the time to really talk to her," Millicent offered.

"She does know everyone. The poor dear has no chance of making a match. I think she realizes that, but she does seem to always be around. I suppose it's quite possible that she saw them together."

"Lady Lynette has been very kind to me every time I've seen her. I told you she paid a call yesterday."

"Yes, yes. I remember that. She's probably a good contact for you. I think we can consider her a reliable source. Tell me exactly what she said to you tonight."

"Let me think." Millicent started putting her belongings back into her reticule now that Hamlet had inspected it all and had settled down again.

"We don't have time for you to think, Millicent," her aunt said impatiently.

"I was taking my leave and . . ." Unexpectedly, she thought of the soft kiss Lord Dunraven had given her in the garden.

"Millicent?" her aunt asked again.

"While Lord Heathecoute was helping his lady with her cloak, Lady Lynette came over and whispered she'd seen the two of them having a private conversation near the front door."

"Perhaps they had planned to meet there."

"I really don't know. Lady Lynette added that Lady Lambsbeth was even more radiant than she had been last year." A wistfulness entered Millicent's voice. "Lady Lynette discreetly pointed with her fan to a lady not far away. From what I could see of her, she was indeed very beautiful." As she said the words, Millicent felt another small stab of—jealousy? Is that what she felt? Surely not.

"As beautiful and as deadly as a jeweled dagger," Aunt

Beatrice said. "Did Lady Lynette by chance overhear anything they said to each other?"

"Not that she mentioned."

"No, of course not. The dear girl wouldn't want to go that far with the gossip."

Millicent again wondered if she and her aunt were even talking about the same Lady Lynette. Millicent found the duke's daughter to be a deep well of gossip, especially where Lord Dunraven was concerned.

"Hurry, get your quill and vellum, Millicent, we must not tarry. If Lady Lynette saw them talking so did others. We will dedicate our entire column to this story."

Millicent squeezed her eyes shut for a moment when she turned away. She didn't like the knot of guilt that coiled and rumbled in her stomach.

What had she done to Lord Dunraven? What would he say if he ever found out what she had done to him?

Would he ever forgive her?

Nine

"Oh, beware, my lord, of jealousy; It is the green-eyed monster which doth mock the meat it feeds on." One has to wonder if Lord Dunraven has so short a memory. Wasn't it only last year that Lord Lambsbeth challenged him to a duel in White's? But this one has just discovered there will be no challenge this Season, for Lady Lambsbeth is a widow.

Lord Truefitt
Society's Daily Column

MILLICENT BREATHED IN deeply as she enjoyed a leisurely drive in the open carriage to the business area located near her aunt's town house. She was properly accompanied by her aunt's housekeeper rather than her own maid, because Mrs. Brown needed to pick up some things for Lady Beatrice.

The housekeeper was as quiet on the street as she was in the house. Millicent had made several attempts at conversation by commenting on how beautiful the day was and how lovely the flowers were in the various parks, but Mrs. Brown had responded with only a brief "Yes, Miss," to absolutely everything Millicent had said.

Giving up on conversing and content simply to enjoy the drive, Millicent fell silent, too. This was her first venture out into the streets of London since she'd arrived in Town and she intended to enjoy every minute of it.

The sky was a vivid blue and the temperature pleasant as they drove past the rows of town homes and the green areas of the squares. Millicent was comfortably attired in a carriage dress of lightweight muslin with a matching three-button pelisse in faille. Her straw bonnet was trimmed with tiny flowers at the crown and banded with stiff muslin the same cinnamon brown as her kid gloves. Her half boots would make any strolling easy.

Millicent found the traffic in the streets shockingly busy for midafternoon. She had never seen so many gigs, phaetons, drays and other types of conveyances in her life. Some of the carriages were quite ornate with elaborate trim and gold crests on the doors. Those were pulled by two or four well-matched horses that were driven by coachmen in handsome livery. As they continued down Oxford Street toward the City, the congestion was further complicated by the addition of street sweepers, the throng of pedestrians going about their daily business, and the rough barrows of the numerous street vendors.

Millicent noticed they passed several shops that sold fabrics, lace and sewing notions, but obviously none of them were their intended target.

The housekeeper was taking Millicent to Aunt Beatrice's favorite place. Her aunt had told her the quaint shop would be the perfect place for Millicent to buy her mother a length of lace, a bit of ribbon, embroidery thread or any number of other things that could easily be sent to her by mail coach.

Millicent had not had much time to think about her mother since arriving in London. She had posted only one short letter to her. Millicent hoped to make up for her lack of attention by purchasing her mother a small gift.

The moment they walked in the shop Millicent saw that Mrs. Brown and the shopkeeper knew each other well. When asked about her employer, Mrs. Brown discreetly told the clerk that her employer's recuperation was progressing as expected, and then she introduced Millicent.

Millicent smiled at the clerk and insisted she needed no help in picking out her purchases. She left the two at the front of the shop and went immediately to the table that held lace and carefully looked over the intricate patterns. From there she walked over to the ribbons, which came in so many different colors and widths Millicent didn't know how she would ever be able to make up her mind.

She heard the door open and close two or three times while she looked over the beautiful fabrics in the shop but paid it no mind. The shopkeeper offered again to help her, but Millicent assured her she would rather take her time and look over everything before making a decision.

The clerk and Mrs. Brown continued to talk as if they were long lost friends who hadn't seen each other in years. Millicent would have sworn that Mrs. Brown wasn't capable of saying so much to anyone, but Millicent had just been proven wrong.

Wanting to give Mrs. Brown time to finish her conversation, Millicent slowly made her way to the rear of the store where the fine fabrics were located. She was pressing her palm over a length of blue velvet when suddenly a hand pressed her back, gently ushering her forward. Her head snapped around and she saw Lord Dunraven at her side. She gasped, but allowed him to maneuver her to the end of the aisle, where large bolts of dark velvets were stacked high.

"Stand here and look at these fabrics," he said as he quickly stacked several bolts of cloth on top of each other. Within moments he had two piles of cloth tall enough for him to stand behind without being seen by anyone in the front of the store.

When he was finished he turned to her and said, "There. That should hide me from your chaperone."

"What in heaven's name are you doing in a fabric shop?"

"Looking for you, of course."

Millicent took a deep breath and said, "I believe you are developing a bad habit of startling me, sir."

"That is because you are so easy to startle, Miss Blair, but why does it have to be a bad habit? Why can't you say I have a good habit of startling you?"

He reached over and added another bolt to the stack closest to Millicent and took a step closer to her.

"Can a startle be good?" she asked.

"Yes."

"How so?"

"I'll show you sometime, but in order for it to work you can't have a guilty conscience."

She lifted her shoulders and her chin. "Whatever do you mean?" she asked and looked over her left shoulder. Mrs. Brown and the shop attendant were still engrossed in their conversation. "A guilty conscience about what?"

"You tell me."

"You are talking in riddles, sir."

"Perhaps I am, but you are a mystery to me, Miss Blair, and of course that intrigues me."

"I have no intentions of being a mystery to you, Lord

Dunraven," she said, wondering if her hat was on straight, because his eyes seemed to be studying her so intently.

"Then why don't you answer any of my questions directly? It makes me wonder if you have skeletons in your closet."

His words alerted her. "Skeletons? You have a vivid imagination, sir."

A devilish grin spread across his face and she realized he was only teasing her, but Millicent had suddenly felt as if she had been caught writing her gossip.

There was no way he could know what she was doing unless—unless he had her real dance card! Could that be? No. She was reacting far too seriously about his offhanded remark because she did have a guilty conscience. How could he know anything about her or what she was doing for her aunt?

She wouldn't say any more about the subject. Surely if he had seen her dance card, he would have to come right out and accuse her, and somehow she felt him unwilling to do that.

Millicent had learned years ago that when she didn't know how to answer a question, or didn't like the direction a conversation was going, it was best to change the subject. That seemed a judicious thing to do right now.

"There is no way this can be a chance meeting, Lord Dunraven."

"Indeed, it is not."

"Rake that you are, you followed me, didn't you?" she asked, a bit miffed, a bit flattered and a bit excited.

"Yes."

"You really are a rogue of the first order."

"Guilty." He paused, then added, "Though only sometimes."

"That's not what I hear."

"I have been known to behave properly when it matters most, Miss Blair."

He smiled and suddenly Millicent felt as if sunlight shone on her face. How could his smile brighten her day and fill her with such pleasant feelings? Suddenly she felt wonderful. She wanted to throw her arms up in the air and twirl around as if she were five years old again.

Standing before her was an admitted rogue who knew how to charm any lady, not just her. Yet, the very sight of him made her heart beat a little faster.

Millicent tried to sound firm while keeping her voice low. She said, "Following me is unacceptable. And standing here talking to me in this shop is even worse. Have you no care for my reputation?"

"Your reputation is safe with me. You left me no choice when you refused again to let me call on you like a proper gentleman. I had to design a plan to see you. I decided to watch Lady Beatrice's house until you came into the garden again. But when I saw you leave the house, I decided to follow you."

"You were watching the house again? That was foolish. I could have stayed inside all day."

"Foolish, yes, but I do have good luck."

"Good luck, indeed. Clearly you are an expert at maneuvering yourself so that you can have a private assignation with young ladies whenever and wherever you wish."

He gave her that warm engaging smile as he folded his arms across his chest in a very relaxed position and leaned a narrow hip against the table. "That's true, but it is also true I have not stooped to such antics lately. I've not had to, and I did it years ago for the fun and the sport of it. Now I'm doing it because you are the first young lady who has refused to allow me to call on her in a proper and gentlemanly manner."

For some reason that truthful admission gave her confidence and freedom to give him a genuine smile. "That should have been a hint that I didn't want to see you."

"A hint? I took it as a challenge. I thought perhaps it meant you didn't want anyone to see us together, giving my dastardly notoriety and your unblemished reputation."

At that remark, Millicent laughed softly, quietly but without restraint. He was so engaging, he was wrapping her up like a gift to present to himself.

"Shhh," he put his hand to his lips. "I don't think anyone knows I'm in here."

Mrs. Brown and the clerk continued to huddle together but had walked farther away from Millicent to look at jars of creams, oils or something behind the front counter.

Millicent cleared her throat and fingered the fabric again. "Nonsense," she said, but asked, "How did you get in without them seeing you?"

"I went to the back alley and slipped in from the rear door." He looked around the bolts of cloth. "I don't think there is anyone else in here right now but you and I, your chaperone and the clerk."

"Thank goodness. You could have been caught."

"Yes."

A shiver of excitement tingled through her. "And that means I would have been caught talking to you."

"Yes."

"Does that not worry you?"

He moved a little closer to her and lowered his voice even more as he said, "For you, yes. For me, some things are worth the risk, Miss Blair."

Millicent picked up an edge of fabric and pretended to study it, when all she wanted to do was look into Lord

Dunraven's seductive blue eyes and tell him she was charmed and flattered that he went to so much trouble just to see her for the second time in two days.

Truly, he must have known how difficult he was for her to resist. His smile, his manner and even his bad reputation perplexed her, worried her . . . and captivated her. But she could never let him know that seeing him today was worth the risk of being caught talking to him in private.

She took a deep, languid breath. But what was she going to do? His pursuing her would make her more visible and jeopardize her work for her aunt. Keeping that secret had to be uppermost in her mind. If Millicent were caught, her aunt might somehow be revealed as Lord Truefitt, and she couldn't risk ruining her aunt's place in Society.

Perhaps she should confess to Aunt Beatrice or Viscountess Heathecoute and ask how she should handle this handsome gentleman rogue, for surely he was way too fast for her country upbringing.

With a fluid grace, Lord Dunraven reached over and took her gloved hand in his and gently pulled her to his chest, concealing her with him behind the bolts of fabric. Millicent gasped softly but didn't pull away from him. How could she when she wanted to feel his arms around her again?

"Did that startle you?"

She looked up into his eyes, so close to hers she felt his breath when he spoke. "Yes."

A wicked half grin lifted one corner of his mouth. "Was it a good startle?"

"Yes."

Most definitely.

Oh, he was a cunning devil. How could she have lied to him and told him that it wasn't? For surely it felt wonderful having his strong arms surround her and to be snuggled so close and so tightly in his arms.

Lord Dunraven's grin turned to a pleasing smile. Millicent wasn't afraid to be in his arms. She felt no danger. He was strong and her will was weak. She merely felt that she was where she wanted to be.

"Do you mind if I kiss you?" he asked.

Surprised, she said, "You didn't ask yesterday."

"Yesterday it would not have been difficult for me to escape had you screamed. Today would be a bit more of a problem."

Millicent smiled. "So I could get rid of you merely by screaming?"

"Or just a loud cough would draw attention to you, Miss Blair. So what will it be?"

"A kiss," she said without hesitating, knowing if she did, her sensible mind would win and she didn't want it to.

Bending his head, he lightly brushed his lips across hers. The kiss was so gentle and brief if she tried hard she could believe it had never happened, yet her heart rate soared and a quickening tightened her abdomen.

She gazed into his eyes, fearing he would kiss her again and fearing he wouldn't. Oh, what sweet torment!

She moistened her lips and said, "I'm glad to know that a rake can ask permission for a kiss."

"I told you that I know to behave as a gentleman—at times. I had a feeling you wouldn't scream if I pulled you into my arms and kissed you, but I didn't want to frighten you."

"You don't scare me, sir."

"I know. So, may I kiss you again?"

"Please do."

His arms tightened around her, pulling her closer to his

chest. He lowered his head again and instinctively her lips parted, her mouth opened, allowing his tongue to slip inside and plunder her warmth. The kiss was long, generous, drugging. Short choppy breaths merged with long whispery sighs. Millicent had no idea which sound emerged from Lord Dunraven and which came from her own mouth.

When he broke the kiss, he remained holding her tightly. He looked deeply into her eyes and said, "I've wanted to kiss you like this since the first night I saw you in the corridor. Remember that night?"

"You blew me a kiss."

"More proof I can be a gentleman at times."

Without letting her go, he turned them around and carefully backed her up until she pressed against the fabric table.

"What are you going to do?"

"Kiss you madly."

Millicent caught her bottom lip between her teeth and formed a protest that never came out.

"Don't be alarmed," he whispered softly. "I can see your maid through the stacks of cloth. I will keep watch. I won't let her or anyone else catch us. If she heads this way, I'll duck under the table."

Millicent nodded as he bent his head toward hers again. She knew what she was allowing him to do was beyond the pale, but where he was concerned she discarded caution and reason. There was something decidedly rebellious, thrilling and a little bit wicked about kissing him in the shop. She had no inclination to stop as she had no inhibitions when she was in his arms.

Her lips parted as his met hers once more. Millicent knew from the first touch that this would be no gentle, tender kiss, and her breathing quickened erratically with desire.

Lord Dunraven's lips bruised hungrily over hers and she matched his furor. His arms wrapped tightly around her back, crushed her to him.

Instinctively she opened her mouth again and accepted his tongue and gave him hers. It pleased her when she heard him swallow soft gasps of pleasure with each probe of her tongue into his mouth.

"You taste so sweet," he whispered against her lips.

"And you are a masterful kisser, sir," she answered breathlessly.

His lips left hers and he kissed her cheek, her chin and her neck. "Do you like the way I make you feel?"

"Yes. I've never felt such intense pleasure with other kisses."

"So you have been kissed before?"

"Of course. I'm almost one and twenty."

"But you haven't been thoroughly kissed, the way I kissed you just now?"

"That's correct. All the kisses I've had up to now have been properly given on the cheek by gentlemen."

"Proper gentlemen? And I am not?"

"You, sir, are not a good matrimonial candidate, and I should not have allowed you so much freedom."

"But you did."

"Your charm is very persuasive."

"You have led me on a merry chase."

"Not by design."

"I think I like the fact that you have been brave enough to allow a kiss or two and discreet enough not to let any man take advantage of you."

There was sudden laughter from the front of the shop and Millicent stiffened in his arms.

"It's all right," he whispered, looking past her through the small opening between the stacks of cloth. "Your maid is quite busy at the moment."

Breathing hard, and needing to see for herself, Millicent leaned her head back and saw the two women opening jars and smelling the contents.

Millicent took a deep, relaxing breath.

"Keep your head back a moment," he whispered. "That's the perfect position for kissing your beautiful neck."

"Necks are not beautiful, sir. They are skinny and bony."

"Yours is lovely and it's sensitive, too. That's why I love to kiss it." He showered her with more kisses.

"Yes," she whispered giving herself over to the pleasure.

Throwing caution to the wind, and her reputation out the window, Millicent did as he asked and allowed the earl the freedom he desired to explore her neck.

Softly he kissed the area behind her ear, and her skin pebbled with delicious goose bumps even though she had never felt hotter in her life. He kissed the lobe of her ear and gently, quickly sucked it into his mouth and out again a couple of times before leaving it to explore his way down the column of her neck to where the hollow of her throat met the stiff lace of her collar.

Shivers of delight threaded tighter and tighter through Millicent, wrapping her in the web he had set for her. She was amazed at how much enjoyment she received from his touch.

"I've never been kissed like this before," she murmured softly.

"Good." He kissed her lips, her chin, then the base of

her throat again. "You shouldn't let anyone kiss you like this—but me, of course."

His lips found hers again and he kissed her passionately. He ran his hands up her back, over her shoulders and down her arms. His hands never stopped moving as their mouths clung together.

Millicent couldn't let her hands be still either. She ran her open palms over the width of his strong shoulders and her fingers up into the back of his hair. She loved the way his lips moved expertly across hers. She loved the taste of his tongue in her mouth. She was eager to enjoy everything she was experiencing, including the touch of the expensive fabric of his coat beneath her hand.

"I like that you enjoy how I kiss you," he murmured softly.

"That pleases you?"

"Very much."

"Me too." Some kisses were soft and warm while others were fierce and passionate. Millicent had thought she had been kissed before, but she hadn't. This was kissing! Weak legs included. If she hadn't been propped against the table, she would have melted to her knees.

Lord Dunraven lifted his head and looked deeply into her eyes as if searching for something. With one hand splayed against her back he pressed her to him. With his other hand he reached up and touched her ear, softly caressing the small lobe. Slowly his fingertips took the same path down her neck that his lips had followed earlier, only this time the journey didn't stop at the lace collar. His hand continued down her chest until his open palm rested on the full swell of her breast.

Millicent was hardly breathing. She felt as though her insides were twisting into a wondrous knot of exciting sensations. No one had ever touched her breasts before, and it was thrilling. His hand slid beneath her breast and lifted it into his palm and he closed his fingers around it, squeezing gently yet firmly. The sensations that shot through her were wondrous.

Her lower body strained to get closer to him, and he answered her invitation by pressing harder against her. Millicent gasped again as she felt the hardness of his body.

For the first time in her life she knew what it was like to want a man to love her. The desirous sensations caused her to press her lips to his and slide her tongue deep into his mouth. He muffled his groan.

"I knew it," he whispered passionately against her lips. "Your breast fits perfectly into my hand."

It feels perfect.

He looked into her eyes. "If only I could remove your dress and look upon your beauty with the desire I feel for you at this moment. I would show you how a man loves a woman."

As if considering the possibility, he glanced toward the front of the shop, where muffled talking could still be heard. He lowered his head to her chest for a moment, then lifted it again.

"But now is not the time and this is not the place. I want to kiss you again. I have good luck, but I'm not going to push it further today."

Slowly he let her go and stepped away. Millicent felt bereft and out of breath. He helped her to straighten her collar, then ran his thumb across her lips and smiled.

"You look like you have been thoroughly kissed."

Millicent touched her lips with her fingertips. "What should I do?" she asked.

"Nothing." He reached up and lowered her hand from her mouth. "The redness will disappear quickly."

She shook her head in worry. "I can't believe I let you kiss me, and, and touch me so intimately here in this public place. I'm afraid I've shocked myself."

As soon as the words were out, she would have done anything to take them back. He probably wanted to hear that she was upset with herself for submitting to his wishes so easily. Her heart was beating so fast and she was so light-headed with desire that nothing more sane would pass her lips.

He smiled. "Don't worry about your reputation. You are safe with me."

"After what just passed between us, that is an absurd remark, sir. I'm safe anywhere but in your presence where I seem to turn into a wanton—"

He cut off her words by placing his thumb lightly against her lips. "We shared some passionate kisses. That is all. No one but us will ever know."

Of course he would say that. He would not want to be caught in such a compromising and unforgiving situation and be forced to marry her. He was a confirmed bachelor. No, it was best they forget this ever happened, and she must stay away from him at all cost.

"I understand." She pulled on the neckline of her dress and moistened her lips. They tasted of Lord Dunraven, and her chest tightened, as she missed his embrace already. Oh, what had she done? What had she allowed him to do, to kiss her so intimately and to touch her in such forbidden places?

"What parties are you attending this evening?"

"We'll be going to the Dovershafts and then to Almacks. Why?"

He stepped away from her and said, "Because knowing where you will be means I don't waste time looking for you this evening. Go back to the other side of the counter before your maid misses you."

Just like that he was ready to be rid of her. How could she have gone so easily into his arms and allowed him to do whatever he wished?

"Clearly, Lord Dunraven, I had not met a rake until I met you. I should have nothing more to do with you."

His gaze stayed on hers. "Perhaps you shouldn't, but the question is, will you?"

Millicent closed her eyes and counted to three.

Angels above! She should be worried about much more than having been so thoroughly kissed. How had she fallen under his enchanting spell so quickly and completely?

She was what she never thought she would be—just like her mother. She was going to fall in love with the town scoundrel and be forced to leave London in shame as her mother had done years ago.

She would tell him he must not try to speak to her again. Yes, that is what she would do.

Feeling resolute, she opened her eyes to tell him, but he was gone.

Ten

"Suit the action to the word, the word to the action." And find the Mad Ton Thief seems to be the outcry from London Society. Acknowledgment is given to Lord Dunraven. Because of his efforts, home soirées must now suffer the presence of ill-at-ease Runners. Why? one must ask, when many of the ton believe the thief is a ghost. One would think the earl would be too busy to bother with the thief, since Lady Lambsbeth is in Town for the rest of the Season.

Lord Truefitt
Society's Daily Column

"*BLASTED DEVILS, ALL* of them," Chandler muttered to himself as he wadded the newspaper clipping Fines had just given him. He looked around the crowded room for a place to throw it but found nothing nearby.

Chandler stood just inside one of the arched alcoves in the ballroom at Almack's. He'd been feeling quite good, looking forward to spending the evening in Miss Blair's company until Fines appeared with a copy of the latest tittle-tattle. He shouldn't have read it. He knew better. It always left him feeling angry and ruined his evening. Tonight was no exception.

It might be worth getting married just so the gossip-mongers would leave him alone.

"You have only yourself to blame, Dunraven," Fines said in a high-handed tone.

"Why the hell do you think I would bring such misery on myself?"

"I tried to warn you last night that Lady Lambsbeth was in attendance."

The orchestra played a tune that seemed to match the slow, strong beat of Chandler's heart. The dance floor was filled with elaborately dressed ladies and expensively clad gentlemen twirling and sidestepping in unison. Chandler was thankful the windows in the large room were open. The gossip along with his tight collar and neckcloth was definitely making him hot.

He'd made an appearance at three different parties tonight, looking for anyone who might not fit in with the usual crowd. At last he'd realized what an ineffectual idea that had been. He was not going to nab the thief at one of the house parties. If that happened, it would have to be one of Doulton's Runners who did it.

He searched the crowd once again for Miss Blair, as he'd done the entire hour he'd been in the ballroom. He hadn't been able to get her out of his mind. He'd felt like an anxious schoolboy as he'd dressed tonight. He couldn't wait to get here so he could see her, talk to her, dance with her. He wanted her back in his arms.

"Did you hear me, Dunraven?"

"Yes," he said, but wasn't sure he had. "I was just

thinking that if I ever get my hands around the neck of
Lord Truefitt, I'll happily strangle him until he begs for
mercy and swears he'll never pick up another quill to put
in ink!"

"All you and Andrew wanted to do was talk about some
penniless girl from the country. What was her name—
Miss Blondel?"

Chandler took umbrage at Fines for speaking of her in
such an ill manner. "Miss Blair. And where did you hear
that she was a penniless girl from the country?"

"I believe Andrew said as much last night when he
alluded to the fact she was in Town only for the Season
and hoping to make a comfortable match."

"He doesn't know as much about her as I do," Chandler
said contentiously. "You can tell by her clothing, her manner of speech and the way she carries herself," *the way
she feels in my arms, the sweetness of her kisses,* "that
she was not raised penniless."

"It could be that her family splurged on clothes just for
the Season. She is lovely. No reason to think she won't
do well for herself."

Finding no place to discard the wadded clipping and
feeling quite provoked by now, Chandler threw the small
paper ball out the open window. He didn't know why he
was so obsessed with Miss Blair. She wasn't the most
beautiful young lady he'd ever seen, but she was the most
intriguing, the most enchanting and the most desirable.

Chandler didn't care a damn about Lady Lambsbeth.
He didn't want to see her or talk to her and he certainly
didn't want his name linked to hers in the papers. There
was only one lady on his mind. Miss Millicent Blair.

Just thinking of her calmed him. Her kisses had been
untutored but responsive. She had been submissive in his
arms, not because he demanded it, but because she wel-

comed his embrace. There was no better aphrodisiac than knowing this lady wanted his touch.

He had tempted many young ladies of the ton into kisses as passionate as those he had shared with Miss Blair in that shop, but none had touched the depths of his soul as she did. He felt restless and his desire to hold and kiss her again was intense.

"Damnation," he muttered more to himself than to Fines.

"Obviously we didn't get you out of the party soon enough. The only thing a gossipmonger needs to know is that you were seen attending the same party as Lady Lambsbeth and the scandal broth is heated to boiling. They don't care that you didn't actually see or speak to the lady in question. It doesn't matter a whit in hell to them if it sells papers."

Chandler didn't comment, so Fines continued. "I found out today that Lady Lambsbeth moved back to London and has rented a town house—not far from yours, by the way. I have it on good authority that her husband is, indeed, dead this time. Some sort of carriage accident in Paris."

"I don't care if she's widow or princess, or if she lives right next door to me. I have no desire or intention of renewing a relationship with her. And after our conversation last night, I don't think Lady Lambsbeth will be seeking my attentions."

"You didn't," Fines exclaimed and stepped closer to Chandler. "Good Lord, Dunraven, are the scandal sheets right? You did talk to her last night, didn't you?"

"Only long enough to assure her I had no interest in her," he admitted, wondering why he hadn't completely ignored her and walked away without speaking to her.

"All you need is a second for someone to see her in your company."

"I could have sworn that no one saw us but the Runner, who works for a Thief Taker named Doulton."

"A Runner? Good lord, Dunraven. Did you take leave of your senses? It only takes one person to see you with her, or God forbid—do you think he could have overheard what you said? Either way, no doubt the Runner made a tidy sum last night tattling on you." Fines paused, then asked, "What exactly did you say to her?"

Chandler's gaze strayed to the door again, looking for Miss Blair. "Exactly what I told you, not that any of it is your concern or the ton's business. I don't intend to pick up where we left off, and she should find some other lackwit to keep her bed warm."

Miss Pennington, Miss Bardwell and Miss Whidmore passed in front of them, walking very slowly. Both gentlemen nodded and bowed. Miss Bardwell winked, but Chandler had no idea if the flirtation was intended for him or Fines. Miss Pennington openly smiled, showing why her beauty made her the belle of the debutantes this Season, and shy-acting Miss Widmore hid most of her face behind a lacy fan.

When he was certain the ladies were out of earshot, Fines picked up the conversation where they had left off by saying, "What you need is a new mistress."

Not that again.

The thought of securing a mistress had no more appeal to Chandler than renewing a relationship with Lady Lambsbeth or starting one with Miss Bardwell.

"Once you get the right mistress settled into your life, Lady Lambsbeth will never cross your mind again."

"She doesn't cross my mind now unless you mention her," Chandler complained.

The only lady on his mind was Miss Blair, and he must be blessed for she was walking in to the ballroom on the arm of Viscount Heathecoute. He hadn't gotten the feel of her out of his mind or the taste of her from his lips. She was an extraordinary lady to have held his attention so long.

He had to find a way to see her again—alone, as he had today. He wanted to sweep her out into the darkness and ravish her until she begged him to show her fully how a man loves a woman.

Sir Charles Wright was the first gentleman to her side. She gave him her hand for an appropriate kiss and curtsy, then smiled at him. A few moments later he signed her dance card. As he walked away, the too-tall and too-thin Viscount Tolby approached her. He stood right in front of her and completely blocked her from Chandler's view.

Chandler was not accustomed to that uncontrollable knot in his chest that made him want to charge over to her and demand she accept the attention of no suitor but him.

"Are you listening to me?" Fines asked.

Chandler swallowed past a dry throat. Had he finally been smitten with love after all these years? No, that couldn't be. But for some reason, she affected him differently from all the other ladies who'd caught his eye.

"Sorry, old chap, I didn't hear what you had to say. What was that?"

"You've been doing a lot of woolgathering lately, Dunraven. Are you feeling all right?"

"I've never felt better. I was just giving serious consideration to your idea of a new mistress."

Fines gave him a pleased look. "Good. At last we're getting somewhere. Excellent to hear. I'll start asking around for you."

"Fines," Chandler said in a warning tone, "I can find my own mistress, if you don't mind."

"No." Fines sniffed loudly. "No. I don't mind at all, but I did hear that—"

"Will you excuse me?" Chandler interrupted. "I see someone I'd like to talk to."

"Who? I'll walk with you." Fines stared in the direction Chandler was looking.

"You know, I don't mind you joining me, but I think you should know I just saw Miss Pennington walk over to the refreshment table alone."

"Really?" Fines pulled on the hem of his waistcoat and sniffed again. "Miss Pennington having to get her own cup of punch? Perhaps she'd like someone to help her."

"That's probably why she walked over alone."

Fines smiled at Chandler. "I think I should go over and speak to her."

"And ask her to dance?"

Fines smiled. "I'm already on the card. Do you suppose there's room for another name?"

"Doubtful. She's been here almost an hour. You'd better hurry. I see Viscount Tolby heading her way."

"I'm off. Should we make plans for breakfast at Whites?" Fines asked walking backward.

"Don't plan on me. I have some things to check on tomorrow."

Fines nodded and turned around and was swallowed by the crowd. Chandler talked to several friends, some acquaintances and even had a dance or two before he finally managed to find himself face-to-face with Miss Millicent Blair. She stood with Lord Heathecoute and his lady.

Chandler joined the group but had eyes for no one but Miss Blair. Her buff-white evening gown had three pale pink flounces, and a pink satin ribbon banded the high waist. The round neck was cut low, showing more of her beautiful breast than he wanted other men to see. He noticed the pearl-drop earrings she wore and remembered taking her dainty lobe into his mouth.

Greetings were quickly dispensed with, and it took only a moment to know that Miss Blair was distancing herself from him fast. Her curtsy was stiff; she wouldn't look him in the eye and she almost jerked her hand away from his after the perfunctory kiss on the back of her palm.

"Lord Dunraven, a pleasure to see you this evening," the Viscount said.

"It's Millicent's first evening here at Almacks," Lady Heathecoute said. "We were so delighted to get the invitation for her to attend."

"I can't imagine anyone you suggest would be denied entrance, Viscountess."

"So kind of you to say, my lord."

Chandler turned to Miss Blair. "Welcome," he said and bowed again. "I hope your first evening here meets with your expectations."

"On all accounts, sir. I'm happy to be here and I'm enjoying myself."

"Millicent knows it is not the building that makes Almacks the place to be seen in Town on Wednesdays. It is the people who frequent it that makes it the most important addition to her first Season in London."

"Of course, you're right," Millicent added. "And I do appreciate all you and Lady Beatrice have done in obtaining the invitation for me."

"I hear you are helping with the search for the Mad Ton Thief," the viscount said to Chandler, clearly bored with the direction the conversation had taken.

"It's more that I insist on staying well-informed of the

progress that is being made by those on Bow Street and the authorities."

Lord Heathecoute lifted his chin a little higher, making his sharp nose appear to be pointing straight up. "I heard they have been going door to door, questioning everyone like common criminals. It's reprehensible the way they are treating all of us as if we are suspects."

"You forget, Heathecoute, one among us *is* a criminal, and they are only doing their jobs."

The viscount continued to demand Chandler's attention when all he wanted to do was talk to Miss Blair and find out what was wrong with her.

At last he was able to turn to Millicent and say, "May I have a dance, Miss Blair?"

She refused to let her gaze meet his but softly answered, "Yes."

Chandler looked up to her ladyship and said, "There is a waltz coming up. Has she been cleared to dance it?"

"My, yes. We've been most select in our care of Millicent, and she has been afforded all the opportunities as if this was her coming-out Season."

Millicent lifted her hand and he took hold of her card and signed his name. Afterward, he took a quick moment to turn it over. The back was blank. But of course it would be, he told himself. He had settled for himself last evening that she was not involved with the Mad Ton Thief. She was merely writing down names and facts about people in order to better remember them. Names and titles could be confusing to anyone new to Town.

When he was finished, he bowed and said, "I shall return at the appropriate time and claim your hand."

"Can you believe it?" Lady Heathecoute said to her husband in as hushed a voice as Millicent had ever heard her speak. "I do believe Lord Dunraven is smitten with her."

"Don't be ridiculous," the viscount answered, surveying the dance floor. "He's never been smitten with anyone in his life, and it's not likely that he will be with her."

"She is lovely. And this is the second time he has sought her out and asked her to dance."

Lord Heathecoute sniffed loudly. "What of it? It's the third time Sir Charles Wright has asked her."

"Sir Charles Wright tries to dance every dance no matter who the young lady is. Lord Dunraven does not. Even given his reputation, he's very choosy."

"Maybe she has caught his fancy for now, but I'm sure that will soon fade. It always does with him. Don't worry. I'm certain the earl has no intentions of being leg shackled anytime in the near future. He's having too grand a life to settle down to the country with a wife and family."

While the Heathecoutes talked about her as if she weren't present, Millicent tuned them out and turned away. She was glad she hadn't told them that Lord Dunraven had asked to call on her several times and she'd refused him. It was best if she kept that information for her aunt alone.

If Aunt Beatrice had reason to suspect the viscount and viscountess wanted to take over the column, Millicent should be careful and not discuss anything of importance with them until she had cleared it with her aunt.

She couldn't deny that Lord Dunraven appeared to be smitten with her, but no doubt it was only temporary. And that was dangerous, since even knowing that, she kept finding herself in his arms. It was time for Millicent to be honest with her aunt and talk to her about Lord Dunraven.

This afternoon she had been a mere glimpse away from her mother's ill fate of being tossed out of London like dirty baggage. She couldn't explain it, she only knew she simply had no will when it came to the earl.

Angels above! If she would let him kiss her in a draper's shop, she could clearly not be trusted in his presence anywhere else in London.

She could not allow herself to become any more enamored of him than she already was, and she must never be alone with him again. But telling herself that didn't keep the minutes from seeming like hours until he came to claim his dance with her.

It was easy to scold herself and be firm as long as she wasn't looking into his heavenly blue eyes, as long as he wasn't caressing her with his mesmerizing gaze, or teasing her with delightful words.

Millicent had seen him several times throughout the evening, but never so closely as when he started walking toward her with that confident stride of a wealthy, titled gentleman. He was devilishly handsome with his hair brushed stylishly away from his face and his neckcloth beautifully tied. His brocade waistcoat and cutaway coat hid most of his crisp white shirt, but she didn't miss the small trim of lace at his sleeves.

Millicent felt a sharp prick to her heart as she thought of the viscount's words. For indeed the man striding toward her had the look of a man who had no intention of settling down to one lady. All the more reason for Millicent to seek the advice of her aunt as to how to rid herself of Lord Dunraven's attentions once and for all.

She took a deep breath to fortify herself as he walked with her toward the dance floor with the ease of a man who has had many years of practice.

Oh, he was so good at being bad.

"I've been waiting for a dance with you all evening."

"I would wager you've said that to all the ladies you've had a promenade with this evening."

He looked at her curiously. "What makes you say that?"

She lifted her eyebrows as if to question him. "Could it be your reputation of knowing just how to charm young ladies into thinking you are madly in love with them, but only calling on them once or twice?"

"So, we're back to that. I fear my reputation will always be between us."

"Something has to be. I need armor, Lord Dunraven, when it comes to you, for my will alone doesn't work."

There was a contrite lift to the corners of his mouth. "I thought I was the one who was in need of help from your charms."

The threat of a smile fluttered at the corners of her lips. She didn't want to be bewitched by him tonight. "You jest, my lord, and I am serious."

"Don't be serious. Not tonight. Let's enjoy the dance, the evening. It must have been wonderful at the Dover-shafts for you to have been there so long this evening."

"It wasn't that we tarried. We had a late start to the evening."

The music started and he took hold of her hand and firmly placed his other hand, open palm, to the lower part of her back. He felt her warmth even through his gloves and her clothing, and it soothed his temper. In one long, fluid step he guided her backward, which led her sweeping into the box step. She faltered once, but he easily covered for her mistake. Something was wrong with her. She usually danced as if she had air between her feet and the floor.

"You seem a bit stiff this evening, Miss Blair."

Without looking at him she answered, "Perhaps that is because I have come to my senses."

"Did you lose them?"

"Dreadfully so."

"We shared a few kisses."

No, it was more than kisses.

"That is all, Millicent. There was no harm done to your reputation."

Millicent wasn't so sure it was only her reputation that she worried about. She now feared her heart was also in danger of being lost to Lord Dunraven.

His impassive attitude caused her to look him in the eye. "I suppose I'm not shocked you take such a cavalier attitude to such inappropriate behavior."

"I don't look at what happened between us that way."

His fingers constantly moved over her gloved hand, rubbing, caressing. It was as if he couldn't get enough of touching her.

"That is because you are a scoundrel, sir. You have done such things on many occasions with many different ladies. It is as natural to you as breathing."

"And that was established before our intimacy this afternoon."

"You would not have been shamed out of Town had we been caught, but I would have."

"Millicent, look at me." When she met his eyes, he continued. "I wouldn't have let that happen. When as a gentleman I take a risk, I'm fully prepared to accept any consequences that might arise from my actions. You must trust me on this."

"Your eyes and your expression are so genuine for a moment I could almost believe you. But I can't. To how many young ladies have you said the same thing?"

"Not as many as you think. You don't know how badly I want to pull you into my arms and kiss you again, Miss Blair."

She looked over his shoulder past him again and said, "I must admit that I am not sorry that we kissed yesterday or today."

"Or the way we kissed so thoroughly?"

Her gaze met his and, for a moment, he thought he saw a hint of a smile on her face. "That's correct. I found it most pleasurable."

"I wonder if you could possibly know how saying things like that affect me? I'm not even sure I'm still following the steps of the waltz. I'm pleased you are not overwrought by what happened between us."

"There will be no shame between us. Not now. It's too late for that."

"Not ever. May I call on you tomorrow?"

"No, sir, you may not."

"Miss Blair you are driving me mad. After what you just told me how can you still deny me? It's clear you don't find me offensive. Why won't you allow me to call on you?"

Millicent's loyalty to her aunt forced her to remain unbending and say, "I am not here in London to be trifled with, Lord Dunraven."

"I hear it in your voice and see in your eyes that you are serious. Trifling is not my intention, Millicent."

"Your reputation says otherwise, and please don't call me by my given name."

"After this afternoon, I don't think it would be appropriate for me to continue to call you Miss Blair."

"You must."

"Why?"

"I'm only here for a few months and then I will go back home. You must stay away from me."

Chandler knew the dance was approaching the end. He

would have to return her to the viscountess. "Did you not come to Town looking to make a match?"

"No. I came to help—" She stopped. "I came to see London, to have a Season and enjoy the parties."

Chandler could have sworn that she started to say something different or something more. But what?

"That is all?"

"Yes. And even if I were seriously looking to make a match, you wouldn't suit."

That was plain speaking indeed, not that he thought for a moment he wanted to marry her. He just wanted to be with her, and touch her, and hold her, and kiss her.

"What makes me unacceptable?" he asked.

A faraway look came to her eyes and her face softened beautifully. "My mother had her coming out Season in London over twenty years ago and she—and I wanted to have a Season, too. That is all I can say."

He was certain now that she wanted to tell him more but wasn't ready to confide in him. If he didn't push her anymore tonight maybe in time she would tell him everything. "And whom did she marry?"

"My father."

He laughed and twirled her around as the dance ended. He bowed. "You delight me, Millicent. How can I give you up?"

She curtsied. "Do not pursue me, Lord Dunraven."

He took her hand and started walking her back to her chaperone. "I will not be denied, lovely lady. If I can't call on you openly, I will have to see you in secret— again."

Eleven

"Modest doubt is called the beacon of the wise" and no wonder. Has anyone, perchance, told the dashing Lord Dunraven this fact, he who seems to be in the gossip sheets daily— and should be. Word has it he is no longer interested in Lady Lambsbeth. He now has his eye on a young lady new to Town but obviously not new in the ways of capturing the heart of a confirmed bachelor. He was seen blowing her a kiss.

Lord Truefitt
Society's Daily Column

$\mathcal{D}$AWN COULDN'T BE more than an hour away as Millicent climbed the stairs to her aunt's bedchamber, her steps slower and heavier than usual. Hamlet announced her with his warning bark, but it didn't seem to be as loud or frantic as usual. She turned out the lamp that was always left on for her and leaned against the back of the door as was her custom. Most nights she was too weary to go immediately to her aunt's room. She usually took a minute or two to unwind before starting the column.

She wanted the privacy of her own bedchamber so she could have some time to think about Lord Dunraven and all the unwanted feelings and emotions he had stirred inside her before going in to see her aunt. But, she couldn't do that. There was little enough time each morning as it was to write the article and get it out to the newspaper on time.

Millicent pushed away from the door and climbed the stairs, stopping short of her aunt's door. She knocked and upon hearing the response, she entered her aunt's room. Aunt Beatrice was sitting up in her bed, looking much better than she had the day before. Once the healing had started taking place in her face it was rapidly returning her features to their normal size and shape.

Weary though she was, Millicent smiled and said, "Good morning, Aunt Beatrice." She stopped at the foot of the bed, knowing Hamlet would not allow her to go further. "Is that a new bed jacket you're wearing? It's lovely and you are looking better each day."

Her aunt smiled. "Thank you, dearie. I'm happy to say that I'm finally beginning to feel better. I was starting to think that day would never come. Tell me about the parties tonight. Was everyone at Almacks? You must have been having a delightful time to be out so long. I do wish I could have been there. I miss seeing everyone."

"My first evening at Almacks was splendid. Thank you for arranging that, Aunt Beatrice. And from what I could tell everyone was there. The place was overflowing with people."

"It's always that way, dear, even on the stormiest nights. It's wonderful to hear you had a splendid evening. It seems like I've been waiting hours for your return. I'm simply faint with wanting to get out of this bed and back to the parties to chat with my friends and listen to what everyone has to say."

"I'm sure it won't be long now. I don't know how the viscount and his lady stay out so late night after night. It's no wonder his lordship sleeps on the drive home." Millicent purposely looked down at the dog. "Good morning, Hamlet. How are you today?" Hamlet barked once. Millicent lifted an eyebrow. Maybe she was winning him over.

"They sleep until it is time to get up and get dressed for the next party. That's how they do it. It's not too bad a life. Remember, this hectic schedule only lasts for the Season. They should attend more luncheons and take more rides in the park, but they do what they can, I suppose."

"I wasn't complaining about them. They are very attentive to me."

"Good. Now, before we begin, I have something for you to read," her aunt said. "A letter for you."

She saw the sheet of vellum in her aunt's hand. "For me?" Millicent's spirits lifted. "Is it from my mother?"

Millicent reached for the letter. She truly felt terrible that she had neglected writing to her mother while she'd been in London, but there had been so little time. She was quite happy with the lace she had picked out for her mother after Lord Dunraven had left her in the shop, and she would see that it was sent to her tomorrow.

"No, but this might make you almost as happy as hearing from your mother. Read it out loud."

Millicent took the sheet and moved closer to the brightly lit bedside lamp. Why would anyone other than her mother write to her?

"Dear Lord Truefitt," she read aloud. She stopped and looked up. "This is not for me."

"But of course it is. My dear Millicent, you are now Lord Truefitt."

Hearing those words spoken stunned Millicent. *She was Lord Truefitt?*

Yes, until her aunt returned to the parties. Millicent must talk to her aunt about Lord Dunraven. There was no putting it off any longer.

"Go ahead," her aunt insisted. "Read it."

Dear Lord Truefitt:

It has come to my attention that we have had numerous comments about your addition of quotes from Shakespeare at the beginning of your column each day. All good comments, I might add. Our readership is growing. We believe the success of your column is one of the reasons our circulation has increased. Congratulations on a splendid job. We hope you will continue your quotes from Shakespeare.

Yours very truly,
Thomas Greenbrier

Millicent looked up from the paper, feeling slightly starry-eyed. "It's a success."

"That is what he is saying, yes." Her aunt laughed low in her throat. "I must admit I had my doubts when you first started helping me, but according to Emery and Phillips everyone on the street is talking about our column."

Millicent didn't like hearing the column referred to as hers. "But why?"

"From what I hear some people are squabbling over

which play the quote comes from or what character has said it and other people are making a game out it. Sales are up on books of Shakespeare's works. There's talk that White's will soon make it available to wager a bet on which work of Shakespeare you will write from next." Her aunt's smile beamed across her face. "It's smashing, dear girl. The attention you have brought to Lord True-fitt's column is simply smashing!"

Millicent couldn't believe what she was hearing. She had overheard a few people mention the quotes, but paid it no mind. "I don't understand. How can this be so popular that it's talked about by everyone?"

"You have mixed the most beloved author of all time with what the ton loves most—gossip! And it has worked beautifully." Aunt Beatrice laughed again. "You are all the rage."

All the rage?

No, she was speechless! What would happen if her mother found out?—or Lord Dunraven?

Millicent forced those thoughts away and politely said what she knew her aunt wanted to hear. "Not me, Aunt Beatrice. You. Remember this is your column and you will return to it soon. If you are pleased, Aunt, then I am pleased and we will continue to give your readers what they want."

"It was a brilliant idea, dearie. To think that all these years I have enjoyed Shakespeare's works divinely but never thought to use his words in my own writings. That was most clever of you."

"Thank you for letting me read this. You brought me here to help you, and I'm glad I have." Millicent handed the letter to her aunt. Hamlet rose to sniff it briefly, but quickly settled back down.

"Shakespeare is all well and good, but it would be boring to most of our readers if we didn't spice it with gossip. Scandal is such a delicious form of entertainment. We must have more, Millicent."

Millicent wasn't shy and she could handle herself at the parties. She just didn't like writing about people's personal and private lives.

"You have been doing this a week now," her aunt continued, hardly catching a breath. "You must get more information on things like the meeting between Lord Dunraven and Lady Lambsbeth, who has danced with whom or who has made a match or who is thinking of making one. What is going on with Miss Pennington and Miss Donaldson? Our readers want to know who slips out into the gardens when no one is looking, which gentleman gets the kiss and which gets a slap. And of course, it always makes excellent gossip if a couple who is suited suddenly decides against marriage and why."

Listening to her aunt talk with relish about the intimacies of other people's lives reminded Millicent why she didn't like what she was doing for her aunt. If anyone had seen her with Lord Dunraven in the draper's shop and then wrote about it, she would be devastated. Suddenly she felt chilled. What would happen if someone had seen them?

Exactly what happened to your mother.

Before she lost her courage, Millicent said, "That brings up a subject I must speak to you about."

Her aunt sat up a little straighter. "Suddenly you look serious. Tell me."

Millicent clasped her hands together in front of her skirt and said, "Against my wishes, it appears that Lord Dunraven is pursuing me."

"What's this?" Her aunt leaned forward in the bed so fast Hamlet scampered to the end of the bed. "The Lord

Dunraven of the Terrible Threesome and the missing raven?"

Is there another?

Millicent hoped she was doing the right thing in confessing to her aunt and seeking help. "Yes. I swear, Aunt, I've done nothing to encourage him." *Had she?* "In fact, I've been quite the opposite and almost rude at times." *Submissive at others.* "But at every turn he rebuffs my rejections and keeps insisting I allow him to call on me. I always decline. And—"

"And?"

"He's been absolutely forward in his manner toward me every time we meet."

"This is most fascinating, Millicent. You must give me details."

Millicent winced. *No.*

She couldn't possibly tell her aunt that she had been so thoroughly kissed and caressed by this man that she had half fallen in love with him already. She must think quickly.

"So far, it hasn't been anything I can't handle, but I need to know how to rebuke him so that he leaves me alone. We can't run the risk of him discovering who I am. He may get curious about what I'm doing."

"The only way for him to discover that is for you to tell him, and I'm sure you won't let that happen. But I agree that it's in our best interest that he not pursue you."

"He's much too charming."

"He is a rake who knows all the tricks, and he's such a worldly gentleman. You must tell me exactly what he has done. Has he compromised you?"

"No, nothing as serious as that," she fibbed. Millicent groped for the right words. "He caressed my hand and squeezed my fingers the entire time we were dancing."

"Botheration, Millicent," her aunt exclaimed. "That's hardly worthy of gossip. What else did he do?"

Millicent looked at her aunt and wasn't at all sure she approved of the gleam she saw her in red eyes.

"He blew me a kiss. He danced the waltz with me. He keeps asking to call on me. I know it doesn't seem like a lot, but he is most persistent. He won't take no for an answer. I don't know what to do."

"I do," her aunt said with all confidence and in the strongest voice she had used since Millicent arrived. "The one thing that will make Lord Dunraven lose interest in a young lady faster than anything else."

"What's that?"

"Having his name linked with hers in the gossip columns. Get your quill, Millicent. We shall write about him and mention you."

*R*ARE LATE AFTERNOON sunshine filtered through the tree leaves and sliced through the open windows in Chandler's book room. He sat at the fine rosewood desk that had been his father's and his father's before him, trying not to look at the empty shelf where the gold raven should be perched.

He was supposed to be going over the array of account books on his vast estates that were spread out before him, but mostly he was brooding. And thinking of Millicent Blair.

Keeping a sharp eye on the management of his estates and holdings was the reason he'd been able to enjoy his extravagant lifestyle these past years. His father had given him a good start, but Chandler had been shrewd with his investments and the lands he purchased. His managers did an excellent job keeping his land prosperous and his tenants happy. He usually paid each of them a visit in the fall before the dead of winter set over the land.

He knew it to be true that in his younger years he had spent too much money gambling and racing horses, and too many nights in debauchery, but he never came close to endangering his wealth or his properties, though he may have endangered his life a time or two.

Today, he couldn't concentrate. A certain young lady had captured his fancy and wouldn't let go. Every time he tried to put her out of his mind, she came back to smile at him, tease him, beckon him. She intrigued him madly. He was sure if she would merely tell him he could call on her properly it would get her out of his mind. It was the chase that no doubt intrigued him.

He swung his chair around and stared out the open window without really seeing anything. It wasn't like him to be so attracted to a woman that he couldn't get her womanly scent out of his mind or the sweet taste of her lips out of his mouth. If he hadn't taken control of himself yesterday afternoon, he would have undressed her right there in that shop—and she would have let him.

There was no doubt that she was as attracted to him as he was to her, yet she refused to have him call on her in a respectable manner. Still, he shouldn't have let things go so far between them in such a public place.

Chandler had done some crazy things in his life, including entering a willing young lady's bedroom window, but he had stopped that foolishness years ago. And even then, he did it for the sport, for the thrill of not getting caught, not because he was in love with the lady. He'd risked Millicent's reputation and his freedom because he wanted to be with her.

He risked a lot for a lady he knew very little about. What was she hiding? He had settled for himself that she had nothing to do with the Mad Ton Thief, but why was she always making notes and being so secretive about her family? He should try to find out more about her before his heart became involved with her.

"Excuse me, Lord Dunraven."

Chandler looked up to see his valet standing in the doorway, impeccably dressed. With thick gray hair smoothed away from his face, Peter Winston, a short broad-shouldered man, had been with Chandler since shortly after finishing his education.

Chandler had been immediately impressed with the older man when he'd interviewed for the job. Winston hadn't cowered or become flustered from Chandler's tough questioning. He'd remained confident and certain that he was the best man to serve Chandler, and Winston had never let Chandler down.

"What is it, Winston?" he asked, turning back to his desk and the pretense of looking at the books before him. Fines was right, he'd done far too much woolgathering recently, and he hadn't spent enough time thinking of ways to capture the Mad Ton Thief.

"I'm sorry to disturb you, my lord, but there's a Mr. Percy Doulton here to see you. I inquired whether he had an appointment. He admitted he didn't but hoped you might be available to see him."

"Maybe at last the man has some news. Show him in."

"Certainly. Should I bring in tea or will you be offering something stronger?"

"No need for either, Winston. I'm sure he won't be long. Ask him to come in."

Chandler stood and started closing books scattered on top of his desk. Within moments, the man walked in.

"How do you do, Doulton. Come in and make yourself comfortable."

"Thank you for seeing me, Lord Dunraven. I have some information that I wanted to share with you right away."

"Good news, I hope."

"No, not at all." He took the winged chair in front of Chandler's desk. "It appears that, despite all our efforts, there was another theft last night."

Chandler sat down. "Damnation! Where?"

"At Lord Dovershaft's."

The name sent a cold chill up Chandler's back. Last night, when he saw Millicent at Almacks, she said she had just come from Lord Dovershaft's. She said they were late because they got a late start. Was that the real reason? Had he exonerated her too quickly?

"It was a small painting, not large at all from what I understand, but apparently priceless. The earl is in a temper, while the countess is having friends in to see the place on the wall where the painting used to hang."

"Damn, this is disturbing news."

"Not according to the countess. She's quite certain Lord Pinkwater's ghost now has the painting."

Chandler was resolute. "She's wrong. A thief has it. Was a Runner there?"

"Yes. He insists he was at his post all evening and no one could have gotten past him with a painting."

"He would certainly insist that. Can he be trusted?"

"He's been with me for two years. I've never had a problem with him, sir."

"Until now. Get rid of him and find another to take his place."

Doulton cleared his throat. "There is hope, Lord Dunraven. The dinner party was a small gathering. Less than one-hundred people. The earl and countess are certain of their guest list. Neither of them saw anyone they didn't know, and together they believe they saw everyone who attended."

"Did anyone offer any clues?"

"No, sir. As I stated before, my man swears he was at the front door the entire evening and no one left carrying anything the size of a lady's small parasol."

"A parasol?"

"The Countess insists the painting was the size of a young girl's parasol when it is open."

"That's impossible."

Doulton remained quiet.

"If your man didn't leave his post, we can assume the thief left by a window."

"My thoughts exactly. Servants would have seen anyone leaving by the rear door. I don't have enough men to guard every room at every party."

"No. I'm not suggesting that, but something more needs to be done. There's been a robbery a week since the Season began, and we're no closer to finding him."

"We're trying to establish a pattern, but so far there hasn't been one. He's taken jewelry, your raven and now a painting."

"Keep working on it. He'll make a mistake sooner or later and we'll catch him."

"I'll be in touch when I have more to report."

Doulton rose from his chair and laid a newspaper on Chandler's, desk open to the Society page. "I don't know if you've had a chance to see this. Good day."

Chandler looked down at the newsprint as Doulton walked out. Chandler's name jumped out at him and the name beside his.

Millicent.

He picked up the paper and scanned it. How could anyone have seen him blowing her a kiss? They were alone in that darkened hallway, he was sure of it. No one knew about it other than Miss Millicent Blair herself.

Something stirred in the back of his mind. He picked up the article and read it again, slower. Could it be?

"Damnation," he whispered to himself.

Twelve

◈

"Tempt not a desperate man," Shakespeare wrote in *Romeo and Juliet*, and the Society papers are writing it, too, as all of London is buzzing about the news that the Mad Ton Thief has struck again and those on Bow Street have no suspects.

Lord Truefitt
Society's Daily Column

"LORD DUNRAVEN," MILLICENT greeted as she walked into the front parlor, her modest afternoon dress swishing across the tops of her satin slippers. Glenda followed her into the sunny room but stayed near the entranceway.

"Miss Blair," he said and strode toward her. "Thank you for seeing me."

Millicent knew immediately that something was wrong. The earl was his usual handsome self, she thought, but something made him appear different. His hair had been ruffled just enough by the wind to make it attractive, but that wasn't it. His collar was straight and his neckcloth simply but superbly tied. His lips, those full, masculine lips were the same as yesterday when he kissed her, so what was wrong?

Ah, yes, she found the problem. The only thing that seemed out of place on the dashing gentleman was the wrinkle of frustration that settled between his beautiful blue eyes.

A hint of worry knocked in Millicent's chest, but she managed to brush it aside, lift her chin and her shoulders a tiny bit higher.

"I've just had another visitor leave, so I'm afraid I don't have much time."

"Yes, I saw Lady Lynette leaving as I arrived."

Oh, dear. "Did she see you?"

"No."

Thank goodness. Lynette would question her unmercifully if she got wind of Lord Dunraven's visit. Remembering Lynette, Millicent looked at the earl's empty hands and realized that he had not brought her apricot tarts. If what Lynette had said about Lord Dunraven always bringing apricot tarts was true, and everything she had told Millicent so far had been, she couldn't help but wonder why there were no tarts for her. And should she see that as a good sign or a bad one?

Millicent relaxed a little and turned to her maid and said, "Glenda, would you mind asking Mrs. Brown to speak to the cook about a fresh pot of tea for us and perhaps some of her delicious *fig* tarts?"

"Yes, Miss."

As soon as Glenda was out of sight, Millicent advanced on Lord Dunraven with purpose. She clasped her hands together in front of her plain day dress and said, "I find it most disconcerting that you have gone against my wishes and called on me after I have repeatedly asked that you not do so. I must ask you to leave at once."

His expression remained sober, and he didn't appear the least bit cowed by her firm accusation. If anything, his shoulders seemed to lift a little higher, too. "Something important made me decide to ignore your wishes and come. I'm not leaving right away."

Determined to keep her aggressive attitude, Millicent said, "What could be that important, sir?"

"This." He took a piece of newsprint out of his pocket and held it in front of her.

Millicent remained unflinched, she hoped. She couldn't let Lord Dunraven know she didn't have to read the piece of paper to know what it said. She had put the finishing touches on it not more than a few hours ago.

Knowing that it was crucial that she remain calm and collected she said, "An old piece of newsprint? What about it?"

"It's Lord Truefitt's column from *The Daily Reader*. You've heard of it?"

Keep your answers short and do not offer anything he doesn't ask for.

"Yes."

"Do you know what this particular column says?"

"I'm not sure which edition you are holding."

"It's today's. Now, do you know?"

If the stakes weren't so high, she would enjoy this question-and-answer game they were playing.

"I believe I do."

"Do you have any idea how it came about that it was written?"

Millicent had to keep her wits about her and remain confident that he did not know she had anything to do with the writing of that column. She didn't know what she was going to do, only that she couldn't fib to him without her conscience bothering her and no doubt he would see through her attempts to blur the truth.

She worded her answer carefully, "What specifically are you referring to?"

"The fact that your name is linked with mine in the title-tattle."

Maybe this is a good time to change the subject.

"Perhaps because we have danced together at the last two parties."

"I dance with many young ladies at every party."

On watery legs she walked past him and over to the window with seeming indifference. She brushed back a sheer drapery panel and looked outside to the street before turning back to him and saying, "How fortunate for you. You are quite the dashing dandy. I'm sure many ladies desire to dance with you each evening, Lord Dunraven."

The furrow between his eyebrows deepened. Flattery was not going to work. She hadn't expected that it would, but that maybe it would buy her a little time to figure out how to handle his questions. She watched him walk across the room with confidence born of knowing exactly what he wanted and expecting to get it. He stopped beside her at the window.

"You know that's not what I meant."

"Nevertheless, every eligible young lady and most of the widows seek your favor and attention."

"Miss Blair, are you deliberately trying to compliment me again?"

His gaze never left her face as he challenged her, still she didn't flinch.

"Lord Dunraven, I speak the truth. If you are flattered by it, then that is your problem or pleasure, whichever the case might be."

"No, I think you are trying, unsuccessfully, I might add, to change the subject?"

"I didn't realize the subject was changing."

"Didn't you?"

"We were and are talking about you and dancing."

He stepped even closer to her. Millicent wanted to retreat, but there was no place for her to go except against the wall. She remained unmoving with her gaze held fast to his.

"No, we were talking about you and I being romantically linked in this column." He dropped the paper to the rosewood table that stood against the wall near him.

She looked up at his handsome face, still marred by the frown of anger. "I'm sorry that it displeases you to have your name so closely linked to mine."

"That's not the problem and I think you know it. I'm not upset to have your name connected to mine."

She made a point of taking a deep breath and a loud sigh of relief. "That is good to hear."

"Millicent, it always displeases me when my name is stewed in scandalbroth, and recently it seems a daily occurrence. Tell me, how do you think Lord Truefitt found out that I blew you a kiss?"

"I suppose he must have seen you," she answered with certain confidence.

"I don't think so."

"You seem sure of yourself."

"I am. Have you forgotten that we were alone in that darkened hallway together when I blew that kiss? Just you and I and the candlelight."

Millicent felt her eyes grow wide. Her heart slammed against her ribs. Angels above! She had been caught, and she had done it to herself.

"How can you be sure?" she asked.

"If anyone had seen us together that night it would have made the papers the next day or no later than the day after. So why has it suddenly shown up today?"

Millicent's mind whirled. Perhaps there was still some way she could save herself and her aunt. She had to try. She couldn't just give up without an argument.

"Perhaps Lord Truefitt is a spiritualist. That would explain why he knows so much."

"A seer? I don't think so."

She hated to feel desperate! "It's possible. There's talk that the Mad Ton Thief is really Lord Pinkwater's ghost."

"I don't believe that for a moment, and you are far too sensible and levelheaded to believe it."

"Of course, I don't believe the thief is a ghost. I'm merely pointing out there is the possibility of more than one way that Lord Truefitt could have known that you blew me a kiss."

She moved to walk past him away from the window and the corner where they stood. Chandler quickly stretched out his arm and braced his hand against the wall, stopping her from passing.

Suddenly he was much too close to Millicent.

He spoke in a low but firm tone. "I'm not going to let you change the subject, Millicent. We are talking about the column, not dancing, not the thief, not a ghost. The column with my name and your name in it. Remember?"

"I believe I do."

"Good." He folded his arms across his chest in a comfortable relaxed manner. "I have a theory regarding how this came about."

"I'm sure the authorities would welcome any conjecture you have on the thief."

His voice remained low and calm. "Nice try, but it's

not going to work. I'm talking about Lord Truefitt's column, not the thief."

"Oh."

"Would you like to hear it?"

"No, I don't believe I would," she answered honestly. "And I think we've said about all there is to say on the subject."

"I think you should hear it. I insist."

She took another deep breath. "All right."

"I think you are a spy for Lord Truefitt and his gossip colum—"

Before he finished the last word, Millicent stepped forward and placed her fingers against his lips, silencing him. "No, Lord Dunraven, please don't say it aloud." She glanced around to see if Glenda had returned and then quickly back to Lord Dunraven. "You mustn't breathe a word out loud about your theory."

While her fingers rested upon his lips, their eyes met and held for far too long. She felt as if he were trying to look into her soul and see the Millicent Blair she didn't want him to know. Millicent felt his warm moist lips against her fingers, and didn't want to take her hand away.

He grasped the palm of her hand and kissed the pads of all four of her fingers before lowering her hand and letting go of her.

"I can't let you tempt me."

Millicent was hardly breathing. Tempt him? She was the one being tempted. Didn't he know how easy it was for him to distract her and make her forget everything but his presence?

"I'm sorry," she said, taking a step away from him and toward the window. "That was impolite. I shouldn't have touched you like that."

"Don't apologize. I don't mind that you touched me, but I can't let it distract me."

"But I shouldn't have—"

"It's all right, Millicent."

She lowered her lashes. "Please don't call me that. You really shouldn't be so informal when addressing me, sir."

"Why? After yesterday afternoon, I feel free to suggest we are intimate friends, and it's quite acceptable for me to call on you and to address you as Millicent. And furthermore, you should call me Chandler."

Her gaze met his again. "No, I was hoping you would forget what happened yesterday afternoon."

"That won't happen."

"I forgot about it until you reminded me just now."

He shook his head slowly and his eyes sparkled with perception. He said, "I don't think so."

How could he be charming even when he was mocking her? "A true gentleman would never remind a lady of an indiscretion."

"We've already established that sometimes I'm not a gentleman."

"Most times, I fear, and no truer words have you spoken."

"And returning to the main subject we have to discuss, it is also true that you are a spy for Lord Truefitt, isn't it, Millicent?"

It was on the tip of her tongue to deny it, but she saw in his eyes that there was no use. He knew.

She acknowledged him with a question of her own. "Were you only guessing when you first suggested it? Did I confirm it by my action?"

"Once I started adding things up, it became an easy answer to see."

"How?" Millicent sighed, knowing how disappointed,

no devastated, her aunt would be to have lost her eyes and ears for the parties. "I have been so careful."

"You were always making notes. I've watched how you walk around the parties and listen to people and then go off on your own to write down what you've heard. When I read what was on the back of the dance card you dropped on the floor, I assumed you were making notes so it would be easier to remember people's names and their titles, since you were new in Town."

"You found my missing dance card."

"Yes, I needed to know what you were doing when you walked off alone."

What must have really happened dawned on Millicent.

"You brute, you deliberately switched my dance card with another just so you could read what I had written, didn't you? You changed cards with me and gave me the blank one?"

"Yes."

"I should have figured that out myself. I've known from before I met you that you were a scoundrel and rake not to be trusted with anything. I knew there had to be a reason you were called one of the Terrible Threesome. You wear your title well, Lord Dunraven."

"I'm not as bad as the tittle-tattle has led people to believe. I only switched the cards because I thought you were working for the Mad Ton Thief."

"What? That's ridiculous."

"Think again, Millicent. It was a plausible idea."

"No sane person could think that. Whatever made you come up with a connection like that?"

"Logic. The first item was stolen just about the time you came to Town. At two different parties, I found you in parts of the house where as a guest you shouldn't have been—making notes on your dance card."

She blinked. "You saw me twice?"

"The first time was the evening we met in the narrow hallway and later that week when you were in a private room in front of the fireplace."

"You saw me in there?"

"Yes, writing on the back of your dance card, again."

"You were watching me, hoping I would lead you to the Mad Ton Thief?"

"More or less that's how it was, yes."

"How could my making notes on my dance cards possibly connect me with the likes of a robber?" Millicent asked indignantly.

"I thought perhaps you were making notes of items in the house that could be easily stolen and hidden under a coat or cloak. Something that could be taken out of the house without notice."

This was unbelievable. "Oh, my heavens! You think I'm a thief?"

"An accomplice. I thought you were giving your notes to the thief so that he could come back later and steal one of the items you listed."

Millicent was almost speechless—almost. "That's absolutely wretched of you. I don't believe this. You were watching me all this time, talking to me, dancing with me, and you kissed me so passionately in that shop thinking that I was a thief. How could you have done that?" The thought mortified Millicent.

"No, I didn't think that of you at the time I kissed you in the shop. By then, I had reasoned that you were merely making notes of names and titles and things about people so you could remember who they were next time you met them. I kissed you because I wanted to and for no other reason."

Millicent shook her head. "This is too inconceivable.

You only spent time with me because you wanted to watch me, get close to me until you discovered who I worked with."

"Not entirely. I find you extremely attractive, Millicent. You must know that. But, I also want to find the thief and recover the raven."

"I think it's perfectly horrible that you thought I had something to do with that contemptible creature who is taking things that don't belong to him."

"It's no more horrible than writing about people's private lives and publishing them in the newspaper."

"Oh but it is, sir," she argued fervently.

"How? You seem overly indignant for a lady who writes gossip."

"I'm not stealing anyone's personal property."

"No, you're only stealing their privacy and their good names."

Millicent opened her mouth to tell him that she was only doing it to help her father's sister, but even though Chandler had found out who she was, he still didn't know who Lord Truefitt was, and, for her aunt's sake, Millicent had to keep it that way. She turned away and said nothing.

"Why do you do it?"

Keeping her back to him she said, "I have nothing more to say on the subject."

"Is it for the money?"

That made her to turn around and face him. "No."

"Is someone forcing you to do this?"

"Of course not." She walked away from him and closer to the settee, but unfortunately he followed her. She glanced toward the door. How long did it take Glenda to ask Mrs. Brown to speak to the cook about a pot of tea?

"Tell me why?"

Millicent wanted to tell him the truth and include the

fact she didn't find any satisfaction in what she was doing, but she dared not. She was caught, not her aunt. Millicent couldn't let him know that her aunt was really Lord Truefitt. She came to help her aunt keep her employment, not expose her and force her to lose it.

"My reasons are of no concern to you and I won't share them with you."

"I suppose that the Heathecoutes and Lady Beatrice are not aware of what you are doing."

Thankfully, he made that a statement and not a question. If she were careful she wouldn't have to tell him any more than necessary.

"Lady Beatrice and the Heathecoutes have been very good to me. I would hate for them to know what you have figured out."

"I could make it known who you are and you would lose your employment."

"I would lose much more than that," she whispered earnestly, loathe to think that scandal would drive her from London like her mother. "I'm sure Lady Beatrice would ask me to leave." She would no longer be of use to her aunt.

Suddenly an idea struck Millicent. She was very still for a moment but turned and looked into his eyes. "I hope I can persuade you not to do anything rash, sir. I think I know of a way I can be of help to you."

His eyebrows rose in question. "You help me? How? You torment me with your writings."

Millicent cringed. He did make what she was doing sound horrible, but she wouldn't let that stop her from telling him her idea. "I can help you find the Mad Ton Thief."

He smiled, then chuckled. "You surprise me and the devil take me if I don't enjoy it, Millicent. I wish I didn't, but I do. How could you help me find the thief?"

"For one, I hear things you don't hear. You are an earl. People watch what they say around you, but with me they are less careful. I am more apt to hear news concerning the Mad Ton Thief than you."

"I am in daily touch with Doulton and others. I would think that would allow me to hear the news before you unless you have an informant on Bow Street."

"No, of course not. But neither you nor your Runners can hear what is said in the ladies' retiring rooms. For instance, I just overheard that there is a certain earl who is looking to make a wealthy match because he has mis-used his fortune and it has run out."

"Really. Who?"

She gave him a knowing smile. "I see there is some gossip I'm privy to that you want to hear."

He frowned again. "You do like to test me."

She smiled. "I feel the same way about you."

"How can a poor blade who's run through his money help me find the thief?"

"Perhaps he is the one stealing the valuables in order to get the money he needs to keep him sound until he can make a desirous match."

"Hmm. That's possible, I suppose."

"It has to be a member of the ton who is pilfering the homes. Everyone agrees to that, except for those who believe the thief is a ghost."

"And that number seems to be growing."

"No one has reported seeing a stranger at any of the parties." She looked at him a little ruefully. "And I believe we've both already agreed that it is not a ghost walking out of the homes with the family treasures."

"We are definite on that point. I suppose you could be of some use to me."

"Lord Dunraven, you do make me sound like a piece of old baggage."

"Old? No. Baggage? Never. Useful? Maybe. All right, Miss Blair, partners we shall be for a time. I won't divulge your secret, and you will report any information you hear that might help me find the thief."

Her chest heaved in relief. Thank goodness, she had kept him from demanding the name of Lord Truefitt. It was too close a call. "You have my word."

"Now, who is this titled gentleman lackwit who's lost his fortune?"

"You'll have to read Lord Truefitt's column tomorrow to find out the answer to that."

"Is that how I will get information from you? Reading the tittle-tattle?"

"Not always, but it seems prudent to start this way. And, now I know why you didn't bring me tarts."

"What are you talking about? Are you changing the subject again?"

"Yes. I've been told that you take apricot tarts to every young lady you call on and that your chef makes the best in all of London."

The wrinkle returned to his brow. "Am I that predictable?"

"Obviously not as far as I'm concerned." She held her hands out palms up and smiled sweetly at him. "I have no tarts."

"With you, nothing is predictable either. I was so worked up when I finally figured out what you were doing that having my chef prepare tarts was the last thing on my mind. Even now, knowing that you do something I despise, I want to take you in my arms and kiss you."

"Angels above, sir. You must be more careful." She glanced over his shoulder to the doorway. "Someone

could come in and catch you saying something like that
to me and we'll end up married. If you'll excuse me, I
really must get dressed for the evening or I won't be ready
when my chaperones arrive."

"Not so fast, dear Millicent." He pulled her into his
arms and cupped her close to him, bringing their faces
close together. "Most business partnerships are sealed
with a handshake, but I would rather we seal ours with a
kiss."

Millicent opened her mouth to protest, but what little
sound she attempted was hushed by warm lips moving
slowly to cover hers. Her mind told her to protest vehe-
mently, and with her mind she did.

He is a rake.

He's not to be trusted.

But he makes me feel so wonderful.

Within seconds her body relaxed into the warmth of his
arms without effort. She thought only of the way he made
her feel, wonderful, desired.

He increased the pressure of the kiss, and as if she'd
always known what to do, Millicent opened her mouth
and accepted his tongue with eagerness. She gave him her
own, and he answered with a soft groan of pleasure. She
slipped her hands around his neck, allowing his arms to
tighten around her and pull her closer to his chest.

His hands slid down her back to her waist. He rested
his palms on the soft flare of her hips for a moment before
sliding them upward until he cupped her breasts, one in
each hand.

At his warm touch Millicent's legs weakened and she
pressed closer to him, needing his strength to withstand
his sensual assault. She didn't know why her breasts were
so sensitive to his slightest touch or why she felt such an

eagerness to explore all these new and wonderful sensations with him.

His warm, soft lips left hers and he kissed her cheeks, her neck, behind her ear. Everywhere his lips touched her she tingled with awareness.

"I can't understand why your kisses make my legs feel weak and my insides feel like they are fluttering."

He raised his head and looked down at her and smiled. "That means you are extremely attracted to me."

"Does it?"

He nodded.

"But how can that be when I think you are a rake and not to be trusted?"

"Perhaps that is some of the allure."

She remembered what happened to her mother. Is this how her mother had felt?

Millicent shook her head. "No. I fear it is deeper than that."

"What do you mean?"

"Nothing. I shouldn't be in your arms. God forbid Glenda or Mrs. Brown should walk in here and see me kissing you."

He gave her a reassuring smile and held her tighter. "No one will see us. I've told you that I have had years of practice avoiding chaperones and maids. They usually make a shuffling sound with their feet or some other noise to alert their charge that they are coming. They really don't want to catch us in a compromising position, you know."

"Chandler, do I make your legs feel weak and your stomach fluttery?"

He laughed softly, seductively, but his gaze never left hers. It was as if he wanted her to see inside him and know that he spoke the truth. "Yes, and it means I'm very, extremely attracted to you."

"But I am not a rake. So where is the allure for you?"

"Not a rake, but you are a seducer."

"And that makes me attractive?"

"It must because I desire you more than any other lady I have ever wanted. Every movement you make, every word you say makes me want to take you into my arms and kiss you like this."

He dipped his head again and captured her lips with his. Gone was the kiss of his lips moving gently over hers. This was a wild kiss that plundered her mouth, bruised her lips and filled her with hunger and passion for more and more. She didn't understand the feelings he created inside her, but she didn't have to understand them to enjoy them.

At the farthest reaches of her mind, Millicent heard a noise—tea cups rattling on a tray. Chandler must have heard it too because he immediately let her go and stepped away.

He swallowed hard. "Your maid, I'm sure, bringing in the tea."

Millicent gasped.

"Don't worry. I'll take care of her and give you a moment to catch your breath."

He strode to the doorway and blocked it by standing in the middle with one arm braced against the doorjamb. "I'm sorry I can't stay longer, Miss Blair. No, no time for tea. Not for me. Do tell Lady Beatrice I hope she is up and about soon. And I will give thought to those apricot tarts. Give my regards to Lady Heathecoute."

Chandler continued talking nonsense for the benefit of Glenda, standing on the opposite side of the door, but Millicent ceased to hear. What was she going to do? She had no will when it came to Lord Dunraven.

He was charming and devilish and his kisses made her forget sound reasoning, made her forget what had happened to her mother. He was bad for her, but he made her feel good.

She walked back over to the window and looked out. Would this alliance with Chandler end up making her one of London's biggest scandals?

Thirteen

"Men at some time are masters of their fates,"
and so it is with Lord Dunraven. Convinced
that it was no ghost that stole the family
raven, he has solicited the help of a private
source, which he refuses to disclose.

Lord Truefitt
Society's Daily Column

CHANDLER PRESTWICK, EARL of Dunraven, sat alone in
a secluded corner of one of the four private gentlemen's
clubs in London that he belonged to, sipping a glass of
claret. He had chosen this club because it was the smallest
and he was less likely to be bothered by anyone wanting
to claim his attention.

He'd spent some time at the gaming and billiards tables,
but it didn't take him long to realize he wasn't in the
mood for the games. He was too distracted by thoughts
of Millicent Blair.

He had dressed for the evening as was usual in one of
his dinner coats and brocade waistcoat. He'd even taken

time to be a bit fancy with the tying of his neckcloth. He'd fully intended to show up at the three parties he'd selected to attend for the evening and had gone so far as to have his driver stop the coach at the first house. But he didn't get out. Instead, he'd told his driver to bring him to this club.

Chandler was in a quandary. For the first time in his life he was smitten by a young lady. Truly smitten, and it was a difficult thing to come to terms with—for more than one reason.

He'd actually expected it to happen one day. He wanted it to happen. He was ready for it to happen, but he never dreamed he'd be charmed by a writer of tittle-tattle. One who spied on his friends.

If it wasn't so outrageous, it would be laughable. He who had always hated the faceless people who wrote the scandal sheets now found himself captivated by one who helped gather the information and write what was written in them.

His infatuation with her was madness.

Perhaps it served him right after all the hearts he'd broken over the years, he quarreled with himself. He supposed he had left many a young lady thinking he would make an offer for her hand only to never call on her again. But still it stunned him that he'd been thunderstruck by a poor, young lady who made her living selling gossip to the highest bidder. It was absurd, downright absurd.

He wasn't fooling himself about Millicent for a moment, but hopefully he was fooling her. He hadn't agreed not to expose her to Society because he thought she could help him find the Mad Ton Thief. That was balderdash, merely a ruse to satisfy her. He agreed because it gave him a reason to continue seeing her. And that in itself was ludicrous, too.

What could be the possible gain for him in continuing to pursue her? She wasn't a suitable wife for him. At the very least he needed to marry the daughter of a baron or a viscount, though an offspring of an earl or duke would be better. He only knew he had not had his fill of Millicent.

Not nearly enough.

"What's this? You're drinking without me?"

Chandler took in a deep breath and looked up from the glass of claret he was staring at to the face of John Wickenham-Thickenham-Fines. Damnation. He'd come to this club, one he seldom frequented, because he'd wanted to be alone. How in the devil had Fines found him?

"Oh, is that what I'm doing here? Clever of you to figure it out."

Fines shrugged his shoulders indolently. "That's a rather rude greeting for your best friend. How deep are you into your cups, Dunraven?"

"Deep enough that I'm not going to be coming out of them tonight," he grumbled.

"In that case, I guess it's good I found you. Any man who has a friend shouldn't drink alone."

"That means you're joining me?"

"Might as well." Fines sat down in a comfortable wing chair opposite Chandler. "I've nothing else to do on this dreary night. It's raining hard enough to drown the fires of hell." Fines brushed water droplets from the sleeve of his evening jacket.

"Why didn't you send word you wouldn't be attending any of the parties tonight and where you would be? I had a devil of a time finding you."

I wanted to be alone.

"Just because I wasn't in the mood for dancing and

playing the gentleman tonight, I didn't want to spoil anyone else's evening."

"You are in a temper. Since when do friends spoil each
other's evening?"

Recently, Chandler thought, but said nothing.

"We used to be part of a threesome and we rarely see
each other anymore. I would have been here earlier, but
this is the last blasted place I thought to look for you. You
seldom come here. Is anything wrong?" Fines asked.

"No."

"Then why are you frowning?"

"Maybe for the same reason you are?"

"I'm frowning because I spent the better part of two
hours looking for you."

Chandler managed a light chuckle. "That should have
been a clue that there are times a man doesn't want to be
found."

"I could believe that if you were with a lady but not
since you are here at the club."

"It's just that I've been to parties and balls every night
for the past few weeks. I needed a change from smiling,
bowing and dancing."

"I guess that means you aren't as interested in that Miss
Blair as Andrew led me to believe, for surely you would
have wanted to see her tonight."

Chandler stiffened. He started to tell his friend that he
didn't want them talking about Millicent, but that would
only make matters worse, so he simply said, "I'm not
interested in Lady Lambsbeth either, in case you're wondering."

"No, I was clear on that. You are still worried because
the raven hasn't been found, aren't you?"

Chandler's mouth tightened. "Don't start on that, Fines.
I'm in no mood for your badgering on a sore subject."

"It's not me, Dunraven."

Chandler raised an eyebrow of doubt before putting the rim of his glass to his lips.

"Truly. There's talk on the streets, in the shops, and in the clubs. Everyone at the parties tonight was talking about it."

"The raven?" Chandler asked incredulously.

"No, no. Not specifically. The Mad Ton Thief. You did hear about the stolen painting that was the size of a large parasol."

"I heard it was a small."

"What, the painting or the parasol?"

Chandler grimaced. "What the damnation does it matter, Fines? It's ridiculous for anyone to think the painting walked out of the house by itself or in the hands of a ghost."

"Of course it is, but you have to admit the rumor is delicious. Can you imagine anyone actually thinking that the thief is Lord Pinkwater's ghost, and he is collecting objects for a house he occupies up on the northern coast?"

"Good Lord. Are you serious?"

"That was the topic of conversation at the parties tonight. According to what I heard it's beginning to be an honor to have something taken by the thief and an affront on the quality of one's possessions if nothing is stolen."

And he thought being enchanted by a lovely gossipmonger was absurd!

Chandler shook his head, mystified. "I'm certain the robber is a common footpad who has managed to find a gentleman's clothing. How do these outrageous ideas get started?"

"It's called gossip, Dunraven. Ever heard of it?"

"Once too often," he muttered, then finished off his drink. He nodded to the waiter, who set a glass in front of Fines, to refill his own glass. After the man walked away, Chandler said, "I'm not worried about the raven."

"Truly?" It was Fines's turn to raise an eyebrow of doubt.

"When the thief is caught, if the raven is not returned, I will simply have another made."

"He says as his gut wrenches with guilt over having lost the original, knowing one cannot simply replace an Egyptian artifact."

Chandler's eyes narrowed. There was a time when Fines's mocking comments hadn't bothered him. He'd rather enjoyed them. Not anymore.

"Sometimes you're a bastard, Fines," he said, but with no real anger in his tone.

Fines laughed. "Yes. Sometimes. Most of the time. But I'm *always* a friend, Dunraven. Never have fear on that account."

Chandler nodded. Was he fortunate or not to have such a dedicated friend?

"What are you doing to find the golden bird of prey?"

"I'm working with Doulton on it, of course, and I'm working with someone else on the thefts, too," he said, as thoughts of Millicent returned to his mind as easily and gently as a late summer breeze.

"Who?"

Chandler picked up his drink as Fines nodded to a gentleman who walked by. "I'd rather not say."

"Since when?"

"In working with this person secrecy is most important."

"More important than friendship? There was a time we told each other everything."

"There was a time we did a lot of things together that we no longer do."

"Yes," Fines smiled wickedly. "Staying out all night drinking, gambling and enjoying our latest mistress, then racing our horses most of the day."

"It's a wonder we didn't kill ourselves."

"Oh, hell, Dunraven! What's wrong with us? We don't do those sorts of thing anymore. Are we growing into our dotage already?"

Chandler grunted a rueful laugh. "No. But, perhaps we're finally growing up, Fines?"

"Good lord! What an ugly thought."

"I suppose it's better than the alternative."

"Which is?"

"Death."

"Yes, so right you are. Forgot about that." Fines finished off his drink and glanced around for someone who could bring him another.

Chandler looked at his friend and it struck him that what he'd said so carelessly was true. The reason he didn't want to spend as much time with his friends anymore was because they'd grown up. He had finally grown up.

The undisciplined life he'd once lived no longer appealed to him. He was tired of Town with its crush of people on the streets, the smells and the carriage congestion. He was tired of the endless parties where people went only to eat, drink, to see and be seen. He wanted to spend more time at one of his estates and ride his horses, not race them. He wanted to sit down to dinner in his own home and eat with his beautiful wife by his side, not dine at the clubs with his friends.

Chandler's thoughts were brought up short when he realized the lovely wife at his side had the face of Millicent Blair.

Andrew must be feeling the call of family responsibility, too, for he'd all but come right out and said that he was looking to make a match before this Season was over. Fines was the one who still seemed to be content as a bachelor.

It also struck Chandler that he didn't want to be sitting here with Fines. He'd rather be dancing with Millicent Blair, which was specifically why he'd avoided the parties tonight. He had to come to some kind of conclusion about her.

He had to think about this logically. He'd never been seriously attracted to a young lady for more than a few weeks before another would strike his fancy. That gave him reason to believe that his obsession, for that was all it could possibly be, for the surprising Miss Blair would be over within the next week or two.

Yes, he would go back to the parties, dance with her, call on her despite her insistence that he not, and take her for a ride in Hyde Park and St. James, too. In short order he would grow tired of her as he had all the other young ladies who had caught his eye over the years. There was no reason to think that Millicent Blair was different from any of the other beautiful ladies in his past. Absolutely none.

Yes, that idea had merit. Given her employment, he couldn't possibly consider her for a wife. He'd see as much of her as possible and, no doubt, the attraction would wear off quickly. It had to, because right now he wanted nothing more than to hold her in his arms and kiss her again.

SHE HADN'T SEEN him all evening thought Millicent as she climbed into the carriage behind Lady Heathecoute. She had danced with several charming young gentlemen and she had enjoyed the parties, but she was constantly searching the dance floor, the supper table, the refreshment table and the front door for any sign of Lord Dunraven. He had never arrived.

The thought of him drove her to distraction.

Not that she was ever in any doubt, but her infatuation with him confirmed she was her mother's daughter. Even thinking about the earl was madness.

Lord Dunraven had proven himself time and time again to be a rake, following her, kissing her so intimately in the shop and again in her aunt's home. He amazed her. He thrilled her. And she was hopelessly smitten by him. She realized now that she had not been prepared to be pursued by a true scoundrel. For surely Lord Dunraven knew all the tricks.

And maybe she was a fool, but she had believed him when he told her he would not leak to Society that she was a writer of tittle-tattle.

The Heathecoutes always took the seat facing the horses. It didn't matter to Millicent which direction she sat in the carriage.

The viscount climbed in behind Millicent and the footman closed the door. As usual, his lordship immediately laid his head back against the squabs and closed his eyes. It was his habit to nap on the ride home each evening.

Millicent wondered why she hadn't seen Lord Dunraven at any of the parties. It was the first night in more than a week that she hadn't seen him.

He's only trifling with you.

Of course, because that's what scoundrels do.

They woo, flatter and kiss innocent young ladies until

they are pining after the rogues, then they move on to the next unsuspecting young lady and steal her heart, too. Millicent knew all this. She should have been able to resist Lord Dunraven's charms, if for no other reason than what had happened to her mother when she'd lost her heart and reputation over a man of the very same ilk.

If only she had been stronger than her mother, but in the end, she found she was just as susceptible to a rake's charms. She had watched for him all evening, hoping he would appear by her side and ask her to dance. Perhaps he didn't intend to have anything to do with her now that he knew what she was doing. A stab of envy struck her at the thought that Lady Lambsbeth was back in Town. Maybe he no longer needed any other diversion.

"Ma'am," Millicent asked, "what do you know about Lord Dunraven and Lady Lambsbeth?"

The viscountess fanned herself. "Oh, that's an old story, and why Beatrice wanted to run it in Lord Truefitt's column I have no idea. It's really passé. There are more appetizing things to be writing about than an old love affair. Perhaps it just shows that Beatrice is having trouble keeping up with the column while she's recuperating."

This was the first comment that Millicent had heard the viscountess make about how her aunt was handling the column. Millicent could only assume that her ladyship hadn't heard that circulation for *The Daily Reader* had increased and Lord Truefitt's column was praised for being one of the main reasons.

Just tonight she'd heard more than one lady mention how eager she was to get the paper each day to see what quote from Shakespeare was used in Lord Truefitt's column.

Millicent decided it would be wise not to express a view one way or the other to the Lady Heathecoute. She would leave that up to her aunt. However, she wasn't shy about asking other questions she wanted answers to.

"Ma'am," Millicent asked in what she hoped was an offhanded manner, "do you think Lord Dunraven loves Lady Lambsbeth?"

"Loves? Good heavens, no. I doubt he's ever loved anyone in his life. I think most everyone considers him a confirmed bachelor. What makes you ask such a question? You haven't set your eyes on him have you? Because I have to agree with my husband that he is quite unattainable."

"No. It's nothing like that. It's just there has been talk about the two of them now that she's back in Town."

"Yes, yes. Everyone assumes they had an affair and it ended badly. Talk about it was all the rage last year. She was married and her husband found out about it. Had it not been for friends of both men one of them would be dead to—" She stopped and chuckled.

The low throaty sound of her laughter sounded ominous in the dark carriage. Millicent noticed the viscount hadn't even blinked an eye since he stepped into the carriage. No doubt he was used to hearing his wife's laughter.

"Ah—that is, one of them is dead, I understand. But of course, not from the challenge. After wise counsel from his friends, Lord Lambsbeth withdrew it and he and his lady left Town the next day. That's no matter now. I don't think anyone in the ton cares whether the earl and lady pick up where they left off. It's old news."

"Yes, I suppose you're right."

"I'm more interested in hearing whether another of the Terrible Threesome, Lord Dugdale, is truly in financial straits. That could account for his sudden desire to make a match before the end of the year."

"Yes, I heard much the same thing," Millicent said, but

didn't mention that she'd heard the story earlier in the afternoon from Lynette.

"Tonight the guests at all the parties seemed to be interested only in talking about the latest news concerning the Mad Ton Thief and the ghost. I wonder if the thief knows how popular he is?"

"With everyone talking about it at the parties, the clubs and on the streets, I'm sure he does. He probably hopes the madness continues so that he can continue to get away with stealing. It appears that this idea that he is a ghost is titillating to them all. I think they want it to be so. Though, why anyone would want to talk about Lord Pinkwater's ghost, I have no idea."

"Oh, I do believe it is newsworthy."

"But it has little to do with gossip," the viscountess said in her don't-argue-with-me voice. "Lady Windham said that she felt deprived when she held a party and nothing was stolen from her home. She said she was thinking of holding another party next week, hoping the thief will show up and take something."

"Do you really think she will do that?"

"Oh, she probably will. The thing is that she has so many lovely things in her home something probably was stolen and she just doesn't know it."

"You think so?"

"Of course, I really have no idea. I'm only saying that the house is filled with paintings, china, pottery and all quite valuable. Now tell me, what other delicious tidbits did you hear tonight?"

It only took a few more minutes to arrive at her aunt's town house. As usual, Phillips quietly opened the door and she stepped inside. She heard Hamlet bark once as usual, alerting her aunt that she was home.

Phillips left to prepare Millicent a cup of tea, and she

took the time to remove her gloves and pelisse before going upstairs. It was then that she heard a light knock on the door. She glanced down the hallway, expecting the butler to come answer the door. When he didn't immediately appear she realized the knock was really too soft for him to have heard it.

Thinking the viscountess must have thought of something else she wished to say, Millicent hurried back to the door and quietly opened it.

Her arm was grabbed and she was whisked outside into the darkness.

Fourteen

❦

"He that wants money, means, and content, is without three good friends." If that is true, it is to Lord Dugdale's benefit that he still has Lord Dunraven and Lord Chatwin as good friends. From what this humble soul hears, money is one of the friends who left him.

Lord Truefitt
Society's Daily Column

"*Shhh. Don't scream.* It's me." Chandler gently pulled Millicent out of the house. He left the heavy door slightly ajar so that it wouldn't throw the latch inside.

It was good he spoke and let her know who he was because it was so dark she couldn't see a thing. She allowed him to usher her to the far corner of the town house, which was hidden from view of the street by a tall shrub. It had rained most of the evening and the moon was completely covered by clouds, making the night pitch-black and heavy with gray mist.

Millicent leaned against the side of the wet house, her

heart pounding with excitement and trepidation. Already the wet grass had soaked through her satin slippers, chilling her with dampness.

"Angels above, Lord Dunraven, what are you doing here, and at this time of night—I mean morning?"

"Shhh. Not so loud." He moved in closer to her, and she could almost make out the features of his face, feel the warmth of his body. "I wanted to see you."

She wished she could see his eyes, but it was just too dark and misty. "Then why, sir, in heaven's name, did you not attend one of the parties tonight? You knew which I would be attending this evening."

"I had other things I needed to do, but I realized I didn't want the night to end without seeing you."

"Phillips has only gone for tea. He'll be right back. I must go inside."

"I'll only keep you a moment. I've been waiting more than an hour for your return. I was beginning to think I had missed you and that you had already come home. Is anyone else in the house awake other than the butler?"

"Of course, My au—" She stopped just before she said the word *aunt*. Heavens! He had her so surprised she almost forgot herself. "Never mind about that. And don't you dare change the subject."

"You can change the subject but I can't?"

"Yes. I can't believe you have once again endangered my reputation by sneaking around to see me. How many times must I insist that you—"

Suddenly he dipped his head and kissed the tip of her nose. Millicent was so shocked that she stopped midsentence. That simple show of affection took away her anger.

"It's hard for me to believe I'm here, too," Chandler said.

"Have you no care for my reputation?" she asked, trying to regain her exasperation.

"I've told you I do. And I mean that."

"Do you want to get caught in a position like this with me and have to marry me?"

"No man wants to be forced into marriage."

The firmness and quickness with which he answered didn't go unnoticed by Millicent. "Then why must you constantly steal around to see me? We are going to get caught and either my character will be ruined for the rest of my life, or we will be obliged to marry by special license. What you are doing is madness."

"I know. Have faith, Millicent. I told you we won't be caught. You have to trust me."

"How can I trust you? Every time I begin to convince myself that you are a gentleman, you do something crazy like this to prove that you are a rogue, a scoundrel, and a rake of the highest order. I'd be a silly fool to trust you."

He moved his body closer to hers, pressing her against the wall. Her vision was adjusting to the black, misty night, and she could make out that he smiled at her.

"Yet, here you stand in the darkness with me while the household sleeps." He stretched out his arms from his sides. "I'm not holding you. You are free to leave me and go inside."

"I don't want to go."

"Then stay a minute longer."

Millicent lowered her forehead to his chest and his arms wrapped around her, pulling her close to the warmth of his embrace.

"I must be one of the silly fools I was talking about," she whispered.

"If that is so, it's only where I'm concerned. You are

quite sensible in all other matters." He paused and moved closer to her. "Except where what you are doing for the gossip writers is concerned. I must admit that, if it is true you are not doing it for the money or by force, I would really like to know why you are doing it."

With her face half hidden in the warmth of his shirtfront she said, "Did you come here to talk about that?"

"No. I came to do this." He kissed the top of her head and pulled her into his warm arms and held her with his cheek against hers. He breathed in deeply as if trying to take in her essences. "I love the way you feel in my arms and the way you smell."

She should be trembling with fear of being caught, but instead she was acutely aware of his every touch and filled with desire to have his lips on hers.

"I don't like being an unwise person, Chandler," she whispered earnestly.

"No, Millicent, you are not foolish. You are intelligent, beautiful, and desirable." He reached up and slowly caressed her cheek with the backs of his fingers as if they had all the time in the world to be together.

"What would you have done if Phillips or one of the maids had come to the door?"

He kissed her cheek, letting his lips travel down her neck as he whispered, "I would have produced your dance card, which I have in my pocket, and said I found it on the floor as you were leaving the party. I rushed to catch you before you departed, but couldn't, so I followed you in my coach. I would have handed it to him along with a guinea. No one would be the wiser."

"That shows how much practice you have had meeting young ladies in secret."

"I have some experience."

"Too much."

"Enough."

"So much that I am no match for your machinations."

"As it should be."

Millicent tilted her head back, giving Chandler freedom to explore the soft skin behind her ear before he moved up to brush his lips across her eyelids and down to her cheekbone. He made her feel sensuous, languorous.

"I knew I wouldn't be able to sleep tonight if I didn't see you and hold you," he murmured across her cheek.

The warmth of his breath on her skin, the strength of his body pressing against her, the seduction of his words made Millicent want to forget everything but this man and the way he made her senses come to life. She loved the way he touched her and soothed her fears.

Wanting like she had never known before filled her. She lifted her mouth to him. The soft warmth of his tongue swept the outline of her lips slowly, teasingly before taking them passionately in a kiss that was meant to weaken the last vestige of her reserve, and it did.

His hand moved up from her waist to cup her breast. Millicent's breath quickened. His palm flattened against her breast and gently moved up and down, causing ripples of pleasure to course through her.

From deep inside herself she found the strength to say, "I must go in. Hamlet barks to let Lady Beatrice know I've come home. She will send Glenda looking for me if she doesn't hear me coming up the stairs soon."

"All right," he whispered. "I'll let you go."

No, don't.

"But only after I have one more kiss. I want to go to sleep tonight with the taste of your lips on mine."

He bent and pressed his lips to hers in a soft, lingering kiss. In the coolness of the night, his lips were warm, his body firmly protective. He circled her in his arms and brought her up tightly to his chest and hugged her to him. It felt wonderful.

Millicent sighed contentedly. She had been disappointed when she hadn't seen him tonight, and while she knew she should be angry that he continued to jeopardize her reputation, all she could think was that she was so happy he took the risk in coming to see her.

"You taste of liquor," she said softly into the warmth of his mouth.

He nodded a little. "I've been drinking, trying to forget about you."

"Obviously, it didn't work."

"No. It didn't. We don't suit, but I can't stop thinking about you. I fear you are in my soul."

Millicent's breath caught in her throat. Did he mean that? When he said things like that, she almost could believe he meant every word.

"You know all the things to say to make a lady lose her head over you, don't you?"

Chandler lifted his head. She wondered if he was trying to look through the darkness into her eyes and read her innermost thoughts. She couldn't allow that to happen. She had to take advantage now while she had him at a weak moment.

"I want to know what pleases you."

"You know how to kiss and tease and make me desire you as I never have any other man. You are a rake. It is what you do, what you are good at and I can't fight you."

"Millicent, you misunderstood me."

"No. I am not ashamed of wanting your touch, or your kisses. I have longed to feel about a man the way I feel about you, but I will not fall victim to believing you care about me, Chandler. Don't try to make me believe you care."

"All right." He stepped away from her. "I guess it is best we know where we stand."

Millicent took a deep breath, wondering where she'd found such courage. It would have been so easy to have believed him. Thank God she hadn't.

"Will you agree that I can call on you tomorrow and take you for a ride in Hyde Park?"

"Why do you insist on pressing me on this matter?"

"I tried to come to a conclusion about that very thing tonight, and I have no answer other than I want to be with you."

"If I agree to see you openly, will you promise not to see me in secret again?"

"No."

He drove her to madness! "You are a mystery, Chandler. Why see me in open and secret?"

"How can I kiss you the way I want to, the way you want me to, if I don't see you in secret?"

"That is the problem. I fear I am only a mad dash away from scandal."

"And so you are. I'll call on you at half past three today. Be ready."

With those parting words he slipped away into the misty darkness.

CHANDLER'S LASHES FLUTTERED against the bright sunshine of midday. He squinted, his eyes not wanting to adjust to the daylight. Had he been dreaming about Millicent or had she really been in his arms?

They were in a room lit only by candlelight. She wore

a low-cut gown of pure white gossamer. Her skin glowed like the finest alabaster and felt as soft as the most expensive silk the Orient spun. She tasted of honey. He was kissing her. Madly. Until the harsh light of reality intruded.

No, it had been only a dream. He had left her at Lady Beatrice's door.

He kept his eyes closed and rolled over. The sheets were cool to his back. The pillow fit snugly under his head. He didn't want to wake from the sweet dream, but had no choice. Even though he hadn't seen his valet, Chandler knew the servant was moving about the room, quietly opening the draperies, laying out his razor, pouring warm water into the washbowl.

Chandler's lashes fluttered again.

"Good morning, my lord."

Chandler remained quiet. He wasn't ready to move or speak. His lower body wasn't prepared to admit that Millicent was not in the bed with him. After a moment or two, reluctantly, he raised his head and looked around. Winston stood at the one window where the draperies were still closed.

"That's quite enough light, Winston," he managed to say and laid his head back down.

"Very well, sir." He left the draperies alone and walked over to the wardrobe. "Lord Dugdale is below stairs wanting to speak to you."

That woke Chandler. He sat up in the bed. "Andrew? At this time of day? That's odd. Did he happen to say what he wanted?"

"No, sir. Only that it was urgent, and he was prepared to wait until you were available to see him."

Something had to be wrong for his friend to pay a call midday. Millicent crossed his mind. He wondered if anyone had seen him with her last night at Lady Beatrice's and had written about it? He grunted a laugh. No, if anyone wrote about them the information would have come from her and he felt sure she wouldn't report on them again. So what was wrong?

"Tell him I'll be down as soon as I dress."

"Yes, sir."

"Take him some tea and scones. That should occupy him until I get down."

As soon as Winston closed the door behind him, Chandler rose. He washed his face and shaved with the warm water the valet left for him and wet his hair before combing it away from his face.

He stepped into the fawn-colored trousers the valet had laid out and pulled the white shirt over his head. He didn't take the time to don a collar and neckcloth, he could do that later in the day. It wouldn't matter to Andrew that he wasn't properly garbed; however, Chandler took the time to stuff the tail of his shirt into his waistband as he headed down the stairs.

He rounded the doorway into the sitting room and saw a splendidly dressed Andrew pacing in front of the unlit fireplace. He took a deep breath and ran a hand over his damp hair before entering the room.

"What has you up and out so early?" he asked as he walked into the parlor.

"It's about time you decided to rise from your slumber. Where the devil were you last night, anyway? I couldn't find you anywhere."

"Fines managed to locate me, and we had a drink together. Sorry you missed it."

"After the third club, I called it a night. The weather was brutish. Where the devil did he find you?"

Chandler looked at the tray of tea and tarts and could

see Andrew hadn't touched it. It was unusual for anyone to ignore his cook's apricot tarts. He knew everyone always enjoyed them, but he'd never realized that he always took them when he called on a lady until Millicent had mentioned it. Now he realized she was right. Since she was a writer of tittle-tattle he wouldn't be surprised to find out that she knew more about him than he knew himself.

"Well?" Andrew asked.

"That's not important, but you being here at this hour is. What's the reason?"

"This." Andrew held out a sheet of newspaper. "Have you seen it?"

Chandler tensed, but he hoped it didn't show. Maybe Millicent had told one of the gossip columnists about their clandestine meeting last night after all.

Instead of taking the paper, Chandler picked up the teapot and calmly poured himself a cup. "My eyes have been open all of five minutes, Andrew. What do you think the odds are I've seen that paper?"

"This is no time to be so damned sarcastic, Dunraven, and I'm in no mood for it, besides."

Chandler returned the pot to the silver tray and asked, "Would you like a cup?"

"No, thank you. You know I don't drink the vile stuff, but I will have a brandy, if you don't mind."

It must be bad. He'd never seen Andrew drink brandy in the middle of the day during their wildest years. But the odd thing was, whatever was written in that paper didn't worry Chandler like it should. He should be furious at even the prospect that Millicent had talked about his late night call on her, but he wasn't.

"Not at all. Help yourself, then stop pacing, sit down

and let me wake up while you tell me what has you stewing."

"The damned gossipmongers are after me again."

"You?"

Relief washed down him. Thank God it wasn't anything about him and Millicent.

"You sound surprised."

"No, it's just that we've been in their columns for years."

"What have you done this time?"

"Nothing, of course."

"Good, then. Don't worry and have a tart. I know you like these." Chandler picked up one and took a generous bite.

"It's that bastard Lord Truefitt. He says I'm hanging out for an heiress because I'm in financial trouble."

Chandler choked on his tart and spilled his tea into his saucer. He coughed and set the teacup down on the table.

"Damnation," he muttered.

"Damn right," Andrew answered.

Millicent was responsible for that being written. She had mentioned to him that she'd heard of an earl who was in financial trouble and suggested he might be the one stealing from the houses, but she had refused to tell him the earl's name. Now he knew why.

She thought Andrew might be the Mad Ton Thief. Damnation!

Andrew poured himself a generous amount of the liquor from the decanter, and turned back to Chandler. "The bastard is trying to ruin my chances with Miss Bardwell."

Chandler cleared his throat again and said, "Wait a minute. You're seriously pursuing Miss Bardwell?"

"Well—er—I'm not sure it is serious, you understand. That's not the point." Andrew took a generous sip of his drink and went back to the rosewood sideboard and poured another splash into the glass.

Andrew was stammering like a street ragamuffin caught stealing a loaf of bread. That was so unlike him. "When did this happen?" Chandler asked.

"The column is in today's paper."

"No. This talk of hurting your chances of a match with Miss Bardwell. Have you made an offer for her hand?"

"Of course not. And I don't know that I will. It's just that if I wanted to—" He paused. "That's not important. It's one thing to write about a gentleman's escapades with the fairer sex, but quite another to write about his pockets. That's going beyond the pale. I have half a mind to hire a Runner to find out who this Lord Truefitt is and give him a taste of scandal. I don't know where he gets his information, but I doubt he'll be writing anything after I get through with him."

Chandler would speak to Millicent and tell her that both he and his friends were off-limits to scandal sheets.

"Hold on, Andrew, what exactly does it say?"

"It all but says I'm ready for the poorhouse, that's what it says."

Wanting to calm his friend, Chandler said, "Here, let me see that."

Chandler took the paper and read the first few lines of the column and looked up. "I don't think it is as bad as you think. In fact, I think it's a play on words."

Andrew walked over to Chandler and looked over his shoulder at the paper. "What do you mean?"

"I think it's one of those things that has a hidden meaning."

His friend gave him an incredulous look. "The only thing that is hiding is your comprehension. What the devil are you talking about?"

"No. I think what he's really saying here is that the three of us don't spend the time together that we used to." Chandler continued to make up his answer as he talked. "Fines and I were just talking about that last night."

"Well, we don't spend the kind of time together that we used to, but what has that to do with what this newspaper says about money no longer being my friend?"

"I'm sure the money aspect was only used so it would fit with the quote from Shakespeare, but the true meaning is that they aren't seeing the three of us together anymore."

"Hmm. You really think so?"

Chandler pretended to study the paper again, knowing he'd have a long talk with Millicent about this later in the afternoon.

"Yes, yes, after reading it again I'm sure of it. You've heard how popular Truefitt's column has become since he's been using Shakespeare. Don't give it another thought. Those who don't know you might think from this that you've fallen on hard times, but no one in the ton will."

"If only you are right," Andrew said, then drained his glass.

Chandler took a long hard look at Andrew and wasn't sure he liked what he saw. Could there be any truth to what was written about his friend? No, Andrew would have told him if there was a problem.

But he couldn't help but wonder where in London Millicent got her damning information.

Fifteen

"To say the truth, reason and love keep little company together now a days," and if that were not true, why would Miss Pennington be spending so much time on the dance floor and in Hyde Park with Lord Chatwin? Her father has made it clear he wants a match before the Season is out. Can he expect an offer for her hand from Lord Chatwin?

Lord Truefitt
Society's Daily Column

WIDE BLUE SKIES dotted by puffy white clouds served as a canopy to the beautiful day as Millicent and Chandler rode in the curricle toward Hyde Park. Bright sunshine caressed their backs and a midspring breeze lightly fanned their hair. It was the kind of day that made Millicent glad she didn't have to be inside, surrounded by dark furniture and heavy draperies.

Chandler had arrived splendidly dressed in his riding coat of dark brown with shiny brass buttons adorning the front lapels and the sleeves. He grinned like a schoolboy when he presented her the predictable box of apricot tarts, which he then made light of when he gave them to her. From behind his back he unexpectedly produced a cutting of fresh Persian lilies from his own garden. She didn't even want to think about what the extra gift might mean.

Before leaving the house, Millicent had asked her maid to see to it that two tarts were sent up to Aunt Beatrice with her afternoon tea and that the rest should not be touched. Millicent would take those to Lynette tomorrow afternoon. After all, she had promised to do so if she should ever receive the highly prized gift. The lilies Millicent had sent to her room so that only she would enjoy their fragrance and their beauty.

Much to Millicent's surprise, and after a long discussion, her aunt had sanctioned her afternoon ride with the most notorious member of the Terrible Threesome. According to Aunt Beatrice, Lord Dunraven would lose interest in Millicent quickly once she became available for him to call on. And Beatrice decided the closer Millicent became with such a notable member of the ton the more gossip she would hear.

Nothing was more important than that. And of course, her aunt warned her that she must be very careful that Lord Dunraven behave as a proper gentleman at all times.

If Aunt Beatrice only knew!

Millicent had worried about Lord Dunraven looking at this afternoon outing in Hyde Park as encouragement, but she couldn't deny the rushing thrill that raced through her chest when she placed her gloved hand in his to be helped into the carriage. And again, when his arm touched hers as he hopped onto the leather-covered cushioned seat beside her, and later his leg brushed the hem of her skirt as a groom handed him the ribbons.

She had tried hard not to be smitten by him but knew she was failing miserably. All he had to do was look at her and her stomach quivered.

Before he'd arrived, she'd vowed to conduct the outing with the utmost consideration for propriety. Many eyes would be upon them and she must be circumspect. She really had no choice in agreeing to see the earl in the polite world. And she had to somehow force him not to seek her out in secret.

Her hope had been that once he started to see her among the ton he would soon become bored with her and seek another conquest. That thought caused a catch in her breath, but given her circumstances, it was the only answer that would be right for her.

Rather than guiding the horses along at a breezy pace, Chandler allowed the grays to clip slowly through the streets of Mayfair. As soon as they left sight of her aunt's house, in typical rake fashion, Chandler moved closer to her on the seat so that with his knees wide apart his thigh was touching her dress.

So much for thinking he might behave like a gentleman.

Millicent could have sworn she felt his body heat through her clothing. She had plenty of room to move away from him in the carriage seat, but had no inclination to do so.

She popped open her delicate parasol, which was trimmed with tiny yellow ribbons that matched her dress and pelisse, and held it with one hand over her shoulder. Chandler looked over at her, winked and smiled that roguish grin that melted her heart and made her wish things could be different between them. If he were not a rake and if she were not a gatherer of tittle-tattle, then perhaps affection could blossom between them.

"I fear you are a rogue even in church."

"I have been. 'Pray you, stand farther from me.' "

Shakespeare again. Chandler delighted her.

She let her gaze stray over his strong profile and dark-lashed eyes. "Indeed, sir. And when we first met you tried to make me believe that all I had heard about you wasn't true."

"It wasn't. At least, not all of it," he amended. "But, no matter, that's in the past now. Since meeting you, I'm trying to mend my ways."

"Heavens above. You can't convince me that is true." She sighed and shook her head indulgently. "I cannot believe that you were once worse than you are now. It's simply unbelievable."

"Scandalous, but true. Perhaps it's best we don't talk about my misspent youth today."

"I think that is probably a good idea."

"For a change, let's talk about you."

No, let's don't.

She turned toward him. His eyes were so clear, so blue, and looking directly at her. "Me?"

He smiled faintly. "Yes."

"That's not a good idea."

There was something challenging in his gaze, and he met her stare-for-stare. "I think it is. I think it's time."

"You already know more than most," she hedged.

"But not enough."

Millicent turned away from him and remained quiet. It was awful, but she couldn't tell him the truth.

She would love to tell him everything about her so there would be no secrets between them. There was nothing about her family or childhood she would keep from him, if not for her aunt. How could she tell him anything about her life? If he knew her father's name, it would be

only a matter of time before he discovered that Lady Beatrice was her aunt.

Millicent knew of her aunt's fear of being exposed and
losing her employment. Millicent couldn't take the chance
that Chandler might follow a snippet of information that
would lead him to Lord Truefitt's door.

"Tell me about your family, Millicent. Who was your
father—other than the man who married your mother?"

"The person who is employing me thought it best if no
one knows about me. For many reasons I can't explain, I
must keep it that way."

Chandler nodded to an acquaintance and a few moments later waved to a friend in military uniform who
passed them on horseback before giving his attention back
to Millicent.

His expression was composed as he said, "You plead a
good case."

"It's not just for me. There are others I must consider."

"Do you know what the rumor is in Town about you?"

Millicent looked at him and laughed softly, playfully.
There was no doubt in her mind that Chandler Prestwick,
the earl of Dunraven, captivated her. If only he wasn't so
charming, she would allow herself to be completely en-
tranced by him and allow him to take her heart. If only
she weren't working for her aunt. If only he wasn't a
rogue. Oh, if only there weren't so many if onlys where
Chandler was concerned.

"Of course I know what people are saying about me. I
wouldn't be very good at my employment if I didn't know
the answer to that. I'm considered a poor young lady from
the country whose ailing mother imposed on an old acquaintance to give her daughter a Season in London in
hopes of making a good match. Did I cover everything?"

"You are in the know."

"It's not difficult."

Millicent slowly twirled the handle of her parasol between her hands and looked at the people and the buildings they passed. How could she not enjoy this sun-drenched afternoon riding in a carriage with Chandler?

"What do you think about what is being said about me? Do you think any of it is true?" she asked with a flirtatious lilt lacing her voice.

He looked at her with a mixture of amusement and cautious insight in his blue eyes. "I think you would marry only for love, not just to make a suitable match."

She laughed again, more sweetly than before. "You are so very good at saying exactly what a lady wants to hear, my lord. You must have had a wonderful teacher."

"Experience was my teacher. But am I right about you?"

"Decidedly so. I've turned down offers because I didn't love the gentlemen who asked me to marry them."

He threw a glance her way. "More than one, I see?"

"Hmm," she answered without acknowledging she had turned down three offers.

"I'll keep that in mind."

They rode in silence for a few moments, listening only to the sounds of the busy streets, the creaks of carriage wheels, and the snorts of the horses.

Chandler said, "You don't have to mention names, but tell me about your family."

He wasn't going to let it go, and she wasn't going to give in. She found it impossible to resist his kisses, but on this subject she must remain firm. She would not jeopardize her aunt's livelihood.

"It's respectable."

"I can see that no matter how hard I press you that's all I'm going to get out of you?"

"Because of what I'm doing anonymity is essential. I honor it and I ask that you do, too."

"All right. I'll accept that, for now, but I don't know for how long."

His last two words were more muttered than spoken, and suddenly Millicent wondered if she should consider them a warning.

CHANDLER GUIDED THE horse through the west gate and onto the lane that led toward the Serpantine. Their curricle fell in line behind a fancy closed carriage that was driven by a liveried driver and drawn by a matching set of bays. The grassy areas of the park were packed with distinctively dressed gentlemen and elegantly fashioned ladies. Those wishing to see and be seen strolled the vast grounds while others rode horseback or drove carriages.

Chandler came to the park only because the ladies enjoyed it. Yet again he had the feeling that he'd much rather be riding in the countryside of one of his estates than the bustling Hyde Park.

The traffic was much too thick for his liking as he queued with the other carriages, so he said, "Let's park over there and take a walk. All right with you?"

"I'd love it," she answered.

As soon as the groom had hold of the horses, Chandler jumped down from the curricle and reached for Millicent. He saw uncertainty in her eyes. He wondered if she was worrying about how he'd behave, or that one day he wouldn't take no for an answer when he asked about her family. And he'd given her plenty of reason to wonder. He wouldn't take no for an answer much longer.

He wanted to encircle her small waist with his hands and lift her down but restrained himself and merely took her hand to steady her on the step. He couldn't remember the last time, if ever, he'd enjoyed being with a woman as much as he looked forward to being with Millicent.

She was seductive, playful, intelligent and loyal to a fault. There was an alluring grace in every move she made, a promise in every smile she gave him.

When she placed her hand in the crook of his arm, he held her a bit too close, but he couldn't stop himself. He wanted to do so much more. He settled for a leisurely ramble, moving away from where most of the crowds had gathered to make sure they were noticed.

Who was she? Why did she spy for the gossips? That plagued him. No one could ever make him believe she was not a highborn, gentle-bred young woman. Yet, for some reason, she was at Lord Truefitt's mercy.

Could he let that go on any longer?

"You're very quiet," Millicent said.

"I was just thinking about what you are doing for Truefitt."

"That could be ominous."

"Does it always work the way it has for you?"

An easy, natural smile curved her lips. "I'm not sure what you mean."

"You told me you were not spying for Truefitt for the money, nor because he was forcing you, so the way I see it, there can only be one other reason you would consent."

"And what would that be?"

"Your family can't afford a Season for you, so Lord Truefitt found someone to sponsor you, someone who had actually met your mother so that you will be properly chaperoned. He takes care of all the expenses for your Season in exchange for the gossip you provide him to write his column."

"It seems you have it well thought out."

"I can see where it would be profitable for both of you. He obtains the gossip he needs and your are afforded the opportunity for a chance at a good match."

"I have no idea how other columnists work. I can only verify that what you just explained is somewhat close to my arrangement with Lord Truefitt."

"Somewhat close you say?"

"Yes."

"So there's more?"

The threat of a another smile fluttered her delectable mouth. "Or, maybe things are just different from the way you have imagined them to be."

Chandler chuckled lightly under his breath. How could he gain her favor, her trust? Why did he want to? They could have no future together.

"For a young lady who listens to everything that is said around her, you know how to reveal nothing."

She smiled faintly, looking into the distance before glancing back at him and saying, "It's a gift of the trade."

There was that seductive grace again. Chandler felt his chest expand with wanting. When she looked at him like that and made a simple statement so innocently, he was knocked off his feet.

"Sometimes you look as innocent as a church mouse, and it drives me to madness, and I think you enjoy every moment of it."

She smiled. "I enjoy you."

Chandler's heart tripped. He saw honesty in her eyes and heard it in her voice. She wasn't just trying to flatter him. And he could have sworn her eyes flashed a "come hither" look that made him light-headed with joy.

He reached over and took hold of her hand that rested in the crook of his arm and gently squeezed. Damn the gloves. Damn convention. Damn Society. He wanted to feel her silky skin without the layers of cotton between them. He wanted to see her beautiful body completely unclothed. He wanted to touch her silken thighs and suckle her firm breasts. He wanted to—no, he had to stop that kind of thinking. It was getting difficult to walk.

He lightly shook his head and cleared his throat. If he was going to get through the afternoon without ravishing her, a change of topic was in order.

"You know, you really should have told me my friend Andrew Terwillger was the earl you thought had spent his inheritance and was looking to make a wealthy match."

"I thought about it, but I couldn't take the chance that you would have warned him."

"What would have been the harm if I had?" He remembered choking on the tart. "It was quite a shock for both of us."

"But true. I have it on good authority."

"I spoke to Andrew about it just this morning, but I didn't mention to him that you hinted he might be the thief among us. I don't think the poor fellow could have stood the blow. You need to keep him out of your column."

"You know I can't do that. If I hear something that is scandalously intriguing, I must write about it."

"I've known him for fifteen years. I think I would know if my best friend had squandered his money. I've seen no change in his lifestyle."

"Perhaps there's a reason there's been no change," she responded quickly.

Chandler was firm. "He did not steal the raven. He would not steal from me or anyone."

Millicent remained calm, unperturbed. "Desperate men attempt dangerous things."

He simply said, "Millicent."

She looked up at him and relented. "However, I apologize if you think I was accusing your friend of being the Mad Ton Thief. I was merely pointing out possibilities."

"In this case, there is no likelihood he's involved. If he were having trouble with his finances, he would come to me. Besides, there must be dozens of titled gentlemen who've been gamblers and spendthrifts with their inheritances."

"But, did they attend your party?"

Chandler stopped and turned her to face him. "You may have something there. My dear Millicent, you are not only beautiful, but clever, too. I'll have Doulton check into who among the ton is in debt, and we'll see if any of those names show up on the lists where there have been robberies."

"That's a very good idea, sir. If there is not a stranger among the ton and it appears there isn't, then the Mad Ton Thief has to be someone's friend."

He looked down at her and an urgent need to possess her filled him. She wasn't right for him. He wasn't good for her, but still he wanted her. "I could kiss you right here in front of everyone within sight of us."

She stepped away and her eyes flashed a warning. "Do not try to do that, Lord Dunraven."

"All right, I'll wait until I get you behind a tree." He took her arm and slipped it through his arm again and continued their walk, but faster this time.

"There are no trees nearby."

"No reason to sound so disappointed." He smiled wick-

edly at her and winked. "There will be in a few minutes.
I know the perfect spot."

"I am not disappointed, sir," she argued, but not with
any real conviction. "And how dare you think to escort
me to a place where you've kissed dozens of girls."

He kept his tone light. "You are hard to please. Now
you sound jealous."

"And you sir, are a cad."

"But a likable one."

She stopped. "Yes. You are incorrigible. It's true and
it's my misfortune."

"And my good luck."

Suddenly Millicent turned away from Chandler and
pulled on the crook of his arm with her arm, forcing him
to turn around and head in the opposite direction.

"What are you doing?" he asked, not using any strength
to stop her from guiding him.

"Not today, my lord. I will not let you endanger my
reputation this afternoon. We are going to make this a
proper outing if it kills us."

He looked down into her eyes with appreciation and
admiration. "All right. Today you win. No matter that I
want to kiss you madly, I will respect your wishes."

She took a solid breath. "Thank you for that small consideration."

"You're welcome." He liked that she didn't try to pun-
ish him for being forward.

Oh, hell, what don't I like about her?

They started walking toward the carriage. "We need to
return to the subject of Lord Truefitt's column, because
there's something else you should know."

"What's that?"

"Andrew is thinking of hiring a Runner to find out who
Lord Truefitt is so that he can expose him."

"Oh, no! That would be disastrous. You can't let your friend do that."

Chandler didn't like seeing real fear in her eyes. Would there be harm to her if Truefitt was revealed? He wondered again what could be between Millicent and the gossip writer. He didn't know, but it was time he did something to find out what hold he had over Millicent.

"You must tell Truefitt to keep Andrew out of the column and perhaps his temper will cool down. I'll do what I can, but Andrew has a mind of his own. I do believe he is serious about this."

"Thank you for telling me." Her voice was soft, uncertain, grateful. "I know you didn't have to confide in me."

What was it he once heard? *A happy, gratified woman knows no bounds in love.* He had to stop thinking of things like that. It took him places he wasn't prepared to go.

"Quite frankly, I don't care what happens to Truefitt, but I don't want you hurt by anything that Andrew might do."

Millicent smiled sweetly at him again. "Thank you. I'm indebted to you."

Wonderful.

"I'll think of some way you can repay me."

"No doubt." She shook her head resignedly. "Why is it every time I convince myself that you are a true rake you do something astonishingly kind like this?"

"I've told you that I know how to behave as a gentleman, at times. Now, if you can't write about Andrew, I assume you will have to put me back in the cursed daily column."

"You are a favorite."

"How about Fines? He's only been in a time or two

recently, or surely there is someone who would love to be mentioned and has felt neglected."

Her eyes brightened like fire glowing in amber. "Chandler, that is a marvelous idea."

"Marvelous? What?"

"Mentioning someone who has never or seldom been in the column."

"Good lord, you're not telling me that the reason my name always shows up is because they haven't thought of naming someone else?"

Her lips twitched into a stunning grin. "Don't try to be dim-witted. You are much too intelligent."

He loved it that she made no effort to hide her teasing. "And you are far too intelligent for your own good."

"Thank you. It's no wonder tittle-tattle is so popular. Haven't you noticed that everyone seems to enjoy talking— about themselves or someone else? All you really have to do at a party is listen to what is being said around you. Maybe I'll ask Lord Truefitt to put in someone new, and to write something flattering."

"Flattering? That would be a first."

"If we can add Shakespeare, why not add nice?"

Chandler looked up at the wide blue sky and the only thing he could think was *"She is a woman, therefore may be woo'd; She is a woman, therefore may be won . . ."*

Sixteen

"I will praise any man that will praise me."
Please allow this one a short indulgence. It has
been heard on the streets and at the best parties that the Shakespeare quotes delight readers. Worry not. Wager if you please. The
quotes will continue and you can hope that
one day you will read your favorite line.

Lord Truefitt
Society's Daily Column

BRIGHT SUNSHINE FELL on Chandler's face as he
walked with Millicent back to the carriage. He was in a
quandary. Should he speak to Doulton about hiring someone to make private inquiries about Millicent's family, her
past, or should he leave it be because they had no future
together? He was certain that she wouldn't tell him about
herself. There was no use in asking again. And he was
certain he didn't like the hold Lord Truefitt had over her.

He'd never intended to get so caught up by her. He
couldn't recall ever having spent so much time thinking

about one lady before Millicent. He hadn't known he was capable of it because he'd never felt serious about any of the young ladies he'd called on. Millicent made him feel different. She challenged him and he liked that.

But there was so much more. He wanted her. Not for sport or fun as it had been with all the ladies in his past. He felt differently about Millicent. It was a growing feeling that he hadn't been able to deny, dismiss, or understand.

Every time he thought about her, he wanted to take her in his arms and kiss her. Every time he saw her, he wanted to lie with her and feel the shape of her body pressed close to his. He wondered how she would feel beneath his hands, with her mouth warmly responding to his kisses and caresses.

"You're quiet again," Millicent said.

Chandler sobered quickly.

He glanced over at her. Wispy strands of golden-brown hair had struggled free of her bonnet and framed her face attractively. She was much too young and too beautiful to wear her hair so severely tight. He liked the way her parasol perched above her straight shoulder and framed her with rows of feminine ruffles and ribbons. Chandler realized he liked walking with her on his arm.

He pulled her closer to his side and said, "No need to worry. Nothing is wrong. I was thinking again."

"I noticed. You seem to be doing a lot of that this afternoon. What took your thoughts off what we were talking about and gained your fancy this time?"

"Hiring a Runner to find out who among the ton might be in embarrassing financial trouble at the moment." He glanced over at her again and gave her a warning smile. "Not that I believe for a moment that Andrew is one of them, but I can see where having that information right now would be useful."

Her deep amber eyes sparkled up at him from the cover of long, dark lashes. She smiled warmly at him. "I'm sure there are other things we can do to help the authorities find the thief if we just put some time into thinking about it. Sometimes I think we are the only two people in London who are convinced the thief is a man and not a ghost."

He shook his head in wary amusement. "It's getting downright ridiculous what some people are saying about Lord Pinkwater's ghost."

"Some members of Society are actually trying to make a game out of it."

"I know."

"And I've heard that at least two of the gentlemen's clubs are considering taking bets on whose house will be the next one robbed."

"As unbelievable as it sounds, it's true."

"I just had a thought. Have you given any consideration to the idea that the thief might be a woman?"

Chandler smiled down at her and slightly raised an eyebrow. "A woman? You jest."

"Absolutely not, sir. I seem to remember only a few days ago you were more than willing to believe that I might be the thief."

"No, no, Miss Blair. I thought you might be an accomplice working with the thief. I've since been enlightened about your real duties and why you take notes."

Millicent rolled her parasol in her hand and said, "We should consider all possibilities. I was just thinking if you and the authorities are going to be looking at gentlemen who might be needing money, maybe you should also look at unattached ladies, too."

"That is another idea to contemplate," he admitted.

"The thief must be tall enough to have reached the items that were stolen without benefit of furniture to climb on. That would have taken too much time. I can immediately name Lady Lynette, Viscountess Heathecoute and Mrs. Honeycutt, all of whom might be of that height." She cut her gaze around to him. "Not that I think for a moment that any of them are capable of such a vile act as robbery."

"But you were more than willing to lay the blame on my dear friend of fifteen years."

"I can see you are not going to let me forget that slip of the tongue."

"It's the slip of the pen that I had problems with."

"It has not yet been proven that Lord Dugdale is in the clear."

"I have no fear that it is only a matter of time and he will be," Chandler said confidently.

"So then, are you going to hold a grudge?"

"Why shouldn't I when I love the way your eyes shine with indignation every time I mention it?"

"You do like to try to put me in a dither, but I won't let you. The day is too beautiful and I'm quite content."

"Hmm. I know. You wouldn't let me kiss you a few minutes ago, even though I'm going mad to do so."

"I've caught on to you and your machinations."

"I'll just have to come up with a new plan."

She laughed softly. "Don't you dare. You have already gone beyond the pale too many times."

"But it's such fun."

"I'll not be so easily caught by surprise again."

"That sounds like a challenge too good to pass on."

Millicent looked up at him with a serious expression on her face. "I do want to help you find the raven, Chandler."

"I know you do, and I thank you for that. You've already helped by your suggestions. I suppose the thief could be a lady. Mrs. Moore is as tall as Lady Heathecoute."

"You're right."

"I'll have Doulton making some discreet inquiries about some of the ladies as well as the gentlemen."

"We might as well include everyone we feel might possibly be a suspect."

"I'll have him check the names he comes up with against attendance at the parties. But there's one thing that bothers me. How would a lady get the object out of the house? The purses ladies carry are so small, and a pelisse fits much too tightly to hide even the smallest of objects—unlike a gentleman's coat, which can be cut much fuller."

"Hmm. You're right. Since we're only thinking in possibilities, I guess if it were a woman she could quickly open a window and place the items outside and come back later and pick them up."

"Or even if it were a man he could do that or hand them to an accomplice who's waiting outside. That would be one way to get them out of the house without anyone seeing him." He stopped and smiled. "Or her."

"Tonight at the parties, let's both make lists of all ladies and gentlemen we think are tall enough to be the thief, and then we can compare notes."

He chuckled. "You and your notes."

They arrived at the carriage and Millicent turned toward him. He was reluctant to let her go. He wanted to continue holding her. When he looked down into her eyes, he realized from somewhere deep inside himself, he yearned for her. And maybe it was arrogant of him, but he sensed she desired him as much as he wanted her.

"Do you know how badly I want to kiss you?"

She sighed peacefully. "I believe you have already mentioned that today. Twice. Chandler, you have wanted to kiss many young ladies in your life."

Her words sobered him. How could he let her know that she was not just one of many? She was special. He couldn't explain it to her, because he didn't understand it himself.

"I suppose it is difficult for me to live down my past."

She gave him a smile filled with pleasure. "It's not necessary. I have enjoyed every kiss, every touch. And we have had very good luck not getting caught, but your antics must end. I must guard my reputation so that I will be able to go back home without scandal. Do not take this foolishness of slipping around to see me any further."

"Millicent."

"Let me finish, for this is important."

He nodded.

"We have teased about a great many things today, and I have enjoyed it immensely. Now, I must insist that you not seek me out in secret again. Let me return home with the good reputation I brought to London."

He had no argument. He wasn't prepared to offer for her hand, so it was time for him to respect her wishes. He cared for Millicent, he admitted to himself, and he didn't want to hurt her or her reputation.

"As you wish, my lovely lady, so it shall be. I will see you only at proper occasions."

He gave her a quick, easy grin and wondered if she realized it was completely false. He reached for her hand and helped her into the carriage.

"Chandler."

Damn.

He took a deep breath and turned to face Lady Lambs-beth. Annoyance pricked the back of Chandler's neck.

With all the people in the park, how did she happen upon them? Chandler had hoped that after their meeting the other evening that Lady Lambsbeth would seek the attentions of someone else. He didn't want Lady Lambsbeth near Millicent.

"What a delightful surprise to see you here. How are you, Chandler?"

"Quite well," he said stiffly.

"So, you've been out for a stroll this lovely afternoon." She looked over his shoulder to Millicent. "And with such a fair young lady by your side. What a dandy you are."

Fair? Chandler bristled. Millicent was more than fair. Millicent's naturally innocent manner and beauty were what men's dreams were made of.

"As I recall," Lady Lambsbeth continued, "you didn't use to enjoy coming to any of the parks. There were *other* places you'd rather spend your afternoons."

Anger shot through Chandler, but he was determined not to let it show in front of Millicent. "If you'll excuse me, Lady Lambsbeth, we were just leaving."

She placed her open hand on his upper arm and gently pressed his muscles. "Aren't you going to introduce me to your companion?"

He lifted his arm away from her touch. "No, I don't believe I will."

"Ah—how rude of you, Chandler. Last year you almost had me convinced you were a gentleman."

"Did I? How clever of me. I seldom consider myself a gentleman."

"Well, if we can't call men like you gentlemen, what exactly are you called?" she asked, pouting her lips suggestively.

"Unforgiving. Good day, madam."

Chandler climbed onto the curricle and took his place

beside Millicent. The groom handed him the ribbons and he immediately snapped them against the horse's rump. The grays took off, leaving Lady Lambsbeth standing alone with her sensuous mouth agape.

Chandler kept the horses at a trot until they were out of the park. The carriage wheel hit a hole and almost bounced them off their seat.

"Sorry about that," he said, without looking over to Millicent.

"I see it didn't take too many words for her to put you in an unfortunate temper. I'm sorry if you are unhappy she saw us together."

Chandler threw Millicent a glance. "Damnation, no. I'm unhappy you saw her."

"Is she a lady you only meet in secret?"

"She's no lady, and I don't meet her at all." He stewed for a minute, then added, "She is Lady Lambsbeth. I'm sure you've heard all the gossip about us so I won't recount a word of it. We didn't part on friendly terms, and I intend to leave it that way."

Millicent remained quiet.

He pulled back on the ribbons and slowed the horses to a walk. He didn't want to hurry the trip home, he'd just wanted to get Millicent away from Lady Lambsbeth.

"You're right. She put me in a foul temper, and I shouldn't have let her. I've told her I have no desire to pick up our relationship where we left off, but I'm not sure she knows I'm serious yet."

"I believe your show of rudeness went a long way toward doing that today."

He looked over at her and smiled. With the most guileless of statements, she could make him feel so good. "You really think so?"

"Without a doubt."

"I might finally be rid of her?"

"I would say, sir, that there is a very good chance you will be called the brute of London by all her friends."

"Will you tell Lord Truefitt about it so he can put it in his column?"

"At the earliest possible moment."

What had gotten into him? He was suggesting she put his name in the gossip column and he was teasing about Lady Lambsbeth. Had he gone daft? And why did he feel it was so important that Millicent know that he was no longer involved with Lady Lambsbeth?

Chandler realized he was changing. His life was changing and it was all because of Millicent.

"Good. Now, what were we talking about before we were interrupted?"

"I believe we were talking about making lists and going over them."

"We had finished that subject. We were talking about how much I wanted to kiss you."

"No, Lord Dunraven, I believe we had finished that subject as well. May I suggest we talk about what a lovely day it has been."

"Why not?" he said with no enthusiasm and turned his attention back to the ribbons.

One unimportant subject was as good as another.

He had promised to behave, and he would, but why couldn't he bear the thought of never kissing her again?

Seventeen

❦

"The robbed that smiles steals something from
the thief." Someone should tell this to Lord
Dunraven. The earl seems to be getting more
ill-humored with each passing day that the
family raven is not returned to its nest. It's on
good authority this one reports that in an outing to Hyde Park, Lord Dunraven rebuffed
Lady Lambsbeth, a lady he once admired, and
left her to catch his carriage dust.

Lord Truefitt
Society's Daily Column

𝓜ILLICENT STOOD IN a far corner of the ballroom, trying
not to watch Chandler. He was on the other side of the
dance floor talking with his good friends Lord Chatwin
and Lord Dugdale, handsome gentlemen with affable
smiles and charming manners. She'd had the pleasure of
meeting both of them earlier in the week.

She had caught Chandler's eyes glancing her way more
than once tonight. Her stomach had quickened each time
his gaze swept over her.

It had been a week since their ride in Hyde Park, and, much to her surprise, Chandler hadn't made any attempts to meet her in secret. She was conflicted with a mixture of gratefulness and disappointment because he had finally decided to respect her wishes and not pursue her. She should have been relieved, but that's not what she was feeling.

They'd managed a few snippets of conversations during the evenings while dancing at the various parties they had attended during the week. Sometimes the dances were so lively it was impossible to talk. Other times it would be a dance where they had to change partners so it was difficult to have a conversation of any merit.

In the end she had a short list of the tallest ladies to keep an eye on each evening, and Chandler had a long list of gentlemen to watch. She hoped to hear tonight that he had news from Mr. Doulton's inquiries into the list of names Chandler had given him, but the evening was growing late and he hadn't approached her.

She scanned the fringe of the room again, hoping no one noticed her eyes lingered on Chandler far too long. She found herself thinking, "If only, if only, if only," in time to the music that filled the crowded room. There was no use in going over the if onlys again. She'd been through them all a number of times and nothing was going to change her position or his.

Chandler was a confirmed bachelor. She'd heard that from several members of the ton. When and if he married, it wouldn't be to a young lady who had spied and written tittle-tattle. He would make a love match with someone like the beautiful Miss Pennington or an astute business match with a young lady like the approachable Miss Bardwell.

Millicent had resigned herself to finishing the gossip

Season for her aunt, who was well on her way to recovering. Each day she looked better and sounded stronger. With Emery's help, she was getting out of bed and spending most of the day sitting in a chair.

In another week or two Aunt Beatrice would be testing her leg to see if she could walk with a cane. Because of her aunt's improvements, Millicent felt sure she would be back in Nottinghamshire by September—and doing what?

She turned away from the area where Chandler stood and started a slow stroll around the crowded room, greeting the people she passed, but hardly seeing them. Millicent hadn't considered what she would do when she returned home. She hadn't wanted to. She couldn't bear the thought of settling down to marriage with any of the eligible gentlemen in her town. After Chandler, how could she accept another man's attentions?

How could she enjoy or even tolerate another man's kisses and caresses when Chandler was the only man who had ever stirred wanton desires inside her? Desires that threatened to—

Someone bumped her arm, breaking her train of thought. And thank goodness, she chided herself.

Her task had been forgotten. She needed to look around and locate Viscountess Heathecoute, Lynette, Mrs. Honneycutt and Mrs. Moore. She truly didn't believe any of the ladies were connected to the Mad Ton Thief anymore than she was, but someone had to be taking the items.

After a quick glance around the room she saw two of the ladies were present. She didn't see the lady Heathecoute or Lynette. Millicent decided to check the ladies' retiring room and the area where the buffet table had been placed and headed in that direction.

"Millicent," Lynette said, coming up behind her. "I saw you looking my way, but when I waved to you, you looked right through me. Are you all right?"

"I'm fine. And I was looking for you," Millicent said with a hurried smile. "I'm glad you saw me. I wanted to thank you for that lovely note you sent thanking me for the apricot tarts I dropped by your house. I'm sorry you weren't up to seeing me when I called on you."

"I was disappointed to have missed you." She rolled her eyes. "There are just three or four days out of every month that I have to go to bed. I'm simply a beast, but as I said in my letter to you, I have been wanting to taste one of those tarts for years. And they did make me feel so much better." She stopped and licked her lips and inhaled deeply.

"I'm so glad you enjoyed them."

"They were heavenly. Truly divine. Didn't you think so?"

"Oh yes," Millicent said, and realized immediately that wasn't the truth. She had not even sampled a one of the tarts. They all had gone to Lynette, except for the two she had sent up to Aunt Beatrice.

Lynette pursed her lips and fanned herself with a lace fan. "You didn't even taste one, did you?"

Millicent opened her mouth to protest but the truth came out instead. "No."

"What a shame, but I understand why you didn't."

"You do?" Millicent wasn't sure she understood why she had had no desire to eat one of the tarts.

"You wanted to be different, didn't you?"

Millicent wasn't sure this was a conversation she wanted to have with Lynette or anyone. "What do you mean?"

"You were hoping Lord Dunraven would treat you differently from every other young lady he has called on.

You wanted him to be so bewitched by you that he forgot to bring the tarts."

He had that first time he came. But he had forgotten only because he was upset because he'd figured out that she was writing the gossip for Lord Trufitt's column—not because he was bewitched by her.

"Sometimes you see too much, Lynette."

"Right you are. Earlier, I knew it wasn't me you were looking for. You were watching Lord Dunraven, weren't you?"

Millicent smiled. "Now that is only partly true. My eyes naturally fell upon him a few minutes ago as I was looking for you and Lady Heathecoute." Millicent made a show of scanning the room again for her chaperone. "I know it's about the time of evening that she said we would be leaving. I was on my way to walk past the refreshment table and the ladies' room looking for her. Would you care to walk with me?"

"That would be nice," Lynette said and fell in step beside Millicent. "You're in love with him, aren't you?"

Millicent stiffened. Lynette asked the astonishing question as easily as she would have asked about the weather. Millicent wasn't prepared to be that honest with her friend.

She was left with no choice but to say, "What? Who?"

"Lord Dunraven of course."

"No, no, no. Does it show?"

Lynette laughed softly. "To me, but probably not to anyone else."

"Angels above, I hope not," Millicent said, feeling more exposed than she would like to be. And was she really admitting that she was in love with Lord Dunraven?

"Remember, I warned you about him that first afternoon I called on you."

They arrived at the retiring room, but the viscountess was not there so they started toward the refreshment table.

"I know, but by then it was too late. I had already met him, had already been besotted by him. You won't mention this to anyone, will you?"

"Of course not. He's a charmer and so engaging it's downright sinful. I know what it is like to love someone who will never be available."

Millicent's attention turned from herself and focused on her friend. "Do you?"

"Oh yes. I knew there was no way he would ever consider me, but it didn't stop me from dreaming about him."

Millicent felt a squeeze at her heart. She should have known that the birthmark would not keep Lynette from feeling love, and it shouldn't keep a gentleman from loving her. She was a warm and delightful person.

"I'm sorry. Is there any possibility?"

"No, no. He's already married someone else and he seems happy." Lynette smiled. "Now tell me, how can I be upset if he is happy?"

"Then I shall look at Lord Dunraven that way, too. If he is happy as a bachelor for the rest of his life, then I shall be happy for him."

"Perhaps some other handsome gentleman will catch your fancy while you are still in Town."

Never.

"Perhaps, Lynette. If it happens that would be wonderful, but if it doesn't, like you, I'll will be content with my reading, writing poetry and my needlework. But, if there is hope for me, there is hope for you."

Lynette laughed and Millicent made a mental note that the viscountess was not at the buffet table. She turned in the direction of the large room, where the majority of the guests had spent most of the evening.

When they entered the crowded room, Lynette said good-bye and Millicent's eyes immediately searched for Chandler and the ladies on her list. Before her gaze had time to cover all the corners, nooks and small clusters of people, Chandler came up beside her. He took hold of her hand and kissed the back of her palm as his blue gaze caressed her face.

Millicent felt the delicious tingles of his touch way down in her soul. Gloves were no barrier to what she felt where Chandler was concerned.

Oh, how I shall miss you.

"How are you this late evening, Miss Blair?"

"Well, sir, and you?"

"Better now that I'm by your side."

Millicent wished her insides wouldn't waken with desire at his flattery, but she had long given up on trying not to be moved by his every word.

"I've noticed that you have been busy dancing and talking with your friends."

"I'm happy that you noticed I had arrived."

"You know I've been waiting all evening for you to tell me what you have heard from your Runner. I fear you've been making me wait on purpose."

"Tsk, tsk. Must we go straight to business?"

"Indeed. We have little time to ourselves in which we can speak privately."

"That is your fault. Just give the word and I will be in your garden tonight waiting for you."

She believed him; therefore, she couldn't agree even in a teasing manner. She looked around and there was no one standing close enough to hear them. The hour was late and the crowd was getting smaller.

"You know I can't do that. Chandler, we must talk while we have these few moments alone."

"Very well. I have a bit of news to report. I spoke to Doulton today. He didn't have any trouble finding out all that I asked him about Lord Dugdale. Your source was correct. Andrew is indeed financially embarrassed at the moment."

It made her feel good that he'd told her. He could have kept that bit of information from her and she would have never known.

"I'm sorry to hear that. I know you were hoping it wasn't true."

"Yes. The good thing is that his situation is not so bad that he would need to resort to stealing in order to get money. His funds are low, but not nonexistent, and according to Doulton's findings, he's taking appropriate steps to correct his mounting debts."

"Well, there is hope for him."

"Yes. Even though he attended every party where there was a robbery, I believe we can safely assume he is not the thief."

She nodded and said, "I'm inclined to agree."

Millicent couldn't help but admire him for at least looking at the possibilities where Lord Dugdale was concerned.

"Doulton also double-checked the guest lists and Lady Lynette, Lady Heathecoute, and Mrs. Moore were all at every home where there was a robbery. Mrs. Honneycutt was not at my party."

"So we can eliminate her from our list."

"Yes."

"What have we learned about the men?"

"That is taking a bit longer." He leaned in closer and smiled. "Perhaps we should meet another time so we can discuss it thoroughly."

"I insist on hearing it all right now."

"You are a difficult taskmaster, Miss Blair."

"That is because you want to play when there is work to be done."

"Very well. I will continue, but I will insist that at a later time we have a bit of idleness all to ourselves even if it is only another ride in the park."

Her pulse quickened at the possibility of being alone with him. She hoped it didn't show how eager she was for him to make good on that promise.

"We've narrowed down the tallest men who attended all of the parties where there were robberies to less than twenty."

Millicent frowned. "That is still a lot of men to consider."

"I know, but better than the near fifty we started with. First thing tomorrow morning, Doulton will be checking the bank records of these men to see if any of them might be under financial pressure."

"That should narrow the field even more. I really can't imagine why a person would steal unless it was for monetary gain."

"I suppose there are those who steal for the fun of it, or because of sickness, but both those reasons seem a bit far-fetched to me."

"Me too. But we are making progress in our elimination game."

"So it seems." He stepped closer to her. "I've noticed all evening that your smile doesn't seem as bright tonight. Is something wrong?"

Yes.

"No, I'm fine." She tried to prove it by smiling at him but felt sure it fell short of her expectations.

"I've missed you. I've wanted to come see you, but I've respected your wishes."

She tried to lighten the mood. "Which has made you a perfect gentleman."

"I've always told you I know how to be one, but it's been a dreadful life."

She laughed. "You are such a delightful rogue."

"You are such a delectable lady."

"And you are trying to change the subject." She started scanning the area in front of her. "I couldn't find Lady Heathecoute earlier. I was looking for her when you walked over."

Glancing over her shoulder, Chandler said, "Look no longer. Here she comes." Suddenly his eyes narrowed. His brows drew together. "Millicent, look at the front of her skirt. Does it not look odd shaped?"

Millicent turned around and looked at the large woman walking into the room. Her gaze dropped to the front of the viscountess's skirt. The dress she wore was high waisted, fitting snugly under her breasts and dropping with a full, heavily gathered skirt. She was walking stiffly as if she were trying not to move, and low in the front of her skirt, the area between her abdomen and knees, there was an unusual bulge.

Chandler was right. Something didn't look quite right under the yards of fabric that was her skirt.

A chill ran over Millicent. She looked up at Chandler. "I think—you don't suppose—"

"That she has something hidden under her skirt?" Chandler finished the question for Millicent.

She looked up into his eyes. "Don't even think it. It can't be possible."

"We've known for some time that the thief had to be someone who is free to come and go at every party," Chandler gently reminded her.

Millicent looked at the lady again and knew for certain

there was something wrong with her skirt. Millicent's stomach knotted with apprehension. "What are we going to do?"

"I don't know, yet, but we'll think of something."

"We'd better come up with it fast because she's heading this way with her husband. I think they are going to tell me it's time to go."

"She's not leaving until we know if she's hiding something under her dress," he murmured under his breath as the Heathecoutes approached.

"Lord Dunraven, how are you this evening?" the viscount asked, his nose held high and not a hint of a smile on his thin lips.

"Well, thank you. How about you and your lady?"

"We're in fine shape, too."

Chandler turned to their prey. "You are looking very nice tonight, viscountess."

She offered a little smile that twitched her lips. "Oh, thank you, sir, but I'm afraid I can tell it's the end of the evening. I'm a little tired and ready to quit the night. Are you ready, Millicent, dear?"

"Yes, of course."

"Good, then we'll take our leave."

"Lord Heathecoute," Chandler spoke up after a quick glance to Millicent, "do you mind if I walk out with you to the carriages?"

"No, not at all, my lord. Pleased to have you join us."

Millicent was quiet and watchful as they stopped for their cloaks. Thankfully, her chaperone didn't try to engage her in conversation. Millicent couldn't help but notice that her ladyship immediately wrapped her large cloak around her body as if she were trying to ward off the harshest of winter nights instead of a pleasant spring evening. Millicent left hers to hang free from her shoulders as was the current fashion.

She didn't want to believe that the woman who'd chaperoned her these past three weeks was a thief. Lady Heathecoute had been diligent in her care and respect for Millicent, and she felt dreadful about what she was going to have to do.

Millicent heard the viscount and Chandler talking as they made their way to the front and waited for their carriage to be brought around. What could she do? Reach out and grab the front of the lady's dress? Demand she lift her skirt? No, the thought of what would happen if she was wrong was too horrible to contemplate, but she must do something.

Their carriage arrived and the driver jumped down and opened the door.

Time was slipping away. Millicent had to do something now. When the lady Heathecoute reached for her husband's hand to be helped into the carriage, Millicent deliberately stumbled and fell into the viscountess, hitting something hard in the front of her skirt that clattered like silver teapots clanging together.

"You oaf!" Lady Heathecoute squealed and shoved Millicent with such strong force she couldn't stop herself from falling forward. She slammed into the carriage door, her head striking the metal handle and cutting a deep gash into her forehead.

Chandler rushed to her aid and kept her from falling. "Millicent, are you all right?"

"Yes," she said, but in truth her head was throbbing with pain and she was a bit dazed. She felt the trickle of blood running down the side of her face.

He threw a hostile glare to the lady. "This roughness wasn't necessary."

"Now see here," the viscount said. "Millicent stumbled into her."

Chandler found a handkerchief in his pocket and pressed it against Millicent's wound. She winced and took it away.

"Chandler, I'm fine. Let me handle this."

"No, we are in this together and you're not all right. The skin is broken and your head is bleeding."

Millicent looked up into his eyes and whispered, "Do not worry about me. I will be well. Let's finish what we have started."

He looked deeply into her eyes. He whispered, "You are more important to me than anything else. Hold this to your wound so it will stop bleeding."

Why did he have a gift for saying things that made her heart beat a little faster, her breath come a little slower?

"Millicent, that does look like a nasty cut and should be seen to right away," Lord Heathecoute said.

Millicent was now certain that her chaperone was hiding something beneath her clothing. She didn't know what was holding the items under her skirt, but the viscountess had deliberately pushed her into the carriage and it was no slight shove. Her head was pounding.

"Ma'am," Millicent said, ignoring the viscount and looking directly at his lady. "I hit something under your skirt. What was it?"

Lady Heathecoute took a step back. Her eyes quickly darted from Millicent to Chandler to her husband. "I don't know what you are talking about. There's nothing beneath my skirt."

Millicent noticed that several people had gathered around. "I felt it," Millicent insisted and took a challenging step toward her.

"She's right," Chandler said. "I heard something clang together when she stumbled into you."

"You're both talking nonsense," Lady Heathecoute huffed loudly. "I don't know what you are talking about." She turned to her husband. "You didn't hear anything, did you, my lord?"

He lowered his eyes and looked down at his wife. "Yes, I do believe I heard some kind of a clanging noise, but I don't know what it was or where it came from."

"You imbecile!" she exclaimed in an earsplitting voice, but then, as if realizing how loudly she had spoken, she lowered her voice considerably and continued. "If there was noise it certainly didn't come from under my skirt! Now, Millicent, get in the carriage at once. We must get you home and see to that cut before you visit with Beatrice. I don't know what made you so clumsy tonight."

Millicent and Chandler looked at her, and so did the six or so other people who had gathered around them. Millicent knew she had to do something. She would be leaving London as soon as her aunt was well. She need never return. This was Chandler's home. She could withstand the talk and embarrassment if they were wrong about Lady Heathecoute. Chandler could not. Millicent had to be the one to press the issue.

It was now or never. She might not get another chance to expose the thief.

"No, I won't leave until you reveal to us what you are hiding beneath your gown."

The viscountess's eyes widened further. "How dare you disobey me."

"I felt something when I hit you. Lord Dunraven and your husband heard something. Now, take off your cloak and show us what you are hiding."

Lady Heathecoute's face contorted into a mask of cold

rage. "Of all the ungrateful chits in London, you are the worst I have ever encountered. You have no right to demand that I do anything, and I will not!"

"Dearest," her husband said in a voice that dripped with boredom over the whole event. "Just open your cloak and show them that you are hiding nothing, then they can apologize to us for being so ungodly rude and we can go home."

"I will do no such thing," she exclaimed again.

Millicent took a deep breath and said, "Lady Heathecoute, I'm afraid I believe you might be the Mad Ton Thief."

Gasps of surprise and horror sounded all around her, but Millicent didn't take her eyes off her suspect. If she was wrong, she would have to leave London and never return—just as her mother had.

Chandler put his arm around Millicent's shoulder and said, "I agree with her. I can't let you leave here until we know that you are not hiding anything."

The viscountess pretended to faint and fell back into her husband's arms, almost knocking him over. She peered up at her husband pleadingly. In a weakened voice she said, "Tell her I don't have to do this? I won't do it. I must go home immediately."

Obviously finding a little backbone, her husband pointed his nose at Millicent and barked, "You accuse my wife of such a dastardly deed after all she has done for you. I'm aghast at your behavior. Have you no shame as well as no manners?"

"It's not just Millicent," Chandler said. "It's me, too, and now these people," he said, pointing to the small crowd that had gathered.

Sneering at Chandler, Lord Heathecoute looked at his lady and said, "You must prove the chit and the earl wrong, my dear, then I will take you home."

The viscountess clutched the front of his coat firmly with both hands. Her face was frantic with fear and rage. "I can't. I won't. I won't!" She screamed and pushed away from her husband.

She tried to scramble into the carriage by herself, but her foot slipped on the wet step and she fell forward, with the clinging and clanging of metal bumping together as she hit the ground.

She tried to pull herself up, and the sound of metal rent the air again. Mutterings of outrage and surprise from the crowd filled the night air. Lord Heathecoute and Chandler hurried over to assist the helpless lady to stand, and there was more clanging.

"What is this?" the viscount asked in horror as he felt down the front of her skirt.

The accused wailed loudly and leaned against the carriage door. Her large eyes seemed to be staring straight ahead but not looking at anyone or anything in particular.

Millicent was chilled by the screeching, pitiful sound that came from the older woman.

"Dear, dear. What is going on?" her husband asked as stiffly as he moved.

Lady Heathecoute started looking through the folds of her large skirt until she came to a long slit in the side that had been hidden in the fabric. She parted the material and reached into a large pocket and pulled out a silver teapot and a silver tray.

For the third time that evening, gasps of surprise rang out in the still air.

Chandler looked at Millicent and something he had never felt before swelled in his chest. They had done it. Together they had found the Mad Ton Thief.

The noise from the crowd grew louder.

"Someone call for the authorities," Chandler said.

Eighteen

"Love looks not with the eyes but with the mind, and therefore is winged Cupid painted blind." Just ask Miss Donaldson. Her father accepted an offer for her hand from Sir Charles Wright.

Lord Truefitt
Society's Daily Column

THE CROWDS WERE still thick around the Heathecoute's carriage an hour later. The authorities arrived and after questioning the viscountess and her husband, they were taken away. Chandler and Millicent had talked to the officers at length and promised to be available later for more questions.

As soon as the officer dismissed them, Chandler saw his chance to get Millicent away from the too-curious crowd. Wanting to be careful of her reputation, he eased around to the far side of his coach with her and helped her inside before climbing in after her. He took the seat beside her rather than opposite her.

He knew taking her to his home was dangerous for more than one reason. If anyone saw her going in or out of his town house, her reputation would be ruined, but he needed a few minutes alone with her. He'd missed being able to spend time alone with her this past week. He would take extra precautions so no one would see her entering his house.

"How is your head?" he asked as soon as the vehicle started moving.

"I think the bleeding has stopped and the pain is almost gone now."

"Good. Let me have a look." He placed his fingertips under her chin and turned her face toward the lamp perched outside the carriage. It wasn't the best light, but he could see enough to know the cut wasn't deep, but it was long. He guessed about two inches. He could see that it was swollen, too. Anger at the viscountess for hurting Millicent rose up in him. The thief deserved whatever punishment she received.

Chandler's eyes drifted past Millicent's cut to her fan-shaped brows and long, full lashes. Her cheeks were glowing from the excitement of the evening. Her lips were moist, parted and beautiful. He was tempted to place a kiss on her lovely eyelids, her flushed cheeks and move down to her enticing mouth and completely cover it with his. He bent his head to do just that as the carriage lurched, stopping him.

He cleared his throat and said, "I'm having my driver take you to my house so I can clean your wound and see to it before I take you home."

"That's nonsense," she said and moved her head away from his touch. "I'm fine."

"Lady Beatrice wouldn't think so if she could see you right now. You look like you've been in a carriage accident, with dried blood in your hair and on your face, even your dress didn't escape the blood."

She turned away from him and glanced out the window. "I'm sure my maid will assist me in cleaning the cut and the dress doesn't matter."

He took hold of her hand and waited until she looked up into his eyes before saying, "It does matter. I want to do this for you. Lay your head back and rest. It will be only be a short ride."

But she didn't lay her head back, instead she continued to look at him in the dim, shadowed light and said, "A gentleman would offer me his shoulder to rest against."

His chest tightened at her offer. "Then allow me." He put his arm around her and drew her back into the curve of his shoulder. She nestled there as if she had always belonged beside him. He softly placed his cheek upon her hair. "Oh, yes, this is a much better idea. I'm glad I have you to remind me how a gentleman is supposed to behave."

"There are certain areas where you need to be coached."

"I'm at your disposal to be taught whatever you wish."

"That could be a challenge."

"You are up to the task."

"Yes, but I very much like it also when you are a rake."

"I know."

Chandler liked the way she snuggled down in the seat and fit herself tightly against him as if she wanted the safety of his arms. He liked the way she didn't hesitate to tell him that she wanted to be held or how she never got truly angry with him when he went beyond the pale. He had no doubt that she was where she belonged—in his arms.

"You proved tonight how brave you are. I was impressed by how you stood up to Lady Heathecoute."

"It wasn't so much bravery as determination. I wouldn't have been so forceful if I had not been certain the viscountess had something under her skirt. But, she would have laughed off my demands had you not agreed with me."

"You give me too much credit."

Millicent sighed into the warmth of his coat. "I still find it hard to believe that she turned out to be the Mad Ton Thief. I've spent so much time with her since I've been in London."

"It's really sad that the poor woman felt she had to resort to stealing to supplement their income."

"Do you believe the viscount was as innocent as he claimed to be?"

"I think so. He was ashen when she pulled the silver teapot out of the pocket she had sewed into the folds of her skirt. And, after all, he kept insisting she show us she had nothing to hide."

Chandler pressed her to him and kissed the top of her head while the carriage moved along at a brisk pace. He wanted to turn her into his arms and devour her with kisses and caresses, but he knew she must have a pounding headache from the wound, so he remained still.

"I hope she told the authorities the truth and that they find all the things she stole where she said they would be. I know how desperately you want to get the raven back."

For some reason the raven didn't seem so important anymore. "I'm sure she wouldn't have told them she had the things if she didn't."

"Imagine, her stealing the jewels, the painting, your golden raven and then realizing she had no idea how to go about selling them to anyone."

Chandler gave a short laugh. "It's our good fortune that

she never made it to the moneylenders to find a trader."

"Yes."

The carriage stopped, and Chandler opened the door and jumped out. He looked up both sides of the street before he helped Millicent down, then held his cloak over her head so if anyone were around they couldn't see her. He told the driver to wait at the coach for him so he could take Millicent home later.

Winston opened the door to his town house, and they quickly stepped inside. A light burned in the front parlor so Chandler ushered her into the room and helped her take off her cloak.

"Winston, Miss Blair has been injured."

The valet stepped forward. "What can I do, sir? Should I get a physician?"

"No," Chandler and Millicent said in unison, then Chandler added, "I don't think it's serious enough for a doctor. Bring me water, some cloths and ointment."

"Yes, sir," Winston said and left immediately to get the items.

"Here, sit on the settee." Chandler turned up the lamp that burned on a table by the small sofa. He then walked over to the sideboard and poured two glasses of brandy.

He handed her one of the glasses. "Drink this. It will make you feel better."

"Thank you." She took the drink and sipped it.

"Are you cold? I can build a fire."

"No, I'm fine. Really, there was no need for you to bring me here to your home, but I'm glad you did. If only for a few minutes. I must go soon. I would hate for news of this evening to reach Lady Beatrice before I get there."

He remained standing, looking down at her. "That won't happen, I'm sure."

"Here you go, sir," Winston said, carrying in a silver

tray containing a bowl of water, cloths and a jar.

The valet set the tray on the round rosewood table beside the settee.

"Thank you, Winston."

"Yes, sir. Can I do anything else?"

"No. I can take care of everything from here. Good night."

"Very well, sir. Good night." Winston walked out and closed the door behind him.

"He seems very capable," Millicent said.

"He is." Long ago Chandler had told Winston when he said the words *good night* that meant he was not to be disturbed again that evening.

"Is the brandy making you feel better?" he asked as he sat down on the settee beside her.

"Yes." She smiled. "For the third time I will tell you, I am fine and I am calm. Even my headache is better. Don't ask me again."

"All right. Let's clean that cut."

Chandler dipped the cloth in the cold water and gently washed the blood away from her wound and face. His face was very close to hers, and he was tempted to kiss her lips, but he silently, tenderly cared for her. When he asked her if it hurt, she merely shook her head and remained quiet until he had rubbed the ointment over the broken skin.

"There. All done. Thankfully, it's not as bad as I thought. There shouldn't even be a scar after it heals. Go on and finish your brandy."

"Thank you," she said as he picked up the tray of water and moved it to a table by the window.

"It's comforting to know that I shall live."

Chandler walked back to the settee and sat down beside her, much closer than he should have, and picked up his drink and took another sip of the amber liquid so much the color of Millicent's eyes. He didn't know if it was the brandy that warmed him or the fact that Millicent was in his house. Suddenly he had a great desire to embrace her. He shouldn't have sent Winston to bed. Being alone with Millicent was just too damn tempting.

"Yes, you will live to tell your grandchildren all about how you discovered the Mad Ton Thief. Now that I think about it, maybe you should have a scar so you can show them how heroic you were."

She laughed. "Oh, you do make the event sound much more dashing than it was, and don't forget you are the one who first noticed that the Lady Heathecoute's skirt didn't look right."

He smiled and ran the backs of his fingers down her cheek. "No, no. You deserve all the glory, and you have the wound to prove it."

"Jealous?" she teased.

"I would take any wound for you. I don't want you hurt."

Her lovely face turned serious. "Chandler, may I ask you something?"

"Of course. Anything."

"Will you make love to me?"

Anything but that!

Chandler's chest tightened at her words. Surely she didn't know what she was saying. It was best to keep the evening playful. He was far too aware of how much he wanted her to allow the evening to turn serious.

"Let me look at that cut on your head again. I fear it's worse than I thought." He pretended to examine the cut more closely.

Millicent reached up and pressed a soft kiss to his lips.

"You said you would do anything," she reminded him, looking as serious as he had ever seen her.

His smile faded. "Anything except that. You are a lady of quality, Millicent. I wouldn't change that. No matter how tempting your request."

He took the empty glass from her hand and placed it on the table in front of them. It was a mistake to give her the strong drink. It had gone straight to her head and had her saying things she would never say otherwise.

"Time to take you home," Chandler said.

She touched his arm and kept him from rising. "I am serious, Chandler. It's not the bump on my head, or the brandy. It's what I feel here inside my heart. I want to be yours tonight."

His lower body immediately rose at her words. "You don't know what you're saying." His voice was so husky with anticipation he could hardly speak. Never in his wildest dreams did he think Millicent would offer herself to him. Even though he was light-headed at the thought of being inside her, he couldn't accept. It wouldn't be right to do that to her. She deserved to be pure on her wedding night.

Millicent picked up his hand and with both of hers placed it open-palm over her heart. She looked up at him with imploring eyes. "Feel how my heart beats for you."

His throat ached to tell her yes. He had long felt unfulfilled. His body was rigid with desire for her, but all he could say was, "Millicent."

She moved closer to him, pressing her thigh against his. "You have pursued me from the moment we met. Why would you refuse me now that you have caught me?"

It was difficult to deny the ache in his loins, but he managed to whisper, "I didn't pursue you to violate you."

She smiled and lifted one arm to cup the back of his

neck with her hand and bring his face even closer to hers. "What a harsh word for what I am asking of you. How could your touch, which pleases me so much, dishonor me?"

Chandler's breaths were so shallow he could hardly get his words out. "You are an innocent and should remain that way."

"No. Do not deny me, Chandler."

He moved his hand from her breast and cupped both sides of her face in his palms. He dipped his head toward hers so that their breaths mingled in heated passion that stirred inside them. His body was painfully betraying him.

"Don't tempt me this way, Millicent." *It's not fair.* "I want you too badly."

"I know this is what I want tonight."

She sounded so earnest, so sincere, so natural. "No. You are a lady. I told you my reputation was far worse than my behavior. I've never taken a virgin to my bed. Yes, there have been unmarried ladies I have taken, but only after I was convinced that I would not be the first."

He looked deeply into her eyes as his desire for her mounted fiercely. He didn't know how much longer he could refuse her.

Chandler knew instinctively that she was an innocent, but his need for her was so strong he asked, "Be truthful with me, Millicent, would I be the first for you?"

"Yes."

"Then I will not presume on your wedding night."

Her eyes glistened and Chandler knew his words wounded her. He thought she would be pleased he'd had the courage to resist her bold offer. It was killing him to do so.

"Why did you pursue me if you didn't want me? Was it only a game?"

"A game? No," he answered with all honesty. It had been a game in his younger years when he'd pursued other young ladies into gardens and in Town, but with Millicent he had done it because he had wanted to see her and be with her. He still did. "Of course I want you. How can you doubt that?"

"Now that I want to be yours for a night, you don't want me?"

"Damnation, no." He took her lips in a long, hard, savoring kiss that left them both breathless and him mad with desire to forget the foolishness of trying to talk her out of what they both wanted and take her now. "I want you more than ever, but I don't take virgins to my bed."

Millicent gave no heed to his words but kissed his eyes, his cheeks, his lips and his neck all the way down to the top of his neckcloth, then started back up over his chin again. When she touched his lips with her own, she whispered, "Then forget the bed and take me here on the settee, for I fear I will faint if you don't return my kisses soon."

All rational thought fled his mind. Chandler gathered her up tightly in his arms and moaned into the crook of her neck. To hell with what was right.

"Yes. How can I resist such a demand when I have wanted to make you mine from the moment you turned and looked at me in that darkened hallway?"

His mouth closed over hers with such fierce hunger he knew it startled her, but he didn't relinquish his hold on her. Their mouths and tongues clung together and the sounds they made were soft and struggling.

He laid her back into the curve of the settee so that her head and neck rested against an arm. She reached up and circled his neck with her arms and threaded her fingers through his hair, teasing him with her light touch.

They were charged by an awakening and neither of them wanted to let go of it. Their bodies pressed, their lips met, their tongues played together, stirring heated passions that were already on fire.

Chandler's lips left hers and he kissed her neck below her ear and down to where her chest expanded with each breath and lifted her breasts up for him. She arched her head back to give him access to wherever his lips wanted to go.

In answer, he slipped the capped sleeves of her gown off her shoulders and exposed the plump swell of her breasts where they rested in the cups of her corset. He gently pulled the rosebud tips from beneath their bindings of cloth. He looked down at her beauty, and though he would have sworn on a stack of Bibles that he could not grow any larger or harder, he did. How could he have thought about resisting her? He must have been a madman.

He looked back into her eyes and whispered through thick, choppy breaths, "You are beautiful, Millicent."

She smiled at him with clear, bright eyes and breathed deeply before saying, "Thank you."

With his lower body he strained against the softness of her womanhood, pressing her farther into the settee. She answered him with a thrust of her own and his body reacted with throbbing, powerful pain. He wanted to bury himself in her, to lose himself in her.

Chandler wanted to say more sweet words, poetic phrases, but he heard her heavy breathing, saw her desire-bright eyes and knew that she didn't want to wait for whispered words, loving touches or lingering kisses. She'd made it clear she wanted him, that she knew what she was doing. All he had to do was accept.

Quickly he pulled her dress and petticoat up past her

thighs and bunched them below her breasts. As his hands left her waist, he pulled her drawers down past her knees. She kicked them off one satin-slippered foot. She parted her legs and supported herself with one foot on the floor.

While Chandler unbuttoned the fall of his breeches, Millicent pulled on the bow of his neckcloth and removed the tight garment and the collar from around his neck and slung them to the floor. Chandler slid an open hand up and down that small area of silky thigh between her stockings and her womanhood before placing himself at her center.

Chandler realized he was trembling, and that stopped him. His need for her was so strong it shook him to the core of his being. His heart was pounding so urgently he had to stop for a moment and try to understand what made Millicent so different from all the other women he had been with. What made her pull at his very soul?

"Is something wrong?" she asked.

He looked into her trusting, eager eyes and knew he had to give her one more chance to stop him. "Are you sure about this, Millicent? I can—I think I can back away if you give the word—damn it, Millicent tell me not to do this."

"No. I don't want you to be a gentleman tonight. I want you to be the rake I know and want."

Millicent slipped her arms underneath his and reached around him. With both hands she grabbed his buttocks and pushed him toward her.

"Oh, damn," he murmured frantically as he shoved into her all at once.

Millicent grunted softly but only a moment. She kept her hands on his hot skin, leading him up and down as he pumped his hips. Chandler gave himself up to the exquisite pain of the indescribable pleasure that was Millicent.

Millicent.

He planted both his hands on her waist and spread his fingers over her hips and joined her rhythm as she arched to meet him. He moved inside her, up and down. Through the fabric of his shirt he felt the heat of her breast rubbing against his chest. He heard her soft sounds of wonderment and his own animal groan of pleasure as he wonderfully slipped over the edge of reality and into a sweet dream, buried deep within her, spilling into her.

Chandler lowered his head and breathed heavily into the crook of her neck and whispered her name as he kissed her damp skin.

His heart lurched with so much emotion he could hardly catch his breath. He knew he must be in love with Millicent Blair.

Nineteen

"Sigh no more, ladies, sigh no more." There
is still time to catch one of the Terrible Threesome before the Season draws to a close.

Lord Truefitt
Society's Daily Column

$\mathcal{M}$ILLICENT LOOKED UP into Chandler's eyes and smiled
at him. She loved him. Loved him madly. There was no
doubt of that and not a trace of regret for what she had
just instigated. She had no fear that she would ever want
another man the way she wanted Chandler.

He was still inside her. They lay half on the settee and
half off. Chandler propped himself up by one elbow on
the settee arm and the other on the back of it. She felt his
weight, his strength and his warmth, and she had never
been so complete or so contented.

With a curious expression he looked down at her and
said, "You're smiling."

"That surprises you?"

"Yes. I'm wondering why you're not angry with me."

She stirred a little so she could see his eyes better. "Why would I be upset for getting what I wanted?"

"This isn't why I brought you here, Millicent. I never imagined we'd end up like this. I didn't plan it."

"I know. I wanted this to happen. It's what I planned," she said as if it was the most natural thing in the world for her to admit this to him.

He returned her smile. "I've never had a lady pursue me quite like you did tonight."

"You've never had reason to. You've always been the one in pursuit."

"I fear I didn't know what I was missing or surely I would have been much easier to catch."

She laughed softly as she looked up into his handsome face. "Well then, you should thank me for awakening you to such wonderful delights."

His long, dark lashes hooded his eyes attractively. He said, "Indeed, Miss Blair. Thank you."

"Would what we just shared have been different if you had planned it?" she asked.

He nuzzled her hair a little and kissed her cheek. "A little perhaps."

"In what way?"

"More words, more caresses, more time."

She smiled at him. "A bed?"

He groaned and adjusted his arms, which were holding up most of his weight. "Most assuredly a bed."

"Would all those things have made what we shared better?"

His gaze locked on hers instantly, piercing her. "It was the best for me. Nothing could have made it better."

Millicent's heart grew in her chest and she smiled again. He couldn't have said anything that would have pleased her more. "Thank you for saying that."

"I mean it, Millicent. It's never been so good for me before."

She nodded and reached up, letting her fingertips lightly caress his beard-stubbled cheek. She wished she could stay here with him for the rest of the night, the day, forever, but knew that wasn't possible.

"I have to go."

"I know. Don't worry, I'll have you home before dawn. I promise."

He thought she was talking about tonight, but she meant she would be going home to Nottinghamshire soon and would never see him again. She would be saying good-bye, not good night. That thought wrenched her heart.

Chandler lifted himself from her and pulled up his breeches with one hand as he rose and pushed down Millicent's dress with the other. In one fluid, sweeping motion he hooked one arm under her knees and the other around her shoulders and lifted her into his arms as if she were weightless.

"What are you doing?" she asked.

"I'm going to make love to you the right way now."

"Why? Did we do it wrong the first time?" she asked, a bit confused.

He carried her over to a thick, sable-colored fur rug that lay on the floor in front of the unlit fireplace.

"It wasn't that it was wrong," he said, kneeling down and gently placing her on the rug. "God no. It was impatient and a bit self-indulgent on my part. I know what we did on that settee was a damn sight more pleasurable for me than for you. I want it to be good for you."

The pliant pelt cushioned her comfortably and felt deliciously soft. Pale yellow light from the lamp cast a golden glow around the room. It was quiet, not even the sound of a clock to disturb the magic of the evening, the thrill of lying half dressed on the floor with Chandler.

Chandler sat down beside her and pulled his shirt off his head, then threw it aside. Her breaths quickened at the sight of his strong chest with firm, rippled muscles filling out his skin. She saw a dark patch of hair low on his stomach where the waistband of his trousers parted invitingly. Her abdomen quivered with anticipation.

She raised up to a sitting position and touched his knee. "I was not disappointed, Chandler. I thought what we did was wonderful."

He reached over and covered her mouth in a brief but deep, tongue-thrusting kiss. "Then wait until you find out what comes next."

"There's more than what we did?" she asked, relaxing a little.

"Yes. And I'm going to take my time and make love to you properly. The way you deserve to be loved."

He untied his evening shoes and took them off, then rose up on his knees. He turned to her and removed her drawers where they hung on one foot. Chandler reached for the hem of her dress, which rested midthigh, but stopped as he looked at her clothing. Her high-waisted dress hung off her shoulders, showing a prim-looking corset.

"But not as much time as I would like. I want to undress you layer by layer, kissing you with each garment I take off, but completely undressing you tonight would take longer than we have."

Chandler slid his breeches down his legs and kicked them aside. He was nude. Beautifully nude. Her heart lurched with love, with wanting. She felt hot and eager when he reached over and gathered her into his arms. His bare skin brushed hers and she tingled, relaxed and melted into his arms, giving herself up to Chandler.

He gently laid her into the softness of the rug and stretched his warm body beside her. He rose on his elbow and slowly inched the skirt of her dress and chemise up to her waist again. He looked into her eyes for a long moment before his gaze drifted down her face, lingered over her breasts, before going on to the junction of her thighs, and looking down the length of her legs.

"I love the way you look, the way you're shaped, and the richness of your satiny skin," he whispered huskily. "You're beautiful, perfect."

Millicent felt hot, flushed, urgent as his gaze continued to roam freely over her.

With an open palm, Chandler cupped her cheek, caressed it. He slid his hand down her neck, over her chest and shoulders with a gliding touch of his fingertips that thrilled her. He let his open palm drift over to her breasts. He lifted first one and then the other, gently squeezing their fullness, feeling their weight, seeming to memorize their shape.

Millicent closed her eyes and savored his gentle touch. She was sensitive to his every move, his every breath. He rubbed each nipple between his thumb and forefinger until she thought she would explode with sweeping, ecstatic sensations that she had never felt before.

She didn't want him to stop, ever, but he moved his hand down to the curve of her waist, over her hip to let his hand rest possessively low on her abdomen. When his hand slipped farther she jerked with surprise, with pleasure. His fingers were still for a moment, letting her get used to the touch of his hand so intimately on her before starting a gentle, slow stroking with his fingers.

Millicent moaned from somewhere deep inside herself but could form no real words. All she knew was that she wanted more and more of what he was doing.

"I love the way you feel," he whispered. "Silky, warm, moist. Beautiful."

Chandler continued to stroke her up and down in her most womanly place as he bent his head and lightly rubbed her cheek with his nose, then he moved on to her chin, down the sweep of her neck, before snuggling his face into the velvety skin at the curve of her shoulder. He breathed in deeply and exhaled slowly, loudly.

"I love the fresh, womanly scent of you," he whispered and inhaled deeply once again.

Millicent felt as if she was about to go over the edge of something and she couldn't stop herself. Without conscious thought, she moved her lower body in rhythm with the motion of his fingers.

Chandler started with her eyes and kissed his way down her cheeks to her lips. She opened her mouth wanting to taste more of him, wanting to be a part of him again. He lingered over her mouth, kissing her, letting his tongue play with hers, occasionally nipping her bottom lip between his teeth.

Slowly he moved to her breasts and covered each rosy peak with his mouth and suckled first one and then the other and back again. Millicent was pliant and dazed with an indescribable pleasure that kept mounting low in her abdomen. All these things he did were so new to her she could hardly catch her breath or stop the contractions of wanting that wracked her muscles.

"I love the way you taste," he murmured against the swell of her breasts. With his tongue he sampled her heated skin. "I can't get enough of you."

Millicent entwined her arms around his neck and pressed her body closer to his. His touch, his words were delicious, but she knew she needed, wanted more. She ached to feel him inside her again.

Breathlessly she said, "I feel the same way, Lord Dunraven. I fear you are teasing me."

"Teasing you?" he questioned between brief kisses that made her body rise up and meet his hand. "I thought I was loving you with words and caresses."

"I don't think I can take many more of your words and caresses. I feel like I'm going to explode if you don't thoroughly kiss me and—" She stopped. And what?

"And fill you?" he finished for her.

She knew he expected her to want the treasured touches and sweet words and, as a lady she should have been satisfied with that, but she wanted more. She wanted Chandler inside her, filling her, taking her. She didn't want the gentleman. She wanted Chandler the man, big and powerful, making her his as he had on the settee.

"Yes, yes, my lord, fill me."

Suddenly Millicent gasped and arched into his hand with a jerking motion. She buried her face into his shoulder as waves of explosive sensations tore through her with gripping speed before fading into pleasant ripples.

"Chandler." She whispered his name softly before collapsing back down onto the rug with no breath left in her lungs, no strength in her muscles.

Without giving her time to catch her breath, Chandler settled his body over the length of her as his mouth covered hers. His lips were moist, hot and demanding as he kissed her deeply, roughly, crushing her body and her lips beneath his. Millicent loved his aggressiveness, welcomed it. She matched him kiss for kiss, touch for touch, breath for breath.

She parted her legs and he pushed inside her. Millicent arched to meet him, taking all of him at once, deeply. She heard his breath quicken, felt him tremble, and she gloried that she could please him in this way. She joined the hungry rhythm he determined with his body moving in and out of her with long, sure strokes that grew stronger, sharper with delicious sensations until she stopped and cried out, breathless with exquisite pleasure once again.

Chandler covered her mouth with his in a bruising kiss that absorbed her cry of pleasure as he pumped powerfully into her. He slid his arms under her back and cupped her to him as her body shuddered with quivering muscles.

He continued to move a moment or two longer before he stopped deep inside her and shakily whispered, "Oh, Millicent, you are too wonderful, too beautiful, too exciting."

"And so are you," she answered and snuggled her nose into the warmth of his neck.

He lay hot and heavy upon her. Her hands made a slow trail over his back, down to his buttocks and up to his shoulders again. She wanted to hold him forever in this moment.

Chandler raised his head and gave her that knowing grin she had come to love.

He said, "Wasn't that better than before?"

"Oh, my, yes! I can't explain it, but I felt such extraordinary feelings. What happened?"

"You just experienced what's called the climax of lovemaking."

"It's really quite breathtaking, isn't it?"

"It stole mine. I don't think I've ever felt quite so satisfied."

"Mmm. That's a good way to describe it. I feel completely contented, too."

He chuckled low in his chest. "So do I."

Millicent sighed, wanting to enjoy a few minutes more

in Chandler's arms before she returned to thoughts of what must be done, but she knew the hour was late. She didn't want to think about going home to her aunt's or to Nottinghamshire. She didn't want to think about never experiencing again this wonderful part of life with Chandler, but she must. Now that their lovemaking was over, the sooner she got on with her life, the sooner she would get over missing Chandler.

She stirred beneath him. "I don't want this to end, but I have to get home. Lady Beatrice will have Phillips out looking for me."

Chandler rose on his elbow and glanced at the window before looking down into her eyes. "Yes, dawn is on the rise." He paused. "Millicent, we need to talk before you go."

She stiffened. She didn't want to hear it. She knew what he wanted to say, and suddenly it angered her that he wanted to ruin what had been the most soul-shattering experience of her life. She shoved his chest, and he rolled away. As she rose from the rug, she pushed down her dress and reached for her underclothes.

"You need not say anything, Lord Dunraven. In fact, I think it would be better if we didn't discuss at all what just happened between us."

"Wait a minute," he said with a queer expression on his face. "What do you mean? We have to talk about it."

She looked down at him. "No, we don't. I know what you're thinking. You believe I orchestrated this so you would feel obliged to offer to marry me, don't you? Well, sir, set your mind to rest. I did not. This was no ploy to ensnare you in a parson's mousetrap."

Chandler sat on the rug, his arms on his knees and looked up at her, clearly stunned. "That's not what I was thinking."

"Good. I wasn't looking to be your wife before this happened and I'm not expecting it now. You need not worry that I will demand your hand in marriage when dawn turns to day."

Frowning, he shook his head and said, "I didn't expect you to demand anything."

"I'm glad we're clear on that." She stepped into her drawers and pulled them up.

"No." While still seated, Chandler grabbed his breeches and shoved his legs into them one leg at a time. "You are not clear on anything, Miss Blair."

"I beg your pardon, sir?" she said in a huff of breath as she tied the waistband of her drawers.

"Damnation, Millicent, you make it sound like you came in here and took advantage of me, and I had no say in what happened between us."

"Yes, that's exactly right."

He glared at her with an incredulous expression on his face. "No, that isn't right."

"What we just shared was all my doing, sir. I asked you to make love to me, remember?"

Chandler picked up one of his shoes and rose from the rug. "You can't take credit for that. And don't pretend you had to twist my arm to get me to agree. I've been wanting to make love to you since I first saw you. When I didn't even know your name, I wanted you."

"I don't remember you ever mentioning anything of the sort to me."

"A gentleman wouldn't come right out and tell a lady he wanted to make love to her."

She pulled the capped sleeves of her dress back onto her shoulders and straightened the front of her gown over her corset. "A gentleman you say? You have behaved like a rake from the moment we met."

"No, not in all things. I keep telling you I do know how to be a gentleman at times, and not telling you that I wanted to take you to my bed was one of those times. Furthermore, it just so happens *I* want to marry you."

Millicent stopped fiddling with her sleeves and looked up at him. Her worst fear had come true. He felt guilt over what they had done.

Her heart pounded slow, hard and sure. Chandler was a gentleman after all. If only he had said that before to-night things would have been so different.

She couldn't bear him thinking she had planned tonight just to force him to propose. That thought chilled her.

"You don't know what you are saying," she managed in a hoarse whisper.

"Of course I do."

"Tell me truthfully, if we hadn't just made love would you be proposing to me right now?"

Chandler hesitated for a second too long and that told her all she needed to know long before he said, "Truth-fully? Right this moment? No."

Millicent let out a shaky breath. "That's what I thought. My point is proven."

"You have no case to prove. I only meant I would have asked for your hand in the proper manner, soliciting your guardian first."

"You can't want to marry me. You don't even know me," she whispered.

He looked pointedly, knowingly into Millicent's eyes. Very quietly he said, "I know every inch of you, my dear."

"Oh! How dare you be so crass about—" She stopped.

"Making love to you?" he asked with a frown settled deep between his eyes as he hopped on one foot while trying to get his bare foot into his other shoe.

"You're hopeless." Millicent looked around for her gloves. Chandler was being deliberately obtuse. "I meant that you don't know anything about my family or the true reason I'm in London."

He stopped trying to step into his shoe and just held it. "That's right, because you have seen fit to deny me that important bit of information even though I have asked about it more than once."

She reached down and picked up one of her gloves, then looked back at Chandler. She opened her mouth to tell him the whole story of her mother's debacle in London's Society and her aunt's double life as Lord Truefitt, but she stopped. If Chandler knew, would it make him love her? Would it make him forget she had spied on his peers and written for the scandal sheets? If none of that would change, then why expose her aunt to ruination?

"I can't tell you because it involves someone else. There's too much at stake."

"What? Why, if no one is forcing you to do this gossip column? Did you lie to me when you said you weren't doing it for the money?"

"No, no. I haven't lied to you."

"Trust me with what you know. Trust me with what you are doing. You can trust me, Millicent."

Millicent looked at Chandler, with his chest bare, his breeches unfastened and only one shoe on. Oh yes, she loved him with all her heart. She wanted to confide in him. And her heart would be overjoyed if she knew he wanted to marry her because he felt for her what she was feeling for him.

When her gaze met his, she knew she had to leave immediately. If not she would give in to his demands and tell him everything. "Don't ruin what just happened between us, Chandler. I want nothing more from you than the sweet memory of being in your arms tonight."

She turned and rushed out of the room.

"Millicent, come back."

She heard him call her name, then a sound like he had stumbled over something and tripped. She didn't stop to find out. She ran to the front door and slung it open. She dashed out into the night, running as fast as she could to the coach that was waiting.

The driver jumped down and opened the door for her. She gave him her address and as she climbed inside said, "Don't stop for Lord Dunraven. I must get away."

As the coach pulled away she looked out the window. Chandler was running down the street after them, his shirt in one hand and a shoe in the other.

Twenty

"Nothing in his life became him like the leaving it," and so it is with great relief London says farewell to the wily Mad Ton Thief. What a disagreeable ending to such a delightful piece of gossip. It would have been far better for the thief to have been Lord Pinkwater's ghost than one of our own.

Lord Truefitt
Society's Daily Column

$\mathcal{A}$S SOON AS Millicent stepped down from the carriage, the front door of her aunt's town house jerked open. Millicent took a deep breath and headed for the open doorway, where her aunt's maid stood waiting for her. She'd refused to allow herself to think about Chandler on the way home. Instead she concentrated on how she would tell her aunt about the sad turn of events involving Lady Heathecoute.

"Where have you been, Miss?" Emery said. "Her ladyship has sent Phillips out looking for you. You've had us all worried sick."

Millicent lifted her shoulders and her chin, trying to act as if nothing was wrong as she neared the doorway. "I'm not so late, am I, Emery?"

"Much too late according to my lady," the maid said with a disapproving glare on her face. "And what happened to you? I see now you've a cut on your forehead and there's blood on your dress. Are you all right?"

"I'm quite all right. I'll explain everything to Aunt Beatrice," Millicent said, walking into the house past Emery. "But I could use a cup of tea, if you don't mind."

"Of course not. I'll be up with it right away."

"Thank you." Millicent went straight to the upper floor. Hamlet barked, and she stopped on the landing and leaned against the rail. There would be so many things about London that she would miss when she went back home.

"Is that you, Millicent?" Aunt Beatrice called from her bedchamber.

"Yes, Aunt, it's me."

"Good heavens! Where have you been? I've been worried sick. Come in right away."

Millicent paused outside the door and took a deep breath. The dream of being in Chandler's arms was over. As she'd traveled the streets to her aunt's house, dawn had arrived and now so had reality.

She walked into the bedchamber talking. "I'm sorry I'm so late, Aunt Beatrice, but you'll understand once I explain everything."

"Well I should hope so." Her eyes rounded in shock as Millicent neared her bed. "My goodness, dear girl, what happened to you? You're hurt and your dress is a rumpled mess. Heaven's gate! Did someone accost you? Oh, your mother will never let me hear the end of it. Don't just stand there, Millicent. Say something."

Her aunt's frantic voice startled Hamlet and he barked

several times before Aunt Beatrice was able to quiet him.

"Please don't worry about me. I'm fine," Millicent said as she walked closer to the bed. "I wasn't attacked. Well—not exactly."

"What does not exactly mean? Something happened? Did you fall? Are you hurt anywhere else?"

"No, no. Really, I'm perfect except for the cut, which doesn't pain me at all, but it has been such an eventful evening my head is spinning at the moment." She sat down in the chair by her aunt's bed.

Millicent touched her forehead and realized it was tender. She had completely forgotten about the cut when she was with Chandler. There was a dull ache inside her, but it didn't come from her wound.

She looked at her aunt, sitting up in the bed, waiting for her to speak. "I find I don't really know where to begin."

"Nonsense! At the beginning, of course," Aunt Beatrice huffed.

"Yes, well you see, I've been trying to help Lord—" she stopped. No, she didn't want to tell her aunt she'd been trying to help Lord Dunraven find the Mad Ton Thief. That would take too much explaining, and it wasn't something her aunt really needed to know.

"That is, I was standing with Lord Dunraven tonight when he—when I noticed he kept looking at Lady Heathecoute with a quizzical expression on his face. So I made a point of unobtrusively glancing at her, too. I noticed that the front of her skirt looked very odd."

"She is very plump, my dear. It is to be expected. What has that got to do with the cut on your head and the unforgivable lateness of the hour? Forget starting at the beginning, I'll need smelling salts before you get to the ending. Give me the high points and you can fill in the details later."

As carefully and as quickly as possible Millicent relayed the events of the evening to her aunt, starting from the time she and Lord Dunraven went with the viscountess out to the carriage. She left out the hour she'd spent at Chandler's house, accounting the story as if she had spent all the time with the authorities, telling them how she and Chandler had pressed Lady Heathecoute to show what was beneath her skirt.

Beatrice pulled Hamlet up to her chest and lay back against her pillows when Millicent finished. "Merciful heavens. This is an unbelievable story. The poor woman a thief? The Mad Ton Thief? I keep thinking it's impossible."

"I assure you it is all true."

"And you say the authorities took her away."

"I watched them put her in the carriage. Her husband went with them, too, but I do feel he knew nothing about what she had been doing."

Aunt Beatrice brushed Hamlet's coat with her hand. "I knew she wanted to take over the column, but I thought it was for the excitement and control of it, not because she needed to obtain money to live."

Something tugged at Millicent. "But that's why you do it, isn't it, Aunt? For the money, to help with your living expenses?"

Beatrice's eyes widened and she hurriedly said, "Oh, yes, my dear, yes. I've said so, haven't I?"

Millicent studied her aunt. She wasn't so sure she believed her anymore.

"Forget that. Tell me what Lord Heathecoute had to say."

"He suggested to the authorities that it might be a sickness with her, and that it was quite possible she was unable to stop herself from doing it."

"Hmm. I have heard of such a thing. No doubt the authorities will sort it out."

"How did it come about that you took her into your confidence?" Millicent asked.

"Oh, it was Mr. Greenbrier from *The Daily Reader* who introduced us. Apparently she had intimated to someone at the newspaper that she was available to obtain information if there was a need. He felt it would be good if I had an assistant, so naturally I was obliged to take her into my confidence when he approached me with the idea."

"Her reputation is ruined and she will no doubt end up in prison. Do you think she will tattle that you are Lord Truefitt?"

Beatrice screwed up her face in a worried frown. "There is that possibility. When Phillips delivers the column this morning, I'll have him give a letter to Mr. Greenbrier and ask him to call on me. Perhaps he can speak to the authorities and the viscountess and work something out to help her so that she would have good reason to stay quiet about me."

"I'll make sure Phillips gets the letter delivered."

"Oh, get your quill, Millicent, we've so much to do and no time to waste. We must get our column to the newspaper and be the first to tell Society that the Mad Ton Thief has been captured."

WHEN HER MAID brought Millicent tea that afternoon, she had a note on the tray from Lord Dunraven saying that he wanted to call on her later that day. She hastily wrote a note back telling him she was unavailable and to please not disturb her again.

It hurt her greatly to refuse him, but she must make sure he knew that she had no intentions of marrying him just because she took him as a lover. It was best they end their affair as quickly as it had begun. Millicent couldn't bear the thought that he would marry her because of duty and honor or because he believed she'd tricked him.

As much as it devastated her to reject his appeal to see her, Millicent had to deny his request. They must go their separate ways. Their partnership was dissolved because the Mad Ton Thief had been caught. She had all hope that the raven would be found unharmed and returned to him without further delay.

She also refused a call from Lady Lynette. She knew her friend wanted to gossip about the events of the previous evening and find out all Millicent knew about the capture of the Mad Ton Thief, but she wasn't ready to start talking with anyone about what had happened. She sent Lynette a note suggesting that she call on her later in the week.

Late that afternoon, unable to stop herself, Millicent walked out into the back garden, hoping that Chandler had not listened to her request to be left alone. She wanted him to burst through the hedge and announce his undying love for her and ask her once again to marry him.

Millicent stayed out in the garden until dusk. Chandler never showed.

Lady Beatrice agreed that Millicent shouldn't attend any of the parties that evening. Her wound didn't look that bad, but her aunt had to have time to arrange a new chaperone for Millicent. Thankfully, they had enough gossip for a couple of days with the capture of the Mad Ton

Thief, and they could always write about one of the Terrible Threesome.

The next afternoon Millicent once again retreated to the garden hoping Chandler would steal through the hedge to see her. The gray sky seemed fitting as she sat on the base of the statue where she'd frolicked with Chandler and remembered their hour together in his home.

Twilight came. Chandler didn't come, and there was no further note from him.

When she went back inside, the latest copy of *The Daily Reader* had arrived. As always, she opened it first to Lord Truefitt's column to have a look at it.

Millicent blinked, then gasped. She turned the pages of the newspaper. Something was wrong. It was Lord Truefitt's column, but it wasn't her writings. What had happened?

She read the words carefully.

> "Beware the ides of March" might be Lord Dunraven's motto, for it seems he may be caught at last by a pretty maiden. It is on good authority this column reports a young lady new to Town, who has danced with the earl at the best parties, was seen fleeing his home in the wee hours of morning, without benefit of a chaperone. The earl himself was said to have been chasing after her carriage in a state of dishabille. Hmm, one wonders what was going on. Do tell, if you know more.

> *Lord Truefitt*
> *Society's Daily Column*

For a moment Millicent was shocked into disbelief. How could her article have been switched with the one about her and Chandler? Who could have seen her leave Lord Dunraven's house so early in the morning?

Only Chandler and the coachman. Could Chandler have replaced her column with one of his own? No, he was a rake and not to be trusted, but she couldn't believe that of him. She had no idea who might have seen her leave his house, but she was certain Chandler would not have done this.

Why would anyone have written about it?

Her hands made fists as she held the newspaper, crinkling the pages tight. She didn't have to ask why. She knew. It was for the gossip. The very thing she had promised herself and her mother that wouldn't happen had happened.

Millicent was the object of scandal!

She dropped the paper and rushed up the stairs to her bedchamber. She would leave immediately. She would run away, so she wouldn't have to look anyone in the eyes. If she were lucky her mother would never find out about this. Millicent hated the thought of trying to explain to her mother, or hurting her. But what could she say to her aunt? How could she explain that being with Chandler was more important than her reputation? She couldn't. Aunt Beatrice wouldn't understand.

There were no words to justify her involvement with Chandler. Millicent went to her wardrobe and jerked down her gowns and threw them on the bed. When she turned back to the wardrobe for the rest of her things, she saw Hamlet standing in the doorway watching her. He wagged his tail and looked at her with doleful, expectant eyes. In the weeks she'd been here, the dog had never ventured into her bedchamber. Did he realize what the clothes on the bed meant?

He continued to look at her and wag his tail. Did he

want her to pat him? She knelt down and reached out her hand. He walked over to her and sniffed her fingers, then licked them. Millicent smiled. She rubbed his warm body and allowed him to lick her cheek affectionately.

"Oh, you smart little dog." Millicent sat down on the floor and pulled Hamlet into her lap so she could brush his coat with her hand.

What a sweetheart he was to come to her when she most needed a friend. Her world had come crashing down around her and somehow Hamlet had known and he had come to comfort her.

No, she was not her mother. Millicent wouldn't flee London, or hide, or be forced into marriage with a man who didn't love her just to save her reputation. She would stay in Town and do her best to finish the job she'd started for her aunt.

There was no way she would be allowed at any of the parties now, but maybe Lynette wouldn't desert her. If Millicent could talk to Lynette once or twice a week, she would be able to get sufficient gossip until her aunt was ready to resume her duties. At that time, Millicent would feel she had fulfilled her commitment to her father's sister.

But first she had to tell her aunt about the column, and she had to do it now. And if her mother, by chance, found out about her liaison with Lord Dunraven, Millicent was sure she would understand. After all, her mother had once been in love with a rake, too.

There was a knock on her bedchamber door. She looked up and saw Emery standing in the doorway, regarding the dog in Millicent's lap.

"So the master of the house has finally come around," Emery said.

"So it seems. Today, Hamlet and I have a new relationship."

"It's about time." Emery paused for a moment, then with a curious expression asked, "Is there a problem with your clothing, Miss?"

Millicent looked at her open wardrobe and her dresses slung across the bed. She smiled at the maid. "No, everything is all right."

"Lady Beatrice would like to see you."

Millicent tensed. Oh dear, she must have already seen the column, and Millicent hadn't had time to formulate what to say, how to explain.

She pulled Hamlet closer for a moment and felt his heart beating solidly against his warm chest. "Tell her I'll be along shortly."

"Yes, Miss. She's in the front parlor."

Millicent looked back to Emery. "What?"

Emery smiled. "Yes, Miss. She said she was tired of her bedchamber. Between Phillips, and me, we carried her down the stairs so she could sit in the parlor for an hour or two. She's so pleased."

"I'm sure she is. Tell her I'll be right down."

"Yes, Miss. Should I send Glenda up to help you with your clothing?"

"Thank you, but I'll speak to her later."

Emery walked away and Millicent hugged Hamlet once more before setting him away from her. She rose and looked down at him and said, "I think this means your mistress is on the mend. No doubt I won't be here much longer."

Hamlet barked once.

"Does that mean you will be glad or sad?" she asked the spaniel.

He barked twice.

Millicent smiled. "I'll take that to mean sad."

A couple of minutes later, Millicent walked into the

parlor. Aunt Beatrice sat on the settee, looking splendidly healthy and happy in a dark green dress. The swelling in her face was completely gone and her bruises had faded to where not even a shadow showed. Sitting so straight in the settee, no one would know that she still couldn't walk without aid.

"Aunt Beatrice, you look wonderful."

"Thank you, dearie. I couldn't spend another full day in bed. For the first time in a long time, I feel good. I've missed so much this Season. I'm ready to get back to my duties. I plan to be down here every day until I'm ready to go out in Society on my own."

"That is good news. By the looks of you, it won't be long." Millicent noticed the paper she'd crumpled and thrown to the floor now lay folded on her aunt's lap. It was clear from the pleasant expression on her aunt's face that she had not yet read the column.

"Aunt Beatrice, I'm afraid I also have some not so good news, too."

"What's this? Have you learned more about what has happened to Lady Heathecoute?"

"No. It's about me."

She picked up the newspaper and turned it to the column and handed the paper to Beatrice. "Read this."

Stunned, her aunt looked up at her after scanning the print. "What is this? I didn't approve this."

Calmly Millicent said, "And I didn't write it."

"I should think not. Someone might think this young lady fleeing Lord Dunraven's house was you." Aunt Beatrice looked over the paper to Millicent. Her eyes widened. "It wouldn't be you, would it? Tell me you were not in Lord Dunraven's house in the wee hours of the morning."

"Yes, I was."

"Millicent!" Her aunt threw her hands up in the air and the paper went flying over the back of the sofa.

"Aunt Beatrice, I can explain."

"How? You can't. Nothing would be acceptable. Oh, dear. Oh, dear. Please tell me this is not true."

Millicent remained quiet but not upset. She had no regrets about what she'd done, and no doubts that she would do it all again.

"Well say something."

"It's true that it was me."

"Heaven above!" Beatrice fanned her chest with her hand.

"Lord Dunraven wanted to clean my cut before bringing me home and I agreed." Thankfully that was the truth and that was all her aunt needed to know.

"Oh, my, oh my no! Your mother will never forgive me. Didn't I tell you not to allow Lord Dunraven to compromise you? Well, no matter. I know what we must do. He'll have to marry you. It's the only thing."

"No, Aunt Beatrice. That is not necessary."

"Of course it is."

"I won't hear of it. I haven't had time to work everything out but—"

A loud knock on the front door silenced Millicent but caused Hamlet to run to the front of the house barking.

"Good heavens, I don't know who that is, but we're not accepting calls right now. Oh, dear. I should have known you were too young and innocent to handle the London blades, especially Lord Dunraven. It's all my fault."

"Aunt Beatrice, please don't be upset for me. I'm not."

When Phillips walked into the room, Millicent walked over to the window and waited for him to present the card of the caller to her aunt. She had to find the words to make her aunt realize she would not be forced into a marriage, not even to the man she loved.

But instead of walking over to her aunt, Phillips walked over to Millicent and said, "I'm sorry, Miss. Lord Dunraven says he hasn't a card with him, but he must speak with you immediately."

Millicent's legs went weak. Her breath caught.

Chandler had come.

After she'd rejected him, refused to see him, he'd come. Her heart lifted and swelled in her chest. But no, she couldn't see him. She wouldn't force him to marry her.

"Send him in," Beatrice declared.

"No. Wait, Aunt Beatrice. I don't want to see him."

"Well, I do."

"I don't want to hear what he has to say. Phillips, tell him that I'm unavailable."

Not waiting to be announced, Chandler strolled through the doorway into the parlor with his hat and gloves in his hand. He looked so confident, so dashing, Millicent's heart skipped in her chest.

"Lady Beatrice." He bowed and kissed her hand. "You're looking well."

"Thank you, my lord," she said tightly. "I do believe you are just the person I wanted to see."

Millicent remained by the window, unable to make her watery legs move closer to Chandler. She was elated, thankful he'd come to see her, and she wanted nothing more than to run into his arms, but she had to remain firm in her decision not to force him to marry her.

Chandler turned to her. "Miss Blair."

"Lord Dunraven."

"I apologize for the intrusion, but I have a special reason for calling upon you this evening."

"I should think so," Aunt Beatrice said.

Millicent took a step toward him. "Don't speak further, Chandler. I meant what I said to you the other night. We have nothing left to say to each other. I think it would be best if you left."

His eyes remained solidly on her face. "And I meant what I said to you, Millicent. We have many things to discuss, but I must take care of first things first. I've brought someone with me who wants to see you."

"Really, Lord Dunraven, you presume too much to come without making arrangements and to bring a guest," Lady Beatrice said. "This is beyond the pale."

"Yes," Millicent added her voice to her aunt's reprimand. "I'm afraid this isn't a good time to receive anyone."

A smile stretched across his face and lit his eyes as if sunshine was sparkling in them. "I think this is one caller you will not wish to turn away."

He strode over to the doorway and reached out his hand.

Millicent's mother walked into the room.

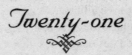

Twenty-one

"Love comforteth like sunshine after rain,"
and so is London comforted that another
splendid Season is drawing to a close.

Lord Truefitt
Society's Daily Column

MILLICENT COULDN'T BELIEVE her eyes. "Mama," she
whispered.

Aunt Beatrice gasped. "Dorothy?"

Hamlet barked.

"Yes, it's me," Dorothy exclaimed with a beautiful
smile on her face. "In London for the first time in well
over twenty years."

Her mother seemed to float into the room on Chandler's
arm. She wore a stylish carriage dress and matching
ruched hat that was the color of dark plum. She looked
down at Hamlet, who had jumped up in Beatrice's lap
and continued to bark. "Oh, my, you are a protective little
doggie, aren't you?"

Chandler stepped away from her ladyship, who looked

at Millicent with a questioning expression. "Do I get a hug from my daughter or just silence?"

"Of course." Millicent ran to her mother and hugged her tightly before kissing her on both cheeks. "It is good to see you, Mama. I'm just so surprised and so happy, I don't know what to say."

"And I'm delighted to see you, my love. You look wonderful." She patted her daughter's cheek affectionately. "I believe life in London has been good for you."

Her mother looked over at Chandler and winked. Winked? What was going on? What was Chandler doing with her mother and what had he told her mother?

"Mama, how did you get here? Why did you come? How did you meet Chandler?" The questions entered Millicent's mind faster than they could tumble from her lips.

"Phillips, take Hamlet upstairs," Aunt Beatrice said, handing the barking dog to her butler. "There's too much going on to settle him."

Millicent's mother completely ignored every one of Millicent's questions and turned to her sister-in-law as soon as Hamlet left her arms. "And, dear Beatrice, how are you? How long has it been since I've seen you? I think it has been at least ten or twelve years since you last visited our home. You look splendid. Millicent's visit must have been just the tonic you needed." She bent down and kissed both of the older lady's cheeks.

"Thank you, Dorothy, but I'm feeling a wee bit overwhelmed with shock at the moment."

"As I am," Dorothy said. "But Lord Dunraven explained everything to me."

"Everything?" Millicent and Beatrice said in unison as they looked at each other.

"Yes, I suppose so," her mother said, glancing from Chandler to Millicent.

"Mama, have you seen the afternoon paper?" Millicent asked, still trying to make sense of why her mother was in London.

"Of course not, my dear, we only just arrived in Town and came straight here."

"And not a moment too soon. Phillips, bring some tea and brandy for our guests," Aunt Beatrice said before the butler reached the door. "When you return, bring my tonic. I think I need fortifying."

Chandler walked over to Millicent with long, confident strides. His blue eyes watched her face so intensely it felt like a caress. "I told you we had a lot of things to discuss," he said quietly. "Do you believe me now?"

Her heart raced in her chest. "I believe I do."

"Are you ready to talk?"

"Most assuredly, sir. I think you have many things to explain to me."

He gave her a curious expression. "Perhaps we should step into the garden and let your mother and your aunt get reacquainted."

"I think that is an excellent idea."

After receiving permission from her mother to stroll with Lord Dunraven, Millicent and he walked to the back of the garden and sat down on one of the benches near the statue. A wispy breeze stirred strands of his hair, and rays from the sun streaked it with shiny bits.

He kept a respectable distance from her on the lawn seat, but she was certain she could feel his warmth and his strength without her touching him.

Earlier in her bedchamber Millicent had prepared herself for being the object of scandal and dealt with it, but she hadn't prepared herself for the arrival of Chandler and her mother.

She had decided the first question she needed to ask

was, "Did you exchange my writings of Lord Truefitt's column in *The Daily Reader* for one of your own?"

"That's the second time you've mentioned the newspaper. Millicent, I've not seen a paper in two days now. I don't know what you're talking about."

Millicent believed him. She hadn't thought him capable of such vile trickery, but what was he doing showing up at her aunt's house with her mother by his side?

"What did my mother mean by saying you had told her everything?"

"As far as she is concerned I did. I didn't tell her you were alone with me in my town house and there is no reason for her to know."

"I'm afraid she will find out quite soon. My greatest fear has been realized."

"What do you mean?"

"Someone saw me leave your house that morning and the story was printed in Lord Truefitt's column today."

Anger clouded his features. "Are you certain?"

"I read it myself only a few minutes ago."

"Damnation, how did it happen?"

"I have no idea. My aunt and I were just talking about it when you came in. Someone must have seen me leave your house. They obviously wrote about it and somehow managed to exchange their column with mine. I can only suppose they paid someone at *The Daily Reader* to make the switch."

A light shown in Chandler's eyes. "I think I might know who saw you."

"Who?"

"Lord Heathecoute."

She gasped. "That would make perfect sense. How do you know he was there?"

"He came to my door shortly after you left. He must have seen you leave."

"What did he want?"

"He brought back the raven and said he had found everything that his lady had stolen. He asked me to help free his wife by speaking to the authorities on her behalf. I must admit I was in a hell of a temper after you left so abruptly with nothing settled between us. I don't remember being sympathetic to his petition."

Millicent shook her head. "Of course it would have been him. He should have been the first person I suspected. He must have bribed someone at the newspaper to exchange my column for his own."

"Does he know you work for the gossips?"

Millicent wondered how much she should admit to Chandler and how much he already knew. "Yes. He and his lady are the only people who know other than my— Lord Truefitt. But, none of that is as important right now as finding out how you met my mother."

A thoughtful expression flowed over Chandler's face. "I went to her home."

"Chandler, this is not the time to play the question game."

"Why? You play it so well."

Her gaze remained firmly on his face. "This is serious. I never told you my mother's name. How did you find out where she lives?"

His expression turned more thoughtful and he said without hesitation, "I had someone make private inquiries about you and your family."

"You didn't."

"I did."

Outrage swept over her. "You spied on me?"

"In a manner of speaking, I suppose you could interpret

it that way. I'd rather you see it as when you wouldn't tell me about yourself, I became worried."

"How could you do that to me?"

"I had to know if anyone was forcing you to do something you didn't want to do. So when I had Doulton looking into the finances of various members of the ton, I asked him to make inquiries about you."

Millicent took a deep breath and looked away from him for a moment. Already her exasperation was fading. It was difficult to be angry with him when she loved him so much and appreciated his concern for her well-being.

She faced him again. "How much did you find out about me?"

"Not everything I wanted to know."

"Good. There is some mystery left me."

"Maybe," he said with a half smile.

Her senses perked up again and put her on guard. "What do you mean?"

"Doulton discovered that your mother was ruined by scandal during her come-out season, and that her father married her off to the earl of Bellecourte, a man more than twice her age. You were born two years later. And I know that Lady Beatrice is your aunt. Why did you keep that a secret?"

"My aunt thought it best that no one know of our relation so they wouldn't be inclined to ask me too many questions. And you, sir, were the only one who queried me at length."

"You fascinated me."

Her heart lifted. "Why go see my mother? It appears you had already found out all there was to know about me."

"Not quite. I knew about your family, Millicent, before you stayed with me in my town house."

"You didn't say a word. You should have told me."

"I wanted you to trust me. I wanted you to tell me what I already knew."

"Perhaps I should have," she admitted, wondering if things would have turned out differently if she had told him.

"I tried desperately to get you to confide in me about yourself that morning we were together and again later that day when I called, but you refused to see me."

"I remember."

"I had to take this matter further without you. That's when I decided to go see your mother. I rode like the devil day and night, changing horses often to get to your mother's house as soon as possible."

Fear gripped Millicent. "Did you tell her what I've been doing?"

"No."

"Thank you. I know she wouldn't understand why I had to do it," she whispered, breathing easier, grateful he hadn't told her mother that she wrote tittle-tattle. There was still hope that she could keep that bit of information from her.

"I quizzed your mother at length, thinking if she knew, she would tell me, but it became clear that she knew only that you were a companion to your ailing aunt and that you had no other mission in London."

"Good."

"It wasn't good for me. I was convinced someone was forcing you to write for the gossips and it was driving me insane. I couldn't bear the thought that anyone had that kind of control over you. Then, on the carriage trip back to London with your mother, I figured it all out."

Millicent stiffened again, but tried not to let it show.

Did he really know or was he only trying to bluff her into telling him what he wanted to know?

"You figured out what?"

A satisfied smile settled on his mouth. "Not what. Who I know who is forcing you to write for Lord Truefitt."

Millicent spoke softly, "Chandler, you need not worry on my behalf. No one is forcing me to do anything."

"You're doing it because someone asked you to?"

"Yes."

"Someone very close to you that you care about?"

"I'm not prepared to say any more on the subject."

"You don't have to. Your aunt is Lord Truefitt, isn't she? The lord is really a lady."

"Yes. How did you figure it out?" Millicent let out a deep breath of relief. It actually felt good to admit the truth to him.

"It was the only logical answer. Lady Beatrice was obviously ill and couldn't attend the parties and events, so she had you attend for her and gather the information."

Millicent leaned close to Chandler. "I must ask you not to tell anyone, Lord Dunraven. After Aunt Beatrice fell and hurt herself, she sent for me to come and take over until she recovered. I didn't want to do it, and I wasn't very good at it."

"Don't be modest. I thought you very good at it. You had me fooled and you had Andrew ready to find you and expose Lord Truefitt."

"Do not make light of this for my aunt's sake. I couldn't refuse my father's sister. I don't care about my reputation. It is ruined anyway, but if the information about her gets out she will lose her employment and be forced to leave London in shame. I don't want that for her."

"Millicent, you don't have to ask. Your aunt's secret is safe with me."

Her breaths became shallow. She believed him. Millicent wanted to melt into his arms. He knew how to calm her with just his expression. "Thank you," she said, then asked, "How exactly did you convince my mother to come to London with you?"

"Oh, that was easy."

"I know my mother, sir, and it would not have been an easy task. What did you tell her?"

"Not tell her, ask her. I asked for your hand in marriage."

"Oh, no. Chandler, why bring my mother into this? She will not force me to marry you, I assure you. I refuse to marry you simply because we had that short time alone together in your parlor."

"I don't want you to marry me because of that, although that is reason enough." His voice lowered. "I want you to marry me because you love me as I love you. You do love me, don't you?"

Millicent opened her mouth to speak, but for a few seconds no words came out. She was too stunned, too elated, too confused. "Yes. Oh, yes, I love you, but I've written for the gossip sheets, and now they have written about me and my reputation has been ruined. I'm not a suitable wife for you, Chandler,"

"Yes, you are. None of the things you mentioned concern me. I love you."

She bent closer to him. "I never thought to hear you say such words. Are you sure you love me?"

"I'm not in any doubt about my feelings for you."

"You aren't just saying this because you feel obliged because of what happened between us, or about what was written in Lord Truefitt's column?"

"I love you, Millicent."

He couldn't have said it any plainer, but still she couldn't believe him. She couldn't believe such an impossible dream could come true. "How?"

"How do I love you? Must I count the ways?"

"How do you know you love me when there have been so many women in your life?"

"It's true, I've never been in love before—not really in love the way I feel about you. You are the first woman I've wanted to be with night and day. I not only want you in my arms and in my bed, I want you in my home living with me, having my children." His eyes looked deeply into hers. "Millicent, just trust me when I say that you are the lady I want forever in my life."

A smile slowly spread across Millicent's lips and joy filled her. "I love you, Chandler."

"That's what I wanted to hear. First thing tomorrow morning I'm going to apply for a special license so we can be married. That's another reason that I needed your mother here. You do want her at the wedding, don't you?"

"Of course." She went into his arms and he held her tightly for a moment, then quickly turned her loose.

"We can't have your mother catching us in an intimate embrace."

Millicent smiled sweetly at him. "What will she do? Make you marry me?"

Chandler laughed. "She's already consented. Your mother happens to think I'm a very good catch."

"No wonder she was in such a good mood when she arrived. She has wanted me to marry." Millicent paused and said, "Chandler, I have a favor to ask of you."

He smiled. "Whatever it is, I'll do."

"Maybe if you could talk with Lord Heathecoute. If you could help his lady by talking to the authorities maybe he won't expose Aunt Beatrice as Lord Truefitt."

"Does he know who she is?"

"Yes. He and the viscountess are the only two in Town who know other than her contact at *The Daily Reader* and, of course, me and now you. Oh, so many people know it will be difficult to keep her identity a secret."

"Don't worry about Lady Beatrice. I meant it when I said your aunt will never be in need for anything. I'll take care of her." He smiled at her. "In a matter of a few days you will be my wife. Your family will be my family."

"Chandler, I am so happy you love me, but you do understand I'll have to continue the columns for my aunt until she's better."

He pressed a finger on her lips. "No."

"Yes, I must," she nodded and talked beneath the light pressure of his finger.

"No, Millicent. She will have to find someone else to do her spying."

"I don't know who—" she stopped. "But of course I do. I'll ask Lady Lynette."

Chandler removed his finger and took hold of her hand. "The duke's daughter?"

"Yes, she loves gossip."

"Millicent, I'm sure all that can be worked out so that you are not involved."

Millicent laughed and squeezed Chandler's hand. "I must write one last column."

"And why must you?"

" 'Love comforteth like sunshine after rain,' and so too can the ton be comforted that the first of the Terrible Threesome has been caught. It is on good authority that I report Lord Dunraven has applied for a special license to wed Miss Millicent Blair."

He scooted closer to her on the bench. "I think I'm

agreeable to you writing that one last column."

Millicent looked up into his eyes. "Are you sure you love me, Chandler?"

" 'Doubt thou the stars are fire, Doubt that the sun doth move, Doubt truth to be a liar, But never doubt I love.' You, Millicent, I love you."

"And I love you, Chandler."

He slipped closer to her on the bench and pressed her hand to his heart. "Will you marry me?"

Millicent smiled up into his eyes. "I thought you'd never ask."

Chandler pulled Millicent into his arms and kissed her thoroughly on the lips.

Millicent thrilled to his touch.